P9-BIO-249

GOOD MORNING, HEARTACHE

A Philip Damon Mystery

Peter Duchin
and John Morgan Wilson

BERKLEY PRIME CRIME, NEW YORK

This is a work of fiction. Names, characters, places, and incidents either are the product of the author's imagination or are used fictitiously, and any resemblance to actual persons, living or dead, business establishments, events, or locales is entirely coincidental.

GOOD MORNING, HEARTACHE

A Berkley Prime Crime book / published by arrangement with the authors

PRINTING HISTORY
Berkley Prime Crime hardcover edition / December 2003
Berkley Prime Crime mass-market edition / November 2004

For information address: The Berkley Publishing Group,
a division of Penguin Group (USA) Inc.,
375 Hudson Street, New York, New York 10014.

Visit our website at www.penguin.com

ISBN: 0-425-19921-5

Berkley Prime Crime Books are published by The Berkley Publishing Group,
a division of Penguin Group (USA) Inc.,
375 Hudson Street, New York, New York 10014.
The name BERKLEY PRIME CRIME and the BERKLEY PRIME CRIME design are trademarks belonging to Penguin Group (USA) Inc.

PRINTED IN THE UNITED STATES OF AMERICA

10 9 8 7 6 5 4 3 2 1

ACKNOWLEDGMENTS

The authors wish to acknowledge the following individuals, organizations, and resources: our agent, Alice Martell, of the Martell Agency; our editor, Natalee Rosenstein, vice president and senior executive editor of The Berkley Publishing Group; Howard Kaminsky, friend, sage, and fellow writer; D. P. Lyle, MD, author and founder of The Writer's Medical and Forensic Lab (www.dplylemd.com), for his assistance with certain details; fellow writers Margie Kase, Larry Kase, Rochelle Krich, and Paula L. Woods, for their help with various aspects of research; two national writing organizations, and their local chapters, for their support: Sisters in Crime (www.sistersincrime.org) and Mystery Writers of America (www.mysterywriters.org). We also wish to acknowledge the value of the following resource books and their authors: *Los Angeles A to Z: An Encyclopedia of the City and County,* by Leonard Pitt and Dale Pitt; *Hollywood and the Best of Los Angeles,* by Gil Reavill; *Los Angeles: An Architectural Guide,* by David Gebhard and Robert Winter; *Behind the Screen: How Gays and Lesbians Shaped Hollywood, 1910–1969,* by William J. Mann; and the *L.A. Musical History Tour,* by Art Fein.

AUTHORS' NOTE

Although many characters in this book are based on real people, living and dead, this story and all its scenes are purely fictional. In addition, some readers may question our spelling of Cocoanut Grove, since many sources list the first word as Coconut, dropping the "a." The correct spelling, as we use it in this book, is Cocoanut, as seen on the awning of the legendary nightclub in archival photographs.

Chapter 1

————

THE LAST THING I wanted to get involved in was another murder, or even the possibility of one. But I faced a knotty problem, and Buddy Bixby seemed like an easy solution.

"I'm not so sure," Anita Loos said, sitting tiny and hunched under her trademark hat and veil, with a gin and tonic poised just beneath her chin. "Really, Philip, I think you've had enough murder in your thirty-four years to last a lifetime. Can't you find a musician who fits the bill, with a past that's less—well, *checkered?*"

"Not as good as Buddy Bixby, Neetsie. He can cover lead trumpet and vocals both. Where am I going to find someone comparable, on such short notice?"

"Yes, darling, I know—the music always comes first." She reached over to pat my hand, acting like the surrogate mother she was. My own mother had died in 1931, three days after my difficult birth; Neetsie—as I'd always called Anita Loos—had selflessly taken her place. "But there's still that pesky problem of the unsolved homicide, isn't there?"

IT was August 5, 1965, a Thursday that was fast approaching midnight.

Anita and I were sitting in a red leather booth at Toots Shor's in upper Manhattan, trying to figure out how I was going to open a six-week engagement at the Cocoanut Grove in Los Angeles, missing two key members of the band. My vocalist, Gloria Velez, had come down with a nasty summer cold, turning her husky contralto into a scratchy whisper. Eddie Sears, my lead trumpet, was caught up in a family emergency that would keep him in New York into next week, at the very least. On Saturday afternoon, my band— the Philip Damon Orchestra—was due to play a fancy Hollywood Hills party, then race back to the Ambassador Hotel to open at the Grove that evening.

Buddy Bixby—Gloria's suggestion as a replacement— was a fine lead trumpet and vocalist, who'd made a name as a young jazz prodigy back in the fifties. The hitch was that Buddy was also a junkie—in and out of jail, his career on the skids. Now he was further tainted as an unnamed suspect in a recent L.A. murder investigation, or so my journalist pals kept telling me that night at Toots's place. So what's a beleaguered bandleader to do?

I ordered another Scotch.

"I didn't say Bixby had been arrested for the murder, Damon." Bob Considine, the star Hearst correspondent and debonair man-about-town, leaned over from the adjacent booth, where he was enjoying a late dinner with his wife,

Millie; Kitty Carlisle Hart; and William Randolph Hearst, Jr. "I'm just saying the cops have a few questions for him, that's all."

"Who's the fellow that got dispatched, Bob?"

"Mexican guy, name of Angel Vargas. Worked night security at one of the L.A. racetracks, watching over the stables. An exercise rider found him early this morning in a stall with his head caved in. Maybe it was a horse that clobbered him, but it looks more suspicious than that. The guy was apparently very careful around the animals."

"How does Buddy Bixby figure in it?"

"My source in L.A. tells me they found Bixby's name and phone number in one of Vargas's pockets. Given the guy's Mexican and Bixby's a hophead, the cops figured there might be a drug connection, maybe a deal gone bad."

"Just because the poor man's of Mexican descent," Anita put in, "hardly makes him some kind of drug dealer. My heavens, Bob!"

"I'm just giving you the cop's take on this, Anita."

"Anyway," I said, "that doesn't sound like the Buddy Bixby I know. He's always struck me as a passive, peaceful kind of guy. Not a thug who'd crush another man's skull, not even for drugs. How come I haven't read about this in the papers?"

"Like I said, it just went down early this morning. Unless they book Bixby, it's just another cheap L.A. homicide. This Angel Vargas was a wetback, no papers. Lived in spartan quarters at the track, sent his money back to his family in Mexico. Not the kind of victim that's going to light up any fires in the cop shop. If it wasn't for the possible Bixby connection, I never would have been tipped to it in the first place."

"Thanks for the information, Bob."

"Sure thing, Damon. Do me a favor, will you? If you hire Bixby, keep me posted. There may be a feature in it yet."

"I hope not—at least not the kind I think you have in mind."

We both laughed, but my heart wasn't in it—I had my own reasons, other than business, for wanting Buddy Bixby to get his life back on track. The waiter arrived and placed a fresh Dewars on the rocks on the linen tablecloth. For the moment, I ignored it. I reached into the pocket of my blazer and pulled out a news item from the July 28 edition of the *New York Times*, which Gloria Velez had passed along to me that morning. While I scanned it yet again, Neetsie leaned close and did the same.

MUSICIAN BUDDY BIXBY
RELEASED AFTER JAIL TERM

LOS ANGELES—Jazz musician Buddy Bixby was released from Los Angeles County Jail yesterday after serving six months for possession of heroin.

Mr. Bixby, 33, a Caucasian, was arrested in January during a police raid on a Los Angeles nightclub, where he was performing with several Negro musicians. According to court records, it was Mr. Bixby's fourth arrest for drug possession since 1961.

In the late 1950s, Mr. Bixby, a trumpet player, was considered one of the more promising young musicians working in the jazz idiom. His distinct, melancholy voice and attractive looks made him popular with young female fans. His records sold well, although he reportedly has not recorded in several years.

"Tsk, tsk." Neetsie straightened up, prim and proper. "He's been out of jail a week, and already he's suspected in a murder."

"He's a first-rate musician, Neetsie. His trumpet solos are fantastic and he sings with real style. He'd be a terrific addition to the band."

"You seem quite intent on talking yourself into hiring him, Philip. I must admit, I'm rather baffled, given his troubled past."

I sipped my Scotch, thoughtful for a moment. "I never told you this, Neetsie, never really talked about it with anyone. But I'm in debt to Buddy Bixby. I owe him."

"Owe him how, dear?"

"You remember how I fell apart back in '61, right after—you know, the incident involving Diana."

"Understandable, Philip. Diana was your wife. We all knew how incredibly close the two of you were. Her murder was nothing less than horrifying."

"After it happened, I was a complete wreck, barely functioning. There was no way I could perform, not for months. Even then, getting back into the swing was tough."

She placed a small, warm hand over mine. "I remember, dear, it was a dreadful time."

"We were scheduled to play an event at Boston University that weekend, then a big wedding the next day, not far from the campus. Gloria was in pretty bad shape herself, given the special feelings she had for Diana. She wasn't sure she could get through a single number, let alone find that sultry voice of hers. We both were devastated."

"And Buddy Bixby helped out in some way?"

I nodded, clouding up with old feelings I hadn't dealt with in a while, and didn't really want to. "He called my office, volunteered to sit in with the band. His name meant something, and his trumpet solos and vocals put back the luster that was gone, and then some. It was a tremendous favor, bailing me out the way he did."

"Maybe he needed the work, dear. You know, with the problems he was having."

"The thing is, Neetsie, he never would accept a paycheck for it. Not one dime." I shrugged haplessly. "That's the Buddy Bixby I know—a decent guy with a good heart. Not a hophead who's a suspect in a murder."

"I see." Neetsie raised her veil to sip at her gin and tonic and meet my eyes head on. "I suppose that changes things, doesn't it?"

"I think it does."

Her veil came back down. "I'm sorry I spoke so harshly of Mr. Bixby. It's just that I worry for you, Philip, and your generous nature." Behind the veil, I could make out the faint outlines of a pained smile. "Always have, always will." She squeezed my hand. "You're like a son to me, you know that."

Toots brought me a phone, and I called Gloria Velez, who'd told me she could probably find Buddy on short notice if necessary. When I reached her, she sounded like a frog at the other end, croaking back at me through her lousy cold. It was only 9 P.M. on the West Coast and she said she'd start making calls immediately. She sounded eager to get on it—almost too eager, I thought—but I was happy to put the matter into her hands.

WHEN I was off the phone, Joe E. Lewis joined us, coming in after his comedy gig at the Copa. A minute later, Toots had crammed his huge body into the booth as well, alongside his diminutive wife, Baby. A minute after that Joe

DiMaggio stopped to say hello on his way out. I congratulated him on his glorious home run off Bucky Walters the previous Saturday in an Old-Timers Game at Yankee Stadium. Joe decided to put off his departure and squeezed into the booth as well. There were more drinks and lots of laughter and some serious conversation as well, the way it always was at Toots's place. The growing mess in Vietnam, the Negro voting rights bill, a controversial new novel, *Midnight Cowboy*—we rambled through all manner of topics. Thankfully, murder was no longer among them.

Before long, I found myself stifling a yawn as the conversation turned to the memoir Anita was readying for publication. Neetsie was best known as the author of glossy Hollywood comedies—most notably *Gentlemen Prefer Blondes*—but her screenwriting days were well behind her. Her attention now was on her life story, *A Girl Like I,* due out in hardcover next year. Kitty Carlisle Hart, always sociable and curious, craned her head from the next booth, wanting to hear all about it. So did I—just not at that moment. Neetsie caught me trying to cover my yawn—I had a morning flight to catch—and immediately called for the check.

A minute or two later, six hundred pounds filled the entrance of Toots Shor's, unevenly distributed between Toots, Neetsie, and me. We must have been an odd-looking bunch as we stepped out onto West 51st Street: Anita Loos, seventy-two and barely five feet, hidden under hat and veil, despite the sultry air; me, not quite half her age, preppy in dress and looming over her at a lanky six-two; and rotund, red-faced Toots, his weight easily topping Neetsie and me put together.

"When you get to Hollywood," Toots bellowed, "tell our

pal Beatrice to start writing some good murder mysteries
again, will you?" Beatrice Gless—with whom I'd be lodg-
ing—was a crony of Anita's, at work on her own autobi-
ography after a career distinguished by several minor film
noir classics. "Tell her they don't make 'em like they used
to. *Detour, Laura, Out of the Past*. Tell her that's the kind of
stuff they need to start making again."

"I'll tell her, Toots."

We bid him good night, turning toward Sixth Avenue
to grab a taxi that would take us uptown. One of those
sporty new Mustangs that Ford had just introduced whizzed
by, a white convertible with red tuck-and-roll upholstery.
It was filled with teenagers and a raucous Beatles tune—"A
Hard Day's Night"—blasted from the speakers. I pretended
to cover my ears until it was out of earshot.

"This humidity," Anita said, slipping her arm through
mine. "Makes me miss Los Angeles, even if the smog out
there is repulsive."

The New York heat index had climbed to excruciating
levels, and I was looking forward to getting out of town
myself. More enticing than the Southern California climate,
though, was the engagement I'd be playing at the legendary
Cocoanut Grove, where my father, Archie Damon, had performed with his own orchestra in the thirties. Six weeks of
rest and relaxation—and a few exhilarating hours on the
bandstand each night—before a return to Manhattan and
the busy fall social season that always kept me hopping.

As Anita and I strolled along 51st Street, Toots hollered
after us. "Remember what I told you, kid. There are more
good-looking broads in Hollywood than there are stars in
heaven. Find yourself a honey and have a swell time."

I turned, waving. "Sure thing, Toots. See you in six
weeks."

*   *   *

"TOOTS is right, you know," Anita said as we approached Sixth Avenue arm in arm. "As long as you're spending half the summer in Lotus Land, you might as well avail yourself of the ladies. Spend some time around the pool at the Beverly Hills Hotel. Work on your tan and your libido."

"I haven't exactly been a hermit, Neetsie."

"No, but you're not really making yourself available, either. These are the best years of your life, Philip. Don't you want to share them with someone special? Diana would want that, dear. She'd never want you to be alone, for her sake."

I have to confess, I'd been preoccupied with similar thoughts. With Diana gone nearly four years, it was time for me to get out more, meet more people, start seriously dating again. I'd had a fling or two in the past couple of years, but I still felt tentative about taking the plunge. Diana's awful murder—even now that it was solved—still hung over my life like a dark cloud, at times keeping out the light.

"I'll keep my options open, Neetsie."

"Promise?"

"I promise."

We stepped aside as a herd of kids thundered past, posting placards along the way advertising the Beatles' upcoming arrival—to my mind, another good reason to flee the city. The British rock group had exploded on the American pop music scene the year before, and if I never again heard "I Want to Hold Your Hand" it would be too soon. I'd be thankful when this latest musical fad faded into memory, along with horror movies and fast-food joints.

"I think the Beatles are cute," Anita said, as if reading my mind, which she often did. "I find some of their more recent tunes rather appealing." Her voice grew playful. "Maybe it's time to update your play list, Philip. Standards and swing tunes are terrific for a certain kind of dancing. But one needs to change with the times, don't you think?"

I gave her a look that suggested I'd rather add "Purple People Eater" to my repertoire.

She sighed deeply. "If I've learned anything while writing this memoir, it's the importance of embracing all the possibilities, instead of fearing them and shrinking back." She lifted her veil and in the glow of the streetlights I suddenly realized how elderly Anita looked, how frail; she was into her seventies, after all, having outlasted the average American life span. "Dying is only tragic, Philip, when one's life has been half-lived."

"I promise, Neetsie—when I get to Hollywood, I'll get back in the swim."

She shook a bony finger at me. "Just beware of the sharks out there, baby. You know the old saying—in Hollywood, a friend is someone who stabs you in the front."

I laughed and raised my hand, hailing a cab.

BY 2 A.M., I was in my apartment high atop Carnegie Hall, across the roof from Bobby Short's place. I set the alarm for 6 A.M. and was about to slip between the silk sheets when the phone rang.

It was Gloria Velez, calling from her pad down in the Village. After numerous phone calls, she said, she'd found Buddy Bixby, who was thrilled at the chance to work again so soon after getting out of the joint. I thanked her, hung up, and switched off the light, exhausted. Before I hit the pillow, however, the phone rang again. This time it was Anita.

"I was thinking about this Buddy Bixby business, Philip."

"Don't worry, Neetsie. It's all taken care of. He's agreed to sit in with the band for as long as we need him."

"That's not what's troubling me, sweetheart. It's that dead man, out in California, who watched over the horses. What was his name?"

"Angel Vargas, I believe it was."

"Yes, Mr. Vargas."

"What about him, Neetsie?"

"Why would an impoverished Mexican who works at a racetrack have Buddy Bixby's name and phone number in his pocket? And then Mr. Vargas turns up dead, possibly by someone else's hand. It seems awfully curious, don't you think?"

"I suppose so, Neetsie. I'm sure that's why the police are looking into it." I covered the phone as a yawn escaped. "To be honest, though, all I'm thinking about right now is getting a few hours' sleep."

"Of course! I shouldn't have bothered you, not so late." She repeated the phrase she'd tucked me in with so many times when I was a toddler. "Sleep tight, and don't let the bed bugs bite."

She told me she loved me, I said the same, and we hung up. I switched off the lamp again and crawled gratefully into bed. But no matter how hard I tried, I couldn't get her troublesome question out of my mind. Why *would* a man like Angel Vargas be carrying Buddy Bixby's name and phone number in his pocket? Then another problematic question popped into my head: Was I making a serious mistake, giving Buddy a second chance like this—and at what risk?

I didn't close my eyes, not for a long time.

Chapter 2

B Y THE TIME we'd landed at Los Angeles International
Airport early Friday afternoon, the pilot had informed
us that Southern California was in the grip of its own
heat wave, with temperatures well into the nineties. But as
we deplaned for baggage claim, the heat I was feeling was
coming from my alto sax player, Hercules Platt, two years
retired from the San Francisco Police Department.

"Buddy Bixby may be out of the slammer," Platt said,
"but he's still got the monkey on his back. And now this
homicide investigation. Stinks, if you ask me."

"Whatever happened to innocent until proven guilty?"
Gloria Velez wedged in beside him, her voice as raspy as a
gap-toothed handsaw. Except for puffy eyes, she was as gorgeous as ever—a dark-haired beauty on the short side, with

an hourglass shape—but her pipes were worthless for singing, at least for now.

Platt fired back, without looking at her, "Whatever happened to hiring a couple of cats who work the Central Avenue clubs and could use a decent paycheck?"

I stepped between them, bringing the three of us to a halt. "We've gone over this already, Platt. Buddy can cover us on trumpet and vocals both, and he's got real promotional value. It's an ideal solution."

Displeasure formed on Platt's dark face. "Seems like a recipe for disaster to me." Platt was a recovering alcoholic as well as an ex-cop—the first Negro to rise to the rank of Inspector in San Francisco, where he'd briefly worked the homicide beat before retiring to join my band. Hard on others, tougher on himself, he had little tolerance for drunks and drug addicts, especially up on the bandstand, as he attempted a second career with music in midlife. It had caused some friction within the orchestra, where alcohol and marijuana were the lubricants of choice. I'd done my best to get Platt to ease up, reminding him that most musicians march to their own beat, and need some leash. He figured that was OK for certain jazz joints, especially after hours, when the rules loosened up. But not for the fancy engagements the Philip Damon Orchestra performed.

"I jammed with Buddy Bixby a few times in the old days." Platt's manner was hard, his speech terse. "Buddy Bixby has a way of attracting trouble."

"I think he deserves a chance." Gloria thrust her chin out, her eyes falling directly on Platt. "It's not like the rest of us haven't had our share of problems."

Platt asked her bluntly if she and Bixby were close. Her eyes faltered a little. "Not exactly," she said. "I met him

years ago, not long after my divorce. From what I understand, he's a low-level user, able to keep his habit under
control."

"A chipper." Platt spat the word out. "I don't begrudge
the man the opportunity to straighten out his life. I just
don't want to associate with hopheads, that's all."

"I'd like you to room with him, Hercules."

Platt looked at me like I'd lost my mind. "You *what?*"

"I called ahead from New York, booked the two of you
into a double. You can keep an eye on him."

"Oh, man."

"The first hint of a problem, he's gone. Sound like a fix?"

Platt shoved his hat on his head, picked up his instru-
ment case and bags. "Funny choice of words," he grumbled.
Without further conversation, he showed us the back of his
plain brown suit, heading out to our hotel limousines.

BY noon, the band members had checked into their air-
conditioned rooms at the Ambassador, happy to get out of
L.A.'s searing heat and suffocating smog. Gloria was immediately on the phone, searching again for Buddy Bixby.
By midafternoon, Buddy and I were connected, working out
the terms of his temporary employment with my orchestra,
which would include a room at the Ambassador.

"I'm really grateful for the opportunity you're giving me,
Mr. Damon." Buddy's voice was soft, pliant, almost child-
like. It was strange hearing a man roughly my own age
address me as mister. "You'll see, Mr. Damon, I won't let
you down."

"You did me a big favor a few years back, Buddy. I'm
grateful." There was silence at the other end of the line. "You
OK, Buddy?"

"Sure, Mr. Damon." I thought I heard a sniffle. "I guess I wasn't expecting something this good to happen so soon."

"You have a tuxedo, Buddy?"

He told me he'd never worn one, not even to his own high school prom, since he'd dropped out of school at sixteen to play his horn in clubs where a tux was considered square. I asked him to meet me for a fitting at Sy Devore's, over in Hollywood, at 3 P.M. sharp.

Chapter 3

S Y DEVORE KEPT his main tailor shop on Vine Street, just off Sunset Boulevard around the corner from the Brown Derby. I arrived a few minutes before three in a Chrysler town car provided by the hotel, parking at the curb and slipping a dime into the meter, which bought me an hour. Sy greeted me at the door, clasping me on each arm with a grin that stretched widely between his big ears.

"So Archie Damon's boy finally comes around for a visit."

Sy was a smallish man in his midfifties, with a receding hairline and warm brown eyes, and impeccably tailored, as always. Born Seymour Devoretsky in Brooklyn, he'd opened a shop in the New York theater district in the '30s, where Dad had been among his many patrons from the music business. Now he was firmly established in Hollywood, where his flashy red matchbooks promoted him in gold lettering as the "Tailor to the Stars," which was no exaggeration. He'd dressed not only the famous Rat Pack—Frank Sinatra and his showbiz pals—but a whole galaxy of celebrities: Milton Berle, Bing Crosby, Nat King Cole, Jerry Lewis, John Wayne—the list went on and on. Even John F. Kennedy had purchased Sy's clothes, and Elvis Presley was known to drop in and scoop as many as fifteen suits off the rack at once. But it was Sy's hand-tailoring that made his reputation—fine fabrics, immaculate detailing, perfect fits. Sinatra, who liked his lapels 2¼ inches wide, had told me once that Sy never missed, not by a fraction of an inch.

"Oy vey!" Sy stepped back, taking in my fading blue seersucker jacket and wrinkled chinos. "A handsome boy like this, dressed like a bum. Come in, come in! We'll get you into something decent."

I explained that I was there to outfit a new band member for our engagement at the Grove, with something off-the-rack and affordable. Sy frowned and led me past racks filled with the hip threads the Rat Pack had made so fashionable—sharkskin suits, fancy dress shirts, skinny ties. We entered a second room that housed more formal wear, where Sy showed me ready-made tuxedos priced in the seventy-dollar range.

"This should do," I said. "I don't expect him to be with the band for more than a week, when I get my regular trumpet player and vocalist back."

Sy looked around. Across the room, Desi Arnaz was picking out cummerbunds in various colors, but otherwise, we were alone.

"So where is this fellow you speak of?"

I glanced at my Bulova, frowning. "Late, I'm afraid."

Sy had his tape measure out in a flash, turning me toward

a full-length mirror. "So we use the time to dress you the way Archie Damon's boy should be dressed."

"Times change, Sy, along with styles."

"That doesn't mean you have to look"—he surveyed my attire, wrinkling his nose—"like *this.*"

Suddenly, in the mirror, I glimpsed a gaunt figure hovering behind us, eyes slightly lowered, as if in supplication.

"Mr. Damon?"

Buddy Bixby's smile was pained, but hopeful. He gripped a well-traveled suitcase with a skeletal hand, a pale ghost of the vibrant young man he'd once been. His narrow, clean-shaven face retained the boyishness that had caused the girls to swoon when he'd first made the scene. But now there was a pallid and wasted look about him, the visage of a man who'd lived too hard too fast.

I glanced at my watch. "Running late, Buddy?"

"Sorry, Mr. Damon. I don't have wheels yet." He hung his head, looking up at me with soft blue eyes under tousled, dark blond hair. "My sister's been getting me around since I got out, but she's teaching school today. I took a taxi."

He set his suitcase down, letting the information hang there awkwardly. I asked him if he needed cash for the driver.

"I guess I do."

I gave him a five spot, watched him hurry out, then followed discreetly to the window, where I saw him stuff the bill into his pocket and kill half a minute for cover. I turned back inside, figuring he'd hopped the bus or walked over from some fleabag hotel in one of the surrounding neighborhoods that were quickly going seedy. It was a small thing, a quick lie to net a few bucks, particularly for an addict. But I needed to trust Buddy, and it rubbed me wrong just the same.

*   *   *

SY spent the next few minutes fitting Buddy in a tux and measuring me for a sport coat, slacks, and shirts that Sy promised to personally tailor by hand. Bob Hope had once joked that in a good year, he had a choice between a Rolls-Royce, a new house in Beverly Hills, or a suit from Sy Devore. When I saw the tab, I got the joke: jacket, $200; slacks, $85; shirts, $25 each. At least the prices were a good incentive not to put on too much weight.

Buddy's pants required taking in so I told Sy we'd need the tux the next morning, for a private party we'd be playing in Bel-Air in the afternoon.

Sy raised his thick brows. "Sid Zell's anniversary bash?"

"That's the one."

"Sid was by earlier in the week, picking up a new suit for the occasion. This party is very important to him."

I grinned. "I guess that's why he hired us. Wants the best." Then: "So, can you do it?"

"Not to worry, Phillie. We'll have Mr. Bixby's pants ready by noon."

Sy excused himself for a moment. When he was gone, Buddy glanced at me, his eyes shifty. "We're playing for Mr. Zell, the big movie guy?"

I nodded. "Is that a problem?"

Buddy shrugged unconvincingly. "Not really."

"You know Zell?"

"I was in one of his movies, a few years ago." Buddy laughed awkwardly. "He told me I was going to be the new James Dean, got me to do the flick for almost nothing."

"I guess that's what producers do—squeeze a dollar for all it's worth."

"Yeah, I guess so." Buddy smiled but his voice had a bitter edge. "Producers—they're all rich but they're always telling you how they don't got enough cabbage to fork over some decent green."

"For what it's worth," I said, "Zell's paying top dollar tomorrow. It's the only way I work. You'll be drawing a nice paycheck."

"Groovy." Buddy's smile brightened. "Very groovy."

A minute later, as we made our exit, Sy held me back, letting Buddy go ahead and speaking low. "This boy, he could be a problem, Phil."

"You look worried, Sy."

"I hate to meddle. It's just that—"

"What, Sy?"

His troubled glance followed Buddy out the front door. "The boy's got needle tracks on his arms. I saw them when I was measuring for the sleeve."

"He's got a history with drugs. I'm gambling he'll stay clean."

Sy raised his thick eyebrows. "A history, you say? *Oy vey.* Some of those marks looked fresh."

I glanced at Buddy out on the sidewalk. "Damn. He's already using again."

Sy shrugged. "I don't want to make trouble for the boy."

I laid a hand on Sy's shoulder, offered him a weak smile. "It's better that I know now, instead of later. Thanks for the nice threads, Sy. I'll let people know where they came from."

Sy slipped a few of his bright red business cards into my pocket, and turned away to tend to Desi Arnaz.

I stepped out into the heat, trying to calculate how many chances you give a heroin addict while weighing the odds against Buddy's value to the band. Maybe Platt had been right; maybe I'd made a mistake, trusting Buddy the way I had. Still, the man had helped me out when he didn't have to, purely from his heart. I couldn't overlook that, and what it had meant to me at the darkest time of my life.

The two of us climbed into the Chrysler from opposite sides, rolling up the windows while I switched on the ignition and the air conditioner, and silently bemoaned the city's rapid decline. Through the end of the Depression, around the time I was born, Los Angeles had been the largest agricultural county in the United States, a paradise of orange groves, clean air, and broad, uncluttered vistas opening up to mountains, desert, and seashore. In the decades since, it had been transformed into a mass of asphalt and concrete, with urban sprawl that looked unstoppable. At the moment, smog shrouded the city in a sulfurous yellow haze; my eyes stung and my lungs ached each time I drew a breath. I twisted the wheel of the Chrysler and pulled into the thick of traffic, surprised by how edgy and irritable I was feeling.

"I'm counting on you to stay straight, Buddy. We'll be playing at the Cocoanut Grove, after all."

"Sure thing, Mr. Damon."

"I expect you to show up on time, in shape to read your music and hit the right notes." I glanced over, trying to find his eyes. "Two shows a night, with Mondays dark, until my regular trumpet player rejoins us and Gloria Velez gets her voice back. Then you're on your own."

"I understand, Mr. Damon."

"By the way, I'm doing this as a favor to Gloria."

"Gloria's a cool chick."

I told him he'd be sharing a room with our alto sax player, Hercules Platt, an ex-cop who didn't put up with any monkey business. Buddy's eyes gave him away for a moment, before he slipped back into his groove.

"Cool, man. No problem. I can dig it."

"One more thing, Buddy, if you don't mind."

"What's that, Mr. Damon?"

"What's the skinny on Angel Vargas?"

Again, the hesitation, the nervous eyes. "You know about that?"

"I know that he was killed, and that your name and phone number were on a slip of paper found in his pocket."

"It was my sister's number, actually. I don't have a place of my own yet. I've been staying here and there, with pals."

"So how did you happen to know the dead man?"

"I went out to the track, Rosewood Gardens. Looking for a guy, that's all."

"Your friend works around the stables?"

Buddy nodded. "He was off that day, so I left my name and number with Mr. Vargas. Asked him to pass it along to my pal."

"That's all there is to it?"

"That's all, Mr. Damon, I swear. The cops already talked to me. It was just one of those things."

"Just one of those things."

He nodded again, eagerly, like a kid who's trying to get off the hook.

I smiled a little. "Sounds like a good song title."

He laughed and sat back, relaxing with his hands behind his head. I switched on the radio, heard the Beatles warbling "Help!" and immediately switched it off again. Buddy closed his eyes and began humming "Time after Time," as if all the problems in the world had vanished, as if everything was very, very cool.

"You can sing it, Buddy, if you want."

As I drove south, back toward the Ambassador, Buddy sang a few of his favorite ballads a capella—"This Is Always," "Sweet Lorraine," "Someone to Watch over Me." On a sentimental whim, I cut through the stately neighborhood of Hancock Park, where the impeccable Nat King Cole had moved his family into an elegant home in 1947, only to have white neighbors burn the word "nigger" on the front lawn. Nat had died the past February and when I passed his former house on Muirfield Road, I slowed to give the place a small salute.

Without being asked, Buddy Bixby started singing "Unforgettable", causing me to get a lump in my throat. For all his flaws and foibles, it was hard not to like the guy.

Chapter 4

B Y LATE AFTERNOON, Buddy Bixby was registered at
the Ambassador's front desk, and I finally had a moment to myself. I decided to stretch my legs with a
stroll around the grounds, taking in the fountains and the
gardens I'd sometimes visited as a child with Anita Loos.
Dozens of guests splashed in the big pool where Buster
Crabbe had once trained for the Olympics or stretched
nearby on chaise lounges, lathered with cocoa butter, turning over from time to time like basted turkeys rotating in
the broiler.

As I came around the south side, I found Hercules Platt
standing alone out front near the circular drive, studying
the Ambassador's extravagant Art Deco entrance while shadows from the tall palms slanted across the broad lawns. Platt
was pushing fifty, a broad-shouldered, rugged-looking fel-

low of medium height with a thick, trim mustache under a blunt nose and thoughtful brown eyes that turned hard as stone when anger was eating away inside him. Even with police work two years behind him, worry lines creased his dark face. He'd stopped straightening and pomading his hair since I'd first met him; he wore it now short-cropped and natural, as so many blacks were beginning to do, but he still used Pink's Luster for extra shine.

"Nice place," he said as I came up, with his customary deadpan delivery. "Though I don't imagine I'll spend too much time working on my tan."

"At least the band gets to stay in the same hotel," I said. "That's progress, I guess."

Platt was the first Negro in my orchestra, which had caused me to reexamine my conscience, along with some of my business practices. I'd started turning down bookings in fancy hotels that had "no colored" policies, not all of which were in the South—the kind that were only too happy to have talented Negroes perform for them, as long as they slept in the "colored" part of town.

"How's your room, Hercules? You OK with it?"

"Better than I'm used to, that's for sure." His eyes took in the palatial, five-hundred-room hotel, which sat on twenty-four acres that had been bean and barley fields when Wilshire Boulevard was just a dirt road. "I imagine this place has some history."

I offered him what little I knew, gleaned over the years from Neetsie: The Ambassador had opened amid much fanfare in 1921, dazzling visitors with its Mediterranean styling, Italian stone fireplaces, and lush garden courtyards. Longtime residents had included Howard Hughes, John Barrymore, Gloria Swanson, F. Scott and Zelda Fitzgerald—who'd run out on their bill—and Jean Harlow, who'd held her wedding reception here. The modeling agency handling a young Marilyn Monroe had kept offices off the lobby. Every President from Herbert Hoover forward had stayed at the Ambassador.

"Nixon broadcast his Checkers speech from here," Platt said.

"How did you know that?"

"I watched it on TV, like most people." Platt shook his head, as if bewildered. "Man almost beat Kennedy. Go figure."

"Some people think he'll make a comeback."

"Nixon?" Platt shook his head. "I don't see that happening. Way that man sweats for no reason, you just know there's something not right about him."

I laughed. "That's the cop in you, Platt—looking for clues to the guilty mind."

Platt didn't even smile. "That's the black man in me, looking into a white man's eyes." Then, with a glance: "Don't mind me, Damon. It's this business with Dr. King that's still going on. The marches, Selma, Bull Conner and his police dogs, all of it. I got history on my mind these days. Stirs a man up some."

"You have family in L.A., Hercules?"

Platt tilted his head southward. "Two brothers, a couple of cousins, scattered here and there. My daughter, Bertha, has a wig salon over in the Crenshaw district. Doing pretty well." His eyes lifted skyward and he seemed to cock his ears, while furrowing his forehead. "Mighty damn hot here in L.A. Let's hope it doesn't last."

"At least it's not the humid kind."

Platt loosened his tie, unbuttoned his collar. "Works at a man, just the same."

"By the way, Buddy's up in your room, unpacking."

Platt's eyes and ears remained fixed, like finely tuned antennae sensing something in the crackling air that was beyond my radar.

Finally, he said evenly, "I'll go up and re-introduce myself to the gentleman, see if there's anything he needs."

JUST before sundown I drove up to Beatrice Gless's house in Laurel Canyon, a deep ravine bisecting the Hollywood Hills just north of Sunset Boulevard. I made a left off Laurel Canyon just before the old ranch house Tom Mix had once owned, winding my way up woodsy Lookout Mountain Avenue until I found the number I was searching for.

Beatrice greeted me at the door, filling most of it. She was a tall woman of considerable heft, formidable in appearance, with an informed intelligence that could sometimes be intimidating. But behind her imposing manner was a warm and affectionate *bubee,* the kind of large, busty woman with wide hips and jiggling arms that knew how to give an old friend a proper hug. Her hair had gone from gray to white since I'd last seen her but her hazel eyes were just as keen and lively. As usual, she wore a long caftan, boldly patterned and colored, which draped her like a tent.

"A sight for sore eyes," she said, standing back after the embrace to look me over. "Get your tush in here, tell me all about yourself. Dewars on the rocks?"

"You said the magic words."

Widowed for nearly a decade, her children grown and dispersed, Beatrice lived with half a dozen cats, a number that increased from time to time as she took in another stray. Several were curled up as we carried our drinks out to the veranda, where we settled into heavily padded rattan chairs. She asked me about New York, people we both knew, and my orchestra business, and I filled her in. When she inquired about my love life, I told her there was none at the moment.

"I guess that means I've got you all to myself." She reached over, placed her mottled hand over mine, gave it a squeeze. "Which is perfectly OK with me."

Beatrice was a fine writer—she'd published several novels and a stage play, to good notices but little money; but her knack, she'd always said, was as a visual storyteller, someone with a unique talent for crafting tales for the big screen. Now, like Anita Loos, she was writing her memoirs, her summing-up, her final statement to the world of who she was.

"It's my last chance," she said. "As a screenwriter, one's vision never reaches the audience intact. It's always altered, compromised, interpreted in some way. Nice way to earn a living, if you're good at it, but hardly a satisfying medium for self-expression."

"You've never seemed shy about expressing yourself," I said. She laughed richly, and I grinned. "I've missed you, Bea. It's good to see you again."

"Six weeks you're here?" Her eyes sparkled. "Time enough to raise some mischief, I'd think."

I marveled aloud at the sense of quiet, and how different it was from the blaring horns and rumble of the subway in Manhattan. Beatrice sipped her martini—gin, never vodka—and I nursed my Scotch, while the tranquil atmosphere settled over us like balm. The air seemed dusted with gold as the fading light filtered through the eucalyptus trees—that special light that had drawn painters here some two centuries ago, when Los Angeles was a Spanish-speaking pueblo. To me, New York was home, the greatest city in the world, with enough art, culture, and commerce for a thousand cities. Yet each time I returned to Los Angeles, it felt right in its own way. New York swept you up, grabbed you and pushed you along, with something always happening; Southern California enveloped you like a warm, protective cocoon, inviting you to slow down, take a breather. I sank deeper into the cushions, listening to the wind stir the brittle leaves as it whispered down the canyon, feeling soothed by the L.A. calm, wrapped in its peculiar bliss.

Everything felt in order now, with the orchestra complete again and Buddy Bixby firmly fixed in position, under the watchful eye of dependable Hercules Platt. I'd been a fool, I thought, to become agitated over problems so easily remedied. I was in Hollywood, after all, the land of celluloid dreams, an industry town where the product was make-believe. Nothing exciting ever happens here, I told myself as I sipped my drink and stretched my legs. Just the illusion.

Chapter 5

SID ZELL LIVED in a nineteen-room mansion high up in Bel-Air, a leafy enclave of the extremely wealthy that looked down on Beverly Hills.

Zell was one of Hollywood's historic figures, a crony of Sam Goldwyn and Harry Cohn, if not nearly of their stature. At times bombastic, abrasive, and charming, he'd been the majority owner and head of production at Premiere Alliance Pictures as long as anyone could remember. I'd first met him back in '52, my final year at Yale, when Premiere Alliance was releasing *The Archie Damon Story,* with Montgomery Clift playing my father in the title role. Not surprisingly, the writers had taken enormous liberties with the truth; perhaps half the story, if that, was based on fact. But my main complaint had been the film's lack of profit— at least what showed up on the books—since I'd been a financial participant through Dad's estate. Somehow, the agents and lawyers had ended up making more money out of the deal than I had.

Now I was back doing business with Sid Zell again. Through my manager, Zell had arranged for me to play at his fortieth anniversary party with a small combo culled from my ten-piece orchestra. He'd wanted us for three hours in the afternoon, which would give us just enough time to get back to the Ambassador and ready for our opening at the Grove. When he'd hired me, Zell had made only one special request: that we play "Begin the Beguine," since it was his wife's favorite number and he wanted her to be happy on their ruby anniversary, above all else.

WE drove up after lunch in two vehicles—my big town car and a Ford Econo-Van—feasting our eyes on the most rarified real estate in Los Angeles: homes like small palaces, lavish gardens, tennis courts, swimming pools, sweeping driveways where Rollses, Bentleys, and Mercedeses were the vehicles of choice. Only one commercial enterprise was allowed inside Bel-Air's four gates: the prestigious Bel-Air Hotel, with its quaint footbridges, floating swans, and five-star cuisine. Up here, one never heard a siren or a horn or the wail of a child. Even the gardeners tending to the lush greenery worked quietly and were often the only human beings one glimpsed from the road.

By two o'clock, we were setting up on Zell's greystone patio in the shade of a spreading olive tree. Beyond the pool, lawn, and terraced gardens stretched a hazy view from downtown Los Angeles to Catalina Island. Tents and awnings had been erected for extra cover, waiters moved among the early arrivals with trays of canapés and champagne, and a violinist strolled the grounds, filling in until we were ready to shift the party into high gear. There were five of us in all, turned out in black tuxedos with white carnations: me, on a rented Baldwin piano; Hercules Platt on alto sax; Buddy Bixby on trumpet and vocals; and a bass player and drummer comprising the rhythm section. On his own, Buddy took a position toward the back, next to the drummer, where he was in the deepest shade and least conspicuous.

Sid Zell came around with a crystal flute of champagne in one hand and a fat cigar in the other. He was a short, trim man—no more than five-five—with jug ears and a prominent nose and taut, tanned skin that belied his sixty-nine years. He talked fast, waving the big cigar for emphasis; his remarkable energy and coiled body put to mind a bull terrier.

When I mentioned that my manager—now away on vacation—had never received the signed contract back, Zell shrugged it off as an oversight, maybe a postal problem.

"We worry about such things later. Today is for celebration." With his champagne flute, he gestured toward the party, where well-dressed guests arrived in bunches. "Such good friends, such beautiful people. I tell you, I'm *kvelling!*"

He brought his three children over to meet me—two daughters and a son, all married, with kids of their own—then introduced me to his wife, Esther. She was a plump little woman with a bobbed nose and not much chin, and kind, patient eyes that suggested the wisdom and endurance of an indispensable wife and mother.

"The love of my life," Zell said, slipping his arm around her soft, pale shoulders. "Me, I'm a *macher,* or so they tell me. But I'm lost without this woman. Take away his family and Sid Zell is nothing, you hear what I'm saying? Nothing!"

"And you'll be nothing," his wife chided, "if you don't start following doctor's orders." She removed the cigar and champagne flute from his stubby fingers, leaving him to savor a kiss instead.

"Bum ticker," Zell confessed, looking sheepish. "My big shot doctors tell me no rich food, no alcohol, no tobacco. *Meshugge,* craziness! What do they know about living?"

He suddenly grew silent, his eyes falling on Buddy Bixby toward the back of the group, as if the sight of Bixby had paralyzed him for a moment.

"Hello, Mr. Zell." Buddy smiled, his gaze placid, maybe druggy.

Zell's eyes came around in my direction; the line of his mouth was grim. "This fellow, this Buddy Bixby, he works for you?"

"Temporarily, in place of my regular trumpet player and vocalist."

"I see." Zell glanced again at Bixby, very briefly. Then, sharply: "So play your music, Damon. That's what I'm paying you for, yes?"

Zell's eyes went uneasily to Buddy Bixby a final time. Then, with a tight smile, he left us, herding his family away with him.

An hour later, the party was in full swing, with champagne flowing and dozens of couples dancing in a pleasant breeze that helped dissipate the heat and smog.

Beatrice Gless, who'd been a contract writer for Sid Zell spanning three decades, was out on the patio twirling with

Rabbi Kaminsky, a husky, bespectacled widower with a luxuriant beard and a black yarmulke perched atop his large
head. Irving "Swifty" Lazar, the famous literary agent, was
also on hand, a diminutive man with a bald pate and owlish,
horn-rimmed glasses, on the arm of his devoted wife, Mary;
both were longtime friends of mine, through my relationship with Anita Loos. Other luminaries were all around us,
some of whom I'd met: Tony Curtis, Esther Williams, San-
dra Dee, Nancy Kwan, Vincent Price, Victor Mature, Angie
Dickinson, Tab Hunter—dozens of stars, a few A-list but
mostly B, some on their way up, others on their way out,
but every one of them basking in that heady aura of Hollywood celebrity, no matter how transitory.

I was having a grand time at the piano, pounding out
"Ain't Misbehavin' "—Fats Waller style, stride tenths in the
left hand—when my eyes strayed across the pool and settled
abruptly on the most beautiful woman I'd ever seen.

In that same moment, her eyes came around toward mine
and made an equally sudden landing.

"MONICA Rivers," Swifty told me when the band took a
break and Mary left him to chat with friends. "Quite a piece,
isn't she? I saw how you were checking her out."

"Is it just my imagination, or have I seen her somewhere?"

"Actress—a couple of dozen movies, mostly B stuff. Under contract to Sid Zell, but ready for the big time. She just
needs the right projects and handling."

I watched Monica Rivers glide around the pool in our
direction, her eyes averted but only slightly: a willowy bru-
nette, leggy and stacked, with a flawless face that brought
Ava Gardner to mind. Because of the confident way she

carried herself, I put her age well into the thirties, though she might have been younger.

"She's stunning. There's no other word for it."

Swifty laughed. "Gives your blood pressure a rise, does she?"

"More than just my blood pressure."

"How about I introduce the two of you?"

"You know her?"

"Phil, sweetheart—is there a pretty lady in this town I don't know?"

"Sorry, Swifty. Stupid question. So fill me in."

"Monica's the last contract player at Premiere Alliance Pictures. As everybody knows, the studio system's been crumbling for years—stars have the power now. Monica owes Zell two more movies, then she's on her own. I'm helping steer her toward the right management. Sid isn't too happy about that. Like a lot of the studios these days, Premiere Alliance isn't in the best of shape. He'd like to hang on to her, if he could."

"He's not so unhappy with you that he kept you off his invitation list."

Swifty grinned. "Nobody keeps me off their invitation list, Phil—I'm the one who keeps them off mine."

He raised a hand, beckoning to Monica Rivers. I felt my knees weaken and my throat go dry—not my customary reaction as I prepared to meet a woman, not even one who qualified as drop-dead gorgeous. When Swifty introduced us, her wide, dark eyes were direct, lively, and—if I read them right—just a bit flirtatious.

"You obviously love to play music, Mr. Damon." Her voice was sultry, her manner playful. "I admire a man who performs with passion."

"What would be the point otherwise?"

She glanced at my hands. "I love watching your fingers—so nimble and sensitive, the way they caress the keys. Perhaps you'll give me a private lesson sometime."

"You'd like to study piano?"

"Not really."

The tip of her tongue appeared briefly, moistening her upper lip. I felt myself swallow with difficulty, feeling like a fuzzy-faced kid on his first date with a girl who might let him get to first base. I stammered something awkward and predictable—"There's always room on the piano bench for two"—and she laughed lightly in a way that wasn't cruel at all, letting me off the hook.

After that, Swifty was filling me in on Monica's career, while I tried to hear his words through the daze I was in. I remember him saying that she had a movie coming out shortly—*Dead Aim,* a remake of a '40s film noir classic that Beatrice had written. It was Premiere Alliance's most ambitious project to date, Swifty said, budgeted at more than a million dollars, counting marketing costs. In Swifty's view, Monica was overdue for major stardom and he said so, while she kept her mischievous eyes on me the whole time, as if all the praise was kind but a little silly.

"Doesn't all this movie talk bore you, Mr. Damon? Promotion costs, box-office figures, all that nonsense."

"I'll admit, there are other subjects I find more interesting."

"Maybe we should explore them sometime." She leaned down, smiling, and kissed Swifty on his bald pate. "When we're alone, without Swifty hovering about."

We joined a cake-cutting ceremony, during which numerous toasts were made and Sid Zell reaffirmed his love and loyalty to Esther, his wife of four decades. He made a great show of slipping a dazzling necklace of blue diamonds around her pale neck, a purchase that must have made a jeweler very happy down on Rodeo Drive. "Remember what Ken Murray said about Rodeo Drive," Beatrice whispered, from our position at the back of the crowd. "It's a place where you spend more than you make on things you don't need to impress people you don't like."

"Zell certainly seems devoted to his wife," I said.

Beatrice stared straight ahead, saying nothing further.

With the toasts finished and the cake sliced, it was time to rejoin the band and get the couples dancing again. I blurted out an invitation to Monica Rivers for our opening that night at the Grove, telling her I'd leave a comp for her at the door if she could make it. After taking my seat at the piano and cueing the band, I launched into a Dixieland version of "Down by the Riverside," hoping that Monica Rivers would get the point.

Never had I played with more passion.

BUDDY Bixby performed like a pro, following his sheet music without missing a note and delivering his vocals flawlessly. That is, until the unexpected arrival of Little Nicky Pembrook.

Pembrook—I didn't recognize him at first—pushed his way into the party like an intruder, looking sleepy-eyed and unkempt, as if he'd just crawled out of bed. The band was in the middle of a lush rendition of "Moon River"—with several dozen couples waltzing languidly in the tepid shade—when Bixby stopped playing for a few bars. I glanced back to find him staring at Pembrook like he'd just seen an apparition. Hercules Platt noticed it as well, and we exchanged a concerned look as we kept playing.

Then Pembrook was gone, toward the cabanas on the

north side of the pool. Bixby picked up the beat, still sounding distracted. As we finished the song, I called for the band to take a break.

"You OK, Buddy?"

"Heat's getting to me, I guess." He looked a bit shaky, with nervous eyes; perspiration beaded his forehead and upper lip.

"Better get something cold to drink."

"Sure, I'll do that, Mr. Damon."

I went looking for Monica Rivers but ran into Beatrice Gless and Rabbi Kaminsky instead. Beatrice asked me if I'd recognized the young man who'd made such a commotion minutes earlier, on his way in. When she spoke his name—Little Nicky Pembrook—I remembered it instantly. Pembrook had been a child star in the '50s—pint-sized, jug-eared, bulbous-nosed, and adorable. Now he was a pale, pimply faced young man who wouldn't be out of place bagging groceries or pumping gas. He hadn't grown much—he stood five-six, tops—with the same prominent ears and nose and a slight, sinewy build. Not necessarily unattractive, just ordinary and not very adorable anymore.

"From what I hear," Beatrice said, "the poor kid hasn't worked in years, at least not in the business."

"I've seen him out at the racetrack," said the rabbi, a reform Jew with a bounce in his step and twinkle in his eye, who brought to mind Tevye in *Fiddler on the Roof*. "Rosewood Gardens, grooming and exercising horses, where I bump into Sid now and then." Rabbi Kaminsky laughed, sounding embarrassed. "I'm always at the two-dollar window—that's my limit. I'm not a high-roller like Sid."

"Sid got him the job?" Beatrice asked.

The rabbi nodded. "With all the money Sid's lost playing the horses over the years, I guess they feel they owe him. At least the boy's gainfully employed, doing something he enjoys. As I recall, he loved horses as a lad. Made quite a few westerns, doing his own riding." He rubbed his sizable behind. "I tried it myself a few times, but my *tush* never found a saddle with the right personality."

"Still," Beatrice said, "it's got to be a difficult transition for the boy. Child stars become famous because the camera loves their natural quality, not because they're consummate actors. Once they hit adolescence, they're suddenly not so cute anymore. Shirley Temple, Bobby Driscoll, the entire cast of *Our Gang*. Seen their names on a marquee lately?" She sighed, shaking her head. "For every kid actor who still has a career after the age of fifteen, I'll show you fifty standing in the unemployment line or stretched out on a psychiatrist's couch."

"Sid seems to be looking after Nicky," Rabbi Kaminsky said. "At least he's got him the job at the track."

Beatrice clucked. "I suppose Sid feels a certain debt toward the boy, now that Hollywood's finished with him and he's saddled with a drug habit."

"I didn't know the lad was on drugs," the rabbi said with a sudden frown.

Beatrice grimaced. "I shouldn't be gossiping—unforgivable. Please, both of you, forget you heard that. I despise gossips, and here I am, doing it myself."

Our attention turned to a nubile blonde, dressed in leather sandals and casual wear, looking apologetic as she approached.

"Excuse me, but I'm looking for Nicky Pembrook. Have you seen him?"

Beatrice told her Nicky had passed through a few

minutes earlier, heading toward the cabana and the north wing of the house. She started off, then stopped, looking sorry again.

"Forgive me—I'm Vicki Hart, Nicky's girlfriend. I'm worried about him, that's all. I hope he hasn't caused a scene."

"A minor disruption." Beatrice beamed a comforting smile. "Nothing so terrible, really. The party's been quite enjoyable."

When Vicki Hart was gone, I paved my own exit. "If you'll excuse me, there's also someone *I'd* like to find."

"A quick request?" Rabbi Kaminsky spread his palms wide. " 'Puttin' on the Ritz'—Beatrice and I plan to show off our Fred and Ginger act."

When he slipped a big hand around her broad waist, I suddenly realized they were a couple. I couldn't have been more pleased.

I grinned. "And what if I play the Black Bottom?"

The rabbi winked. "We were hoping you would."

Beatrice gave him a peck on the cheek while I went in search of Monica Rivers.

I bumped into any number of attractive women along my route, the kind whose photogenic faces on glossy eight-by-tens fill thousands of casting office files, but Monica was not one of them. As I rounded the southeast corner of the big house, continuing my search, I found myself drawn by familiar voices coming from a small patio camouflaged from the rest of the grounds by a six-foot hedge.

As I peered over, I saw Vicki Hart speaking earnestly with Sid Zell, who took the opportunity to hold her hand and stroke her bare arm. After a moment, she gently removed his hand, but it soon found its way to her bubble-shaped behind, where it lingered until she removed it again. She couldn't have been more than eighteen, I thought, which put roughly fifty years between them and told me something about Sid Zell's sexual predilections—affirmations to his dear wife Esther notwithstanding. His hand was beginning to stray again when Nicky Pembrook appeared through open French doors behind them, coming down the tiled steps. Zell quickly withdrew his hand, stepping back to put an extra foot or two between him and the young woman. A flurry of angry words followed, as the two men argued over Pembrook's demands for money.

A moment later, Monica Rivers appeared in the doorway, beseeching them to stop. Zell barked at her to go call someone named Johnny Langley. "Have him come get the kid!" She disappeared back inside. Zell turned back to Pembrook. "I told you never to come up here! You stay away from my home, you hear?"

"Or what?" Pembrook said, sounding like a petulant child.

Zell raised a finger an inch from the boy's nose. "I'm warning you, Nicky. You don't come near my family again. You got business with me, you come see me at the studio."

Vicki Hart grabbed Pembrook by the hand, begging him to come away with her. He wasn't budging. "At least let me have the gun," she pleaded.

Zell threw up his hands. "He's got a gun now? He's going to do what, shoot me?"

"You gave it to him, Mr. Zell." Vicki Hart was nearly in tears. "For protection, years ago. That's what Nicky told me."

"Oh, that. I don't give a rat's fart about that *cockamamie* gun."

Nicky Prembrook pulled away from his girlfriend, going nose to nose with Zell. "I want what I'm owed! Or I swear I'm going to make trouble!"

"You already made trouble, you little *schlemiel*. You come into the sanctity of my home with this *mishegoss?* On today, of all days? I should rip your heart from your chest, you little punk, for insulting Sid Zell like this."

"Nicky, please!" Vicki was wailing, her hands pressing her blonde head as if to keep it from exploding.

Monica Rivers reappeared, hurrying down the steps. She wedged herself between Zell and Pembrook, shoving a wad of cash into the younger man's hands.

"Take it, Nicky, and go!" Her eyes, wide and dark like his, flashed with equal fury. "This isn't the time or place!"

"You've got your money, Nicky, come on." Vicki pulled at him again. As he came around, I saw the handgun tucked in his waistband. She pulled his shirt down to cover it and dragged him away, out a gate at the patio's west side, but not before he'd leveled a last blast of expletives at Zell.

Zell threw up his hands, glaring at Monica. "*Kvetch! Kvetch!* After everything I've done for him. Nothing but *kvetching!*"

"You created this," Monica told him angrily.

"We *both* created this!"

Zell's jaw was set and his small eyes were fierce when he suddenly spotted me eavesdropping over the hedge. Without another word, he took Monica Rivers by the elbow, turned her up the steps and inside, and shut the double doors firmly behind him.

Chapter 6

⌒

THE BAND PLAYED a final, forty-minute set that included
Rabbi Kaminsky's special request. He and Beatrice did
a fine job of putting on the Ritz, moving their bulk with
admirable rhythm and enviable grace. Then we picked up
the tempo, building to a crescendo of high-octane swing
music that kept the energy high and the patio filled with
athletic dancers, with George Chakiris and Juliet Prowse
leading the way.

"Stompin' at the Savoy" took us to 5 P.M. and left the
dancers gasping for air, collapsing with laughter, and maybe
a little more in love, the way it should be. Then we were
packing up. I was hoping Sid Zell might present me with
a check, but he was nowhere in sight. His wife, Esther,
explained that her husband was upstairs, resting from the
strenuous day.

"He doesn't like to admit it, but his heart's seriously weak." Her smile was brave. "That's why you didn't see us up and dancing, the way we love to. His doctors absolutely forbid any strenuous activity."

She thanked us for our fine work and assured me that someone from her husband's office would be in touch first thing Monday to take care of the bill.

OUT front, on the circular drive, valets were taking tickets and jockeying cars up from the road for a line of guests that grew longer by the second. To save time, the band members collectively decided to hump the instruments down the long drive and find our two vehicles on our own.

As we made our descent, we realized we needed our keys, and I volunteered to go back up while the guys lugged their instruments to the two vehicles. I collected the keys and was about to start down again when I encountered a knot of people engaged in urgent conversation: Nicky Pembrook, Vicki Hart, and a brawny young man who appeared to be in his late twenties. He was bronzed and muscular, with shaggy, sun-bleached hair and the standard uniform of the hard-core surfers who rode the waves along the Southern California shoreline: faded jeans and wrinkled T-shirt, rubber thong sandals, and a narrow string of rawhide knotted around one ankle. Although he glowed with vitality, he also seemed high-strung and jumpy, as if he couldn't stay still inside his own skin.

"Time to split, Nicky." The surfer snapped his fingers three times in quick succession, like a hipster finding a fast beat. "Time to make some dust, man."

"I want my money!"

It quickly became clear that Nicky Pembrook wanted

back in the house, to have it out with Sid Zell. Vicki had resumed her pleading, but it was obviously futile, so the surfer stepped forward and took over. He put one hand on Nicky's skinny neck and the other on his sinewy arm.

"Nicky, cool it." The surfer's voice was deep, masculine, firm. "Let's blow this joint. We got waves to catch."

His words had an instant calming effect on Pembrook, whose head came around quickly. "You mean it? You'll take me surfing with you?"

"I'll show you how to walk the nose." The surfer's blue eyes were kinetic, the pupils huge. "But we got to get moving, Nick."

"This is great!" Pembrook kissed Vicki Hart on the mouth. "He's taking me surfing with him, honey."

"Great, Nicky," she said, forcing a smile. "That's fantastic."

The surfer led Pembrook to a wood-paneled station wagon parked at the edge of the drive—a Woody, in surfing nomenclature. Vicki Hart followed, looking relieved, if not very happy. Moments later, the surfer burned rubber and sped off, while his radio speakers blasted "Let's Go Trippin'," one of those pulsating numbers by guitarist Dick Dale, who'd invented the reverb surf sound a few years earlier.

"Johnny Langley." The pleasant female voice came from over my left shoulder. I turned to find Monica Rivers standing there, looking as alluring as the moment I'd first laid eyes on her. "Something of a surfing legend down in the beach towns."

"You know him?"

"Not really. He's works on Sid's movies from time to time. Stunt driving, stand-in for the star on surfing shots, that kind of thing."

"You mean Frankie Avalon doesn't ride those twenty-foot waves all by himself?"

She smiled. "Only in the script, I'm afraid."

"I'd hoped to run into you again, Monica. Gives me a chance to say good-bye."

"Good-bye—or just good afternoon?"

I smiled haplessly. "I don't imagine someone like you has much time for—"

She pressed a finger to my lips. "Don't assume too much, Philip. Finding out can be so much more fun, don't you think?"

"Like I said, I'll leave a comp for you at the door tonight."

Her eyes left mine, as if drawn upward by instinct, to a second-story window where Sid Zell looked down. When she glanced back in my direction, her eyes had lost their warmth and playfulness.

"I'll see what I can do." She said it crisply, before shaking my hand like someone ending a business conversation. "It was nice meeting you, Philip."

BY the time I caught up to the others, Beatrice Gless and Rabbi Kaminsky had also collected a set of keys and trudged down the hill, tired of the wait. I handed out mine and the guys began wedging their instruments into the trunk of my car and the back of the rented van.

"You and Monica Rivers seem to have hit it off," Beatrice said. "We saw you up at the house, schmoozing like old pals."

"She's hard not to like."

"Just remember where you are, honey. Things out here are never quite what they seem."

"I'm going on thirty-five, Beatrice. I hope by now I can read the message in a woman's eyes."

Just then, Monica appeared at the foot of the drive, behind the wheel of a new Jaguar. It was a series 1 E-Type Roadster, long and sleek, creamy white, with the top down. She looked fantastic in it, svelte and sexy, and I wanted nothing more than to hop in beside her. Impatiently, she turned into the road, which was clogged with other cars, pulling out and maneuvering for position. As she became stuck in the congestion, a photographer stepped suddenly from the foliage, as if he'd been waiting in ambush. He fired off a flash directly into her face. She threw up a hand and cursed him but he paid her no attention, ejecting his spent bulb and screwing in a fresh one.

I dashed over, getting a better look at him as I drew close: He was on the far side of fifty, I guessed, an absolute slob from head to toe—scruffy, unshaven, draped in a cheap suit that probably hadn't seen a dry cleaner in years. As I came up, I noticed a distinct purple birthmark on the left side of his neck, about the size of a quarter, amoeba-like in shape. I was more accustomed to the well-behaved paparazzi in Europe, where I'd played some dates. They worked in packs but they were also well dressed and well groomed, professionals who first asked politely if they might take your picture, a request that was granted more often than not. The creature before me was of an entirely different breed— pushy, boorish, and seriously in need of a bath.

I put a hand on his arm. "Leave the lady alone."

"It's a free country, pal." The photographer sneered, showing remnants of his lunch in a mouth that needed scrubbing. "She's a celebrity, out in public—fair game."

He raised his twin reflex to fire another shot. I stepped

around in front of him, one hand in front of his lens and the other on his chest. Traffic opened just then and Monica's tires squealed. She raced off down the road, showing the photographer her upraised middle finger as she went. I grinned, liking her more than ever.

The photographer glared a moment, cursing me silently with his dull brown eyes, then turned away to look for other prey.

"HUDLEY Pinkston," Beatrice informed me upon my return. "Hollywood's most aggressive and despised paparazzo. Hudley's got an identical twin named Hedley—dead opposites and sworn enemies. Hedley Pinkston handles Monica's publicity. If you intend to chase after her, you'll probably have to deal with them both."

"How will I tell them apart?"

"Hudley's the one with the birthmark, the bad hair and the bad breath. Hedley's the slick one, put together like a mannequin at Brooks Brothers."

"And no birthmark?"

"No birthmark."

I stared with longing after Monica's disappearing Jag as it became a speck down the canyon. In my mind was a vivid memory of the moment we'd met, when she'd moistened her lip while smiling at me so mischievously. I was enjoying it when a flash of light shattered the spell—Hudley Pinkston's Rolleiflex, its double lens aimed directly at my face. He lowered the camera, showing me a smirk.

"Did I forget to say cheese?" His smirk turned downright nasty. "Maybe next time."

"There won't be a next time, Pinkston."

"Don't count on it, sweetheart."

I drove off feeling angry and resentful, and just a bit unsettled. I'd come to La La Land to relax and play a great gig—not to get my mug in *Confidential*.

Chapter 7

WHEN WE OPENED that night at the Cocoanut Grove, I could almost feel Dad's presence in the big room.

I'd worked here once before—splitting the bill with Rosemary Clooney—and considered a gig at the Grove to be a privilege. Not just because the most popular big bands had performed here in the old days, including Dad's, but because of the individual names etched indelibly into the Grove's legacy. According to legend, Carole Lombard, Joan Crawford, and Loretta Young had been discovered dancing here. Gloria DeHaven had gotten her big break the night of her high school graduation, when classmates had pushed her up on the Grove's stage to show her off. Bing Crosby had made his mark here as a crooner decades ago, and it had been the site of Barbra Streisand's recent West Coast debut. For years, Howard Hughes had dropped in nearly every night, to do the rhumba. Even the artificial palm trees that decorated the club's interior were linked to Rudolph Valentino, salvaged from the set of his 1921 classic, *The Sheik*. When you performed at the Grove, you became a bit player in a starry history. It dripped with kitsch—a funny-looking boat hung suspended from the ceiling—but it also epitomized glamour, the nightclub by which all others were measured.

At 8 P.M., my tenor saxophonist raised his horn. I sat at the Steinway in an island of light, a fresh burgundy carnation pinned to my lapel, nodding the downbeat. The orchestra broke into our usual opening number—"Make Someone Happy" by Styne, Comden, and Green—and the infectious tune got the evening moving in a hurry.

BUDDY Bixby, thankfully, was back in form.

We'd grabbed an hour to rehearse before the show, and it was paying off. He played earnestly and competently, if not quite fluidly, looking down at the music on the tunes with which he was less familiar. I gave him the spotlight on several vocals and the crowd ate it up, seeing Buddy Bixby with microphone in hand again. "My Funny Valentine," "Moon Love," "Isn't It Romantic?"—he knew just how to croon a syrupy ballad with the quality of a lost little boy, making it sound like it was directed personally to each and every lady in the place. As always, he was especially effective on his signature tune, "Good Morning, Heartache," the melancholy ballad by Irene Higgenbotham, Ervin Duke, and Dan Fisher that had first been recorded in 1946. Buddy's plaintive voice brought to mind Billie Holiday's classic version—even if it lacked the richness and timbre— and I saw more than a few misty eyes among the women in

the audience who must have been teenagers a decade ago
when Buddy had first gained notice.

In general, however, the crowd skewed older, as it customarily did. Roz Russell, Kirk and Anne Douglas, Mitzi
Gaynor, Gene Kelly, Jack and Mary Benny, Greg and Ve-
ronique Peck—from the low stage, I could see them all on
the dance floor or making their way to their tables. Many
of those in attendance were one-time film people who'd
turned to TV to survive, now that the boob tube had de-
voured eighty percent of the movie audience, leaving the
film business floundering in search of new formulas. Directly
out front, Ronald Reagan, the affable B movie actor now
hosting TV's *Death Valley Days*, was two-stepping with his
wife, Nancy, who seemed to be leading. Broderick Crawford
had shown up early but thoroughly potted, and was passed
out facedown on his table while his entourage talked around
and over him. Merv Griffin, who'd performed at the Grove
as a young singer with the Freddie Martin Orchestra, was
head to head with Eva Gabor, giggling impishly. Bette Davis sat nearby with a male escort, dining on caviar and roast
pheasant while slipping her hand beneath the table to stroke
the young man's thigh. There wasn't much you missed from
the bandstand if you didn't want to.

I kept my eyes on the prowl for Monica Rivers, but she
never showed. To my consternation, it was her mother who
came instead, claiming the comp at the door.

LORNA Draper approached me during our final break, putting out her bejeweled hand to introduce herself. She was
an attractive but hard-edged woman in her fifties, with her
daughter's dark eyes. For the evening, she'd dressed in a

showy emerald green silk gown and matching shawl, with glittering jewels at her ears, throat, and wrists that looked like paste.

On her arm was a man I took to be Hedley Pinkston, the twin brother of the obnoxious photographer I'd encountered earlier that evening.

"Hedley T. Pinkston," he informed me with a faint drawl when I asked. He extended a well-manicured hand. "I apologize for any unpleasantness Hudley might have caused up in Bel-Air. I'm afraid I have no control over my brother, despite the mere seconds that separated us in birth. We never got along, not even as children. The experts say that twins are invariably soul mates. I suppose Hudley and I are the exceptions that prove the rule."

Hedley Pinkston appeared to be everything his unpleasant twin was not: polished, charming, well groomed, smartly dressed, and missing the purple birthmark so visible on Hudley's neck. Beatrice had been right—it wasn't at all difficult telling them apart.

"Hedley's a personal publicist," Lorna Draper explained. "He's molding Monica's public image, doing a wonderful job. Show him your family snapshots, Hedley."

Hedley opened a fancy alligator wallet with a plastic accordion photo file to display head shots of his most famous celebrity clients: Rock Hudson, Lana Turner, Robert Mitchum, Monica Rivers, and Sal Mineo among them.

"I think of them as my children," Hedley said, with a reverence that sounded utterly sincere. "Anytime, night or day, whatever they need, I'm there for them."

I laughed. "I should get a publicist like you, Pinkston."

He smiled, winking. "No offense, Mr. Damon, but I'm not sure that you could afford me."

"Hedley's been named Hollywood's top publicist of the year an unprecedented five times," Lorna put in. "We're so happy to have him watching after Monica."

My smile grew tighter. "When I met her, she struck me as someone who can take care of herself."

Lorna's voice became cool, her speech more clipped. "A successful Hollywood career demands careful tending, Mr. Damon, not to mention a healthy dose of luck. Being blessed with mere talent, as I was, is hardly enough. I'm not letting Monica make the same mistakes I did. I'm leaving nothing to chance."

"I take it you're also an actress, then."

"Was." She said the word as if it tasted sour in her mouth. "I brought Monica along slowly, waiting until her time was right. They can eat you alive in this town when you're young, you know."

"And we feel Monica's time is now," Pinkston added.

"I may have waited too late," Lorna admitted. "Monica's hardly an ingénue. I hadn't counted on television having such an impact on the feature film business. That's why every moment is crucial now, every move."

"I was hoping Monica might drop by tonight." I did my best to keep the disappointment from my voice. "I find her quite captivating."

"If Monica led you on, Mr. Damon, I apologize." Lorna Draper's smile was lukewarm at best. "She can be thoughtless that way, especially with impressionable young men."

"Monica had a previous social engagement," Pinkston explained, his tone more genial. "With someone who's become rather important in her life."

Lorna leaned in, putting it more bluntly: "Monica is spoken for, Mr. Damon."

"I see."

Lorna Draper extended her hand again, looking pleased. "Then we have an understanding. I love your music, by the way. It reminds me so much of the old days, when class and decorum were still in vogue, when people still had manners."

"I hear that a lot," I said, but they were already showing me their backs, waving to a small group across the room.

I was on my way to find a drink when Gloria Velez beckoned me to join her in conversation with an attractive older woman who looked awfully familiar.

"Philip, I want you to meet Claudette Colbert. She's been singing your praises to the skies. Miss Colbert, Philip Damon."

I hadn't seen anything of Claudette Colbert in years, though Diana and I had watched all her classics on the Late Show—*It Happened One Night, Imitation of Life, The Palm Beach Story,* so many others. I guessed her age now at around sixty. She was a small woman with dark, wavy hair and expressive, dewy eyes, and a sense of strength and will that belied her slight stature.

"I've been telling Miss Velez that with her looks, she really belongs in front of the camera." Miss Colbert's eyes fell fondly on Gloria. "The face, the figure, the poise—she has it all. And, of course, such a lovely voice."

"When I'm able to find it," Gloria croaked, laughing.

"I have a few of Mr. Damon's records, dear. I break them out for dancing when I have friends over." Miss Colbert laughed broadly. "In Barbados, they always make a huge hit!" She touched Gloria lightly on her bare shoulder. "Your vocals are absolutely first rate." Gloria flushed beneath her dusky skin. "Really, Gloria, you should give it serious consideration. I'm not as active in the business these days, but I still have connections. I could help."

Gloria clasped Colbert's tiny hands. "It's flattering, but I'm afraid I wouldn't fit in too well in Hollywood. Even if they wanted me, they'd try to cast me as maids, whores, and red-hot mamas. It happened to Rita Moreno after *West Side Story*. That's not for me."

"You could change your name, dear, give yourself a new hair color. Look at Rita Hayworth, before she acquired that flaming red hair—born Margarita Carmen Cansino. The change worked for her."

"I prefer being myself." Gloria smiled awkwardly. "I think I'll stick to singing."

"If you should change your mind—"

"It's kind of you, Miss Colbert."

"Call me Claudette, will you?"

I asked Miss Colbert if she'd come with anyone, and if we might be keeping her.

"I'm single, actually, and I often go out alone." Her eyes moved quickly back to Gloria. "It's been lovely chatting with you, Gloria. I'll be in touch, if that's all right."

"Of course. I'd like that."

When Claudette Colbert was gone, Gloria was suddenly transformed from a sophisticated band singer to a gushing fan. "My god! I just talked to someone who won an Academy Award!"

"What about my Grammy? Doesn't that count for any-thing?"

Gloria rolled her dark eyes. "Philip, *please.*"

ßY midnight, the orchestra was playing "Chopin's Nocturne in E Flat," my father's theme song and the one I always closed with. Then people were calling for their checks and I was signing autographs, chatting with fans, and posing for photographs. On the way out, one of the younger guests hollered a suggestion—start playing some Beatles tunes—that caused me to grimace. After that, Buddy Bixby hit me up for an advance and I gave him all the cash I had in my pockets, about thirty bucks. He was about to hop a cab out to the suburb of Hermosa Beach, he said, to sit in with the Cannonball Adderly Quartet, which was appearing at the Lighthouse. Bixby invited me along, but I told him I was bushed and maybe another night. I thanked him for filling in with the band at the last minute and told him to keep up the good work.

"You made the right decision," Buddy said, "giving me a shot like this. I'll do right by you, Mr. Damon. You'll see."

"I'm counting on it, Buddy."

It was close to 1 A.M. before I had a well-deserved night-cap in my hand. I took it out on a balcony, where I found Hercules Platt loosening his bow tie and collar in the stifling air, which lacked the relieving breezes of the night before. He seemed brooding and uneasy, as if sensing trouble in the relentless heat. I suggested he lighten up, go out on the town; I reminded him that we were in Hollywood, after all, where half the waitresses were pretty enough to be in the movies, and the other half once had been.

Platt laughed, but it died fast. He'd been divorced for years, I knew that much, but if he was dating anyone, I wasn't aware of it. He kept a lot to himself, Hercules Platt.

"What about you, Damon? You still have your sights set on that Rivers woman?"

I sipped my drink, smiling for effect. "It seems she's taken."

"Ain't that the way it always is."

Not half a minute later, the concierge found me and informed me that I had a phone call at the front desk. I bid Platt good night and left him staring out into the night, looking as fretful as ever.

In the lobby, the concierge led me to his station, pointed me to a phone, and departed. I finished off my drink as I picked up the receiver.

"Philip Damon here."

Monica Rivers was at the other end, lonely and sulking after what she called a "dreadfully boring" date arranged by Hedley Pinkston.

"Meet me for lunch tomorrow, Philip." Her languid voice washed over me like a lullaby. "We'll have a nice interlude, just the two of us."

"If you're sure you want to, Monica."

"Musso and Frank—I'll reserve a booth."

"As I recall, their booths are rather private."

"Yes, aren't they though?"

I slept easily that night in Beatrice's spare bedroom, with the windows open to the clean canyon smells and a couple of her cats curled up near my feet.

At ten the next morning, Hercules Platt woke me with a phone call to tell me that Buddy Bixby hadn't returned from his jam session at the Lighthouse the night before, that Buddy's bed remained unused. Platt wasn't alarmed, he said, he was just taking note of events. "He could have shacked up with some cutie, I guess."

To be honest, I was too intent on my lunch date with Monica Rivers to pay much attention.

Chapter 8

MUSSO AND FRANK was situated on the north side of
Hollywood Boulevard in the decaying heart of a movie
capital that was more a memory now than the real
thing.

Out front, along the Walk of Fame, city workers repaired
and regularly polished the stars and names imbedded in the
marbled sidewalk. But the drug dealers and street prosti-
tutes had moved in—runaway kids seemed to be everywhere—and most of the studios and real stars had departed,
heading west where the air was cleaner and the crime under
control, or north over the hills to the San Fernando Valley
where real estate was cheap. The studios that remained
rented more and more of their soundstages to TV production
companies that ground out up to three dozen episodes of a
single program each year, adding a canned laugh track to

the comedies in a feeble attempt to replicate the audience at the neighborhood movie theater. It was an uneasy time in Hollywood, especially for those who made their living in the feature film business.

Still, Musso and Frank hung on, an old-fashioned, wood-paneled grill awash in Tinseltown history that billed itself as the oldest operating restaurant in Hollywood, dating back to 1919. Anita Loos had eaten here since the thirties, bringing me with her when I was a little boy; once, we'd bumped into two irritable screenwriters named Faulkner and Fitzgerald, whose names, of course, had meant nothing to me at the time. The neighborhood had deteriorated in the decades since, but the only thing that had changed at Musso and Frank were the prices on the menu, which kept going up.

I left my car with the valet in back and stepped down into the restaurant to the bustle of waiters and clatter of heavy silverware on porcelain platters. Monica Rivers sat in a small booth enclosed by dividers in the restaurant's west half, near the long counter. I slipped in across from her, intending to get right to the matter of the other man she was seeing. Before I could open my mouth, she pushed a menu into my hands.

"Let's order, Philip. I'm starving."

A waiter came around and we placed our drink orders. When we were alone again, Monica gazed at me with her suggestive dark eyes, as if we'd known each other intimately and forever.

"I heard your music playing all night long in my head— even in my dreams." Her smile was radiant. "Sweet dreams, thanks to you."

"I'm delighted I made an impression."

"You're very handsome, Philip. You have a boyish, self-effacing charm. You know, you could be in the movies, if you wanted to."

I paraphrased Gloria Velez, from the night before: "I think I'll stick to piano playing."

"Never thought about acting?" I hesitated; Monica smiled. "You see, it's not such a far-fetched idea."

"I'm sure lots of people entertain fantasies like that," I said. "It's natural enough. That doesn't mean you let it preoccupy you."

"What does preoccupy you, Philip?"

I thought about it a moment, unaccustomed to being so forthright and open. Years of hiding my deepest feelings had taken their toll—I wasn't used to confiding in people like this, not even stunning women capable of turning me into putty. Monica surely sensed it, because she reached across the small table and touched my hand.

I took a deep breath. "My late wife, I suppose. Trying to keep Diana a part of me but also to move on, start over. Then there's my music, of course. Without my music, I'd be rather lost."

"I read about your wife's death in the newspapers a few years ago. Terrible, the way it happened. As I recall, someone broke into your Manhattan apartment and strangled her. It took two years before you solved her murder. Up in San Francisco, wasn't it? Where the two of you had met and courted before you were married."

"You have quite a memory, Monica."

"It was a sensational case. When the murder occurred, wasn't she listening to 'Blue Moon'?"

"Yes, 'Blue Moon.' Her favorite." I shrugged haplessly. "It's been four years now. The worst of it recedes, little by little."

"A San Francisco police detective helped you figure out

who killed her. A black man, wasn't he? I vaguely remember seeing his picture on the news."

"An inspector, homicide division," I said. "Hercules Platt. Retired now—plays alto sax in my orchestra. You heard him yesterday, up at Sid Zell's place."

Her eyes widened. "The sax player—?"

I nodded. "He's let his hair go natural, put on a little weight." The drinks arrived and the waiter took our lunch order. Lamb stew for me, a grilled cheese sandwich and small salad for Monica.

"And your parents?" she asked when the waiter was gone.

"My mother died shortly after my birth, my father when I was twelve. I was raised by my godparents, Barclay and Isabel Harrington of New York."

"The former governor?"

"That's right."

She looked down her nose at me with great effect. "*Veddy* upper crust."

I smiled. "And you?"

"Very lower crust, I'm afraid."

We both laughed.

"Mother grew up south of here, down near San Diego. I don't know much about my grandparents, really."

"And your father?"

Her eyes dropped and she pretended to be interested in her drink. "I never met him. Mother wasn't particularly good at choosing or keeping men."

"I'm sorry, I shouldn't have pried."

"No—I was the one asking questions. Fair's fair."

"It's obviously a tender spot for you."

"Mother and I have each other. We're very close. That means a lot."

"You never married?"

"No, and if I'm going to, I should do it soon."

"You're on a timetable?"

"I'd like to have children, and I'm already thirty-six." She laughed easily. "A woman's not supposed to admit her true age, especially in this town. But there it is."

"I would have guessed younger."

Her smile was coy but cute. "Are you trying to flatter me, Mr. Damon?"

"A woman like you doesn't need flattering, Monica. A woman like you—"

She suddenly pulled back, withdrawing her hand, as a figure loomed over us. I looked up to see Hedley Pinkston standing there, tapping a folded newspaper against his open palm.

"Monica, Mr. Damon. What a surprise."

"Is it really?" Monica's voice was cool, displeased.

Pinkston glanced at his watch. "It's half past noon, Monica. We have three press interviews this afternoon, beginning with Chuck Champlin at two."

"I told you, I don't like to work Sundays."

"No days off, Monica, when you have a premiere coming up." Pinkston forced a smile that he beamed in my direction. *"Dead Aim* opens this week. The premiere's Thursday night. We've scheduled it early, around seven, because of the big party we have planned afterward."

"I can make it then, and still have time to get back to the Grove. Beatrice Gless invited me, by the way. She worked on the screenplay." I glanced across the table. "Perhaps I'll run into Monica again."

Pinkston pointed to his nose. "Monica, I believe you're a bit shiny."

"Excuse me." Monica slid from the booth, not quite looking at me. "I'll be in the powder room, just for a minute."

When she was gone, Pinkston took her seat. "Have you seen this morning's *L.A. Times,* Damon? Specifically, Hedda Hopper?"

"I'm afraid I don't follow the gossip columns."

His smile was all charm. "Not even if you're in them?"

I served up a shrug. "Maybe then."

He unfolded his newspaper, found the entertainment section, and opened it to an inside page. The *Los Angeles Times* tended to be thin, without much substance—more real estate and swimming pool ads it seemed, than articles—and it didn't take Pinkston long to find what he was looking for. He folded the page back and placed it on the table, positioning it for my benefit. Hedda Hopper's column was front and center. My eyes went directly to the lead item:

Everyone who's anyone is talking about the sizzling new romance between Rock Hudson and Monica Rivers, the latest beauty to catch his eye. Rock's about to start filming *Seconds* in New York with director John Frankenheimer, and Monica's got *Dead Aim* about to open. But the two lovebirds have still found time to be together whenever possible, and sources say this is the real thing for these two terrific kids. I'm especially happy for Rock, who's still getting over the pain of divorce from his beloved Phyllis Gates. If it weren't for Frank Sinatra and Mia Farrow stirring up headlines, I'd cast my vote for Rock and Monica as Hollywood's hot new couple to watch.

"You see my problem," Hedley Pinkston said.

I knew a bit about Rock Hudson's private life, and tried hard not to laugh. "I see a lot of problems, Hedley."

"Sid Zell has made quite an investment in Monica's career. A Hollywood career depends enormously on popularity and public image."

"And since you represent both Rock and Monica, you're able to kill two birds with one stone. Or should I say—lovebirds?"

Pinkston's smile was strained. "I'm sure you can appreciate the situation."

"I believe Monica likes me, Hedley, and I know that I like her."

"It's like Lorna told you last night, Damon—her daughter's spoken for."

"Maybe Monica needs to tell me that herself."

"Unfortunately, Monica can be—shall we say, impetuous. Which is not always in her long-term interests."

He cut the chatter and turned on a smile as she approached, sliding out to let her slip back in, then standing over us with the Hedda Hopper column in full view. He reminded Monica that the interviews would take place at his Beverly Hills office and asked if she preferred to ride with him or drive herself. She explained that her Jag was in the garage for a tune-up—she'd come to lunch by cab—and that she wanted to go home first to change into something more formal. Pinkston said he'd be happy to drive her home, wait while she dressed, then take her on to her interviews. She told him she planned to call the studio and have a car and driver sent out to pick her up. Growing flustered, Pinkston offered to call a cab immediately, to keep her on schedule.

"I haven't eaten yet," Monica said, "and I won't be needing a cab." She ended the volleying by slamming home the winning shot: "Mr. Damon will be driving me home, thank you."

*   *   *

LORNA Draper was waiting at the front gate of her Mulholland Drive house when I pulled up out front, no doubt tipped off by Hedley Pinkston that we were coming. She didn't look at all pleased. Monica sat beside me in the front seat, her hands folded rather primly in her lap.

"Your house," I asked, "or your mother's?"

"I bought it. We both live here. Mother's rather high-strung. Sometimes she needs"—Monica broke off, searching for the right words—"special attention."

Lorna glared at me as I came around to open the door for Monica, but immediately turned her chilly voice on her daughter. "You don't want to keep these people waiting, Monica. The *Los Angeles Times,* the Associated Press, UPI. These interviews will reach millions—*millions.*"

"There's such a thing as being fashionably late, Mother."

Lorna Draper steered Monica through the gate, but lingered behind. "Leave her alone, Mr. Damon. This is her big moment, her big chance. Let her have it."

"Her big chance, Lorna, or yours?"

Her dark eyes turned to daggers. Then she pivoted on her heel and went in, shutting the gate sharply behind her. A moment later, as I reached my car, Monica reappeared at the gate. She dashed over, whispered to me that she kept a room at the Chateau Marmont down on the Sunset Strip, gave me the room number, and made a date for late Wednesday night.

I drove away on Mulholland Drive, taking in the views of the Los Angeles basin on one side and the San Fernando Valley across the road, feeling like my life had just taken a wonderful seismic shift. I had a date with Monica Rivers—a clandestine date with a beautiful actress whom I found fascinating, in one of L.A.'s more legendary trysting places. Finally, I'd met a woman who seriously excited me. In my elation, I switched on the radio, punching preprogrammed buttons to find some appropriate music. I landed on local radio station KFWB, which seemed to have the strongest wattage. A deejay named Bill Ballance announced that in two days the Top 40 station would begin carrying live half-hourly updates on the Beatles' upcoming U.S. tour, with two of KFWB's "rock jocks" aboard the group's private jet. More Beatles—I wanted to scream. As I reached to push another button the regular newscast came on, introduced by the exaggerated clatter of teletype. As it died down, the newscaster began reading the lead story. I pulled immediately off the road, shut off the engine, and listened with a growing sense of dread.

Buddy Bixby was dead.

Chapter 9

THE NEWS REPORT on Buddy Bixby's death was brief, and went something like this: Shortly after sunrise that morning, a fisherman had come across the body along the shore in Hermosa Beach. Evidence at the scene indicated that Buddy had probably died of a drug overdose. Local police were investigating.

It might sound cold, but my thoughts turned quickly from Buddy to the band. We had a dead lead trumpet player and vocalist on our hands but somehow we also had a show to do that night. Grief and funeral arrangements notwithstanding, the old cliché held fast: The Show Must Go On.

Word travels fast when someone in the music community passes. By midafternoon, after hearing the news, several agents had called me to offer their clients as temporary solutions. We ended up with Wesley Turner, a black crooner in the smooth Joe Williams style who doubled passably on trumpet, and I was grateful to have him. We dedicated the night's performance to Buddy Bixby and after that just tried to do our job, to remember him best by playing with feeling and losing ourselves in the music. We ended the night rousing the crowd with "Heat Wave," the sensual, hard-driving song Peggy Lee had made famous. It was an appropriate choice, given the blast of hot air still baking the landscape, sucking every bit of moisture from the atmosphere, and fraying plenty of nerves.

THANKFULLY, the Cocoanut Grove was dark the next night, Monday, which gave us time to cope with Buddy's death.

Luckily, my regular trumpet player, Eddie Sears, had dealt with his family emergency and hopped a jet from New York to rejoin the group, so we were covered there. Wesley Turner continued subbing for Gloria Velez, who was swilling gallons of hot tea with lemon and honey, certain she'd have her voice back by the end of the week. Frankly, I was more concerned with her emotional state, the burden of guilt I sensed weighing her down. She'd been the one, after all, who'd urged me to bring Buddy back into the spotlight—maybe too soon.

"I should have let Hercules have his way," she said. "I wish I'd never—"

I put an arm around her, pulled her close. We were in the hotel coffeeshop, divvying up tasks that needed handling in the wake of Buddy's death. "You gave Buddy one last chance to perform before his time ran out," I told her. "We should all be so lucky to go out like that."

She looked up at me, smiling; her big, dark eyes were moist, vulnerable. Gloria Velez was a genuine beauty and we were often seen cozying up to each other like that. There had been more than a few false rumors about the two of us from the lips of silly people who had no understanding of her deeper feelings and private life. She stretched up, pecked me on the cheek.

"Thanks for being a good guy, Philip."

"Same to you, kid," I said, and pecked her back.

ACCORDING to the news reports, Buddy had sat in as planned late Saturday night with the Cannonball Adderly Quartet at the Lighthouse. Sometime around 2 A.M., he'd left alone. Several hours later, a fisherman had spotted Buddy's body near the municipal pier, just above the tide line, a hypo still in one of his arms.

We were all curious for more particulars. Hercules Platt had a call out to an old buddy of his, Ray Verdugo, who was working homicide with the county sheriff's department. I spent much of the day dealing with press inquiries and providing quotes about Buddy for the ongoing news reports. The calls came in from all over the world—France, Japan, Germany, the Netherlands, Brazil—anywhere that modern jazz was popular and Buddy had been well known. I felt awkward talking about someone I was barely acquainted with. But it struck me that the least I could do was to say a few nice things about a kid with all kinds of potential who'd gone so sadly wrong.

By nightfall, I wanted to do nothing more than slip into a double Dewars on the rocks, have a nice dinner with Beatrice at Scandia, and catch Harry Belafonte at the Greek Theater. Hercules Platt, however, had other ideas.

*   *   *

PLATT had been brooding through the early evening about Buddy's death, his old detective's instincts kicking in. He was bound and determined to drive out to Hermosa Beach, to see for himself where Buddy had died. For one thing, he said, Buddy had only thirty bucks on him when he'd left the Ambassador Saturday night—the cash he'd cadged off me just before splitting. By the time he'd gotten some dinner, a pack of cigs, paid for the long cab ride to Hermosa Beach and his club cover, Platt figured, Buddy would have been tapped out.

"So how did he pay for the smack?" Platt pondered, sitting at a table in the empty Cocoanut Grove over a cup of coffee going cold. "If the heroin was a gift, shared with a fellow junkie, why did they give him enough to kill him? Buddy was just a chipper, strictly small time. At least that's the skinny I've always heard."

"Let's leave those questions to the cops," I suggested. "You're a sax man now, remember?"

Platt reminded me that he'd kept his California private eye's license current, then pointed out that he didn't have a car at his disposal, as I did.

"We came out for a pleasant working vacation, Platt. Not to get entangled in another criminal investigation like that nasty business up in San Francisco."

Platt leveled his brown eyes on me, his voice maddeningly neutral. "True enough, Damon—why should somebody like you give a damn about Buddy Bixby?"

I put up a hand. "Don't even try it, Hercules—"

"I guess it's easy for someone like you to just toss Bixby aside and forget about him."

Someone like you. "Damn it, Platt—"

"Get on with your fancy engagement at your fancy hotel, in front of your fancy audience, in your fancy two-hundred-dollar tux." Platt shrugged. "Who was Buddy Bixby, any-way? Just some blue-collar kid with a horn who'd never even owned a tux before Saturday."

"If I remember right, you were the one opposed to the junkie joining the band."

"But now the junkie's dead." Platt stood as if to go. "No use to you anymore, is he, boss?"

"Listen here, Platt——"

"And don't worry about putting Buddy in the ground, Damon. Me and the other cats will see to that. We take care of our own."

But he didn't leave just yet. He stood there, hat in hand, pinning me with his implacable eyes, knowing exactly what he was doing.

I sighed in reluctant surrender. "I'll need a drink first, and a decent dinner."

"You buying?"

"Don't I always?"

We ate nearby at Perino's and were on our way to Hermosa Beach by half past nine.

Chapter 10

H ERMOSA BEACH WAS a densely populated community of about sixteen thousand that hadn't changed much in recent years, except for a small influx of bohemians and a growing flock of surfers drawn to a sport that had suddenly caught the public's attention.

The town was situated roughly fifteen miles southwest of downtown L.A., where modest family homes and small apartments were tightly stacked on low hills overlooking the ocean. The many new freeways spreading across Los Angeles County in a tangle had all bypassed Hermosa Beach, leaving it isolated and somewhat overlooked. By the time we reached the city limits by way of surface streets, it was nearly half past ten.

We found the Lighthouse on Pier Avenue, half a block from the beach. Converted from a Chinese restaurant, it had become a jazz mainstay during the fifties, when some of the top musicians migrated from New York to the West Coast, with their music achieving classic dimensions among a dozen or so small clubs along Central Avenue in downtown L.A. A bassist named Howard Rumsey had put together the Lighthouse All-Stars and set up shop in Hermosa Beach, where his little jazz joint became legendary for jam sessions that often ran from 2 P.M. to 2 A.M., drawing appreciative audiences starved for soulful jazz out in the white suburbs. Because of Jim Crow laws, black musicians had to leave town each night to find a place to stay, heading east into Los Angeles to bunk at places like the historic Hotel Dunbar, a situation that hadn't changed all that much as Platt and I rolled down dimly lit Pier Avenue.

I parked the Chrysler across the street from the club, in front of a colorfully painted bookstore called the Insomniac that was closed and boarded up. Nearby, in the shadows, two uniformed cops—both white—were rousting a couple of effete bohemian types, giving them grief about their goatees and longish hair. As we climbed from the Chrysler, the air was salty and bracing. The two cops glanced over, first at me, then at the nice car, then they settled their unfriendly eyes on Hercules Platt and left them there as we turned to cross the street.

A small crowd of young people was gathered outside the Lighthouse, listening for free through a narrow side door that was customarily open for ventilation on warm nights.

We gained entry through the main door twenty feet away, paying the two-drink minimum and entering to a rocking version of George and Ira Gershwin's "Who Cares?" The house was full, even on a Monday, with lots of youthful white couples packed knee to knee at tiny tables, while no-nonsense waitresses hustled drinks and cigarette smoke hovered above like an atomic cloud. The stage was about the size of a postage stamp, dominated by the huge form of Cannonball Adderly, who seemed to engulf his alto sax as he played. The quartet sounded fantastic—incredibly tight after years together—and I got so into their music that I forgot my dark thoughts about Buddy Bixby and the purpose of our visit.

Platt and I squeezed in at the bar. He ordered a Coke and I requested a Dewars on the rocks. When he was able, Platt got the bartender's ear and peppered him with questions. The bartender was a tall white guy in his late twenties named Kevin Cody who had the kind of square-jawed blond looks and solid chest that probably made picking up girls in a place like this as easy as batting his baby blues. He told Platt that Buddy had come in sometime after 1 A.M., huddling at the end of the bar smoking and nursing a bourbon and Coke as if he might be out of money. A woman had joined him, ordering a Virgin Mary and engaging Buddy in earnest conversation before slipping something furtively into his hand, which he'd quickly pocketed. Platt asked the bartender if he could describe the woman.

"On the tall side for a chick, pretty enough but definitely square."

"Why square?" Platt asked.

"First, there was that Virgin Mary—no alcohol. Then the old-fashioned look—horn-rims, skirt below the knees, sensible shoes, ponytail from the '50s. Carried herself kinda funny too. Reminded me of that tomboy chick on *Dobie Gillis.*"

Cannonball Adderly came around at the break, recognizing me and offering his condolences. I introduced him to Platt, who quickly turned the subject to music. Adderly was a jovial guy, heavyset and nicely turned out in a dark suit and tie, with black horn-rims that made him look intelligent, which he was. In short order, he and Platt learned that they'd jammed with some of the same musicians, up in San Francisco, back when Cannon was playing with Miles Davis. When the two sax players had their reminiscing out of the way, Platt brought the conversation back around to Buddy Bixby's final hours.

According to Adderly, Buddy had climbed onto the stage sometime before 2 A.M. and slipped easily into a groove. At some point, though, he faltered with the beat, missing a few notes, when he glanced out the open side door and into the small crowd of onlookers gathered on the sidewalk. Platt recalled a similar break in music when Buddy had spotted Nicky Pembrook barging into Sid Zell's party Saturday afternoon.

"In my experience," Platt told me, "that kind of reaction in a junkie often means he's just spotted one of three people—a cop, a connection, or a fellow user." Then, to Adderly: "You didn't happen to see who was out there beyond that door, did you?"

"Bunch of kids, probably locals, like you usually have when you play the Lighthouse in summer, with the side door open. Beyond that, I can't help you much." Adderly added that he had his doubts about an accidental overdose being the cause of Buddy's death. "I've seen the cat play all night long when he was high, man, never missing a beat. Buddy had discipline when it came to putting the horse in his veins. He didn't like the heavy spike. Everybody who knew him knew that."

"Suicide?" I suggested.

"I don't think so. With that nice gig you gave him at the Grove, he figured he was right back in the action again. He was talking about doing studio sessions, maybe putting together his own group. No, I don't see Buddy Bixby catching an easy flight to the Big Broadway, not when he had so much to look forward to."

Adderly asked us if we wanted to sit in for a set but we opted for a rain check. We shook hands and thanked him and he took the stage again. I glanced at my watch. It was exactly half past eleven.

PLATT and I strolled west a half block, past a sad-looking bar, a couple of surfboard shops, and a corner burrito joint. A skinny boy in a T-shirt and cutoff jeans whizzed by on a skateboard made from an old pair of skate wheels screwed to the bottom of a flat, narrow section of one-inch plywood. He pushed hard with his right foot, the rough wheels clattering along the hard pavement of a strand lined with old-fashioned lampposts that glowed through frosted globes.

We crossed the strand directly onto the municipal pier, which smelled of dead fish and crusty brine, and kept walking. As we reached the end, just beyond a small bait house, we had an unobstructed view of the dark ocean. On either side of the pier, open shoreline ran for miles. The beach was wide and clean, with gentle waves lapping along the edge of a broad, moon-shaped bay.

"Right there." Platt pointed north toward a stretch of sand near the water, deserted at that late hour, midway between two lifeguard towers. "That's the spot Ray Verdugo told me Buddy's body was found."

"Verdugo's your source with the county sheriff?"

Platt nodded. "Sergeant, homicide."

"His department's handling the case?"

Platt explained that like most small towns in Southern California, Hermosa Beach depended on the sheriff's department to investigate homicides. "But the county only comes in if the local department specifically requests it. In this case, the deputies initially sent out a crime scene team, which included a photographer and a coroner. How much deeper it goes will be up to the Hermosa Beach Police Department."

We heard the shuffle of heavy shoes and the jangle of handcuffs behind us. When we turned, we found ourselves facing the two uniformed cops we'd seen earlier. Each had his gun hand close to his weapon. The taller cop asked if we could read. I said that we could. He pointed to a posted sign signifying the pier was off-limits after midnight.

I glanced again at my watch. "Unless my timepiece is off, it looks like we've got twenty minutes."

"Your timepiece?" The cop smirked, turning to his shorter colleague. "The gentleman wears a timepiece. I guess a watch isn't good enough for him."

"We'll be gone by twelve," Platt said evenly.

"You'll be gone before that." The shorter cop pointed to another posted sign: *No Loitering.* "That applies particularly to fruits, beatniks, and Negroes who stray too far from their own neighborhood."

I saw Platt swallow with effort and his chest expand as he took a deep breath, the usual symptoms when he was doing his best to keep himself under control. When he spoke, it lacked the slightest hint of anger. "For what it's worth, officers, I'm San Francisco PD, retired. Rank of Inspector, two years ago."

The taller cop cocked his head grandly. "You don't say. . . . I guess they do things a little different up there. Here in Hermosa, a Negro has about as much chance of joining the force as a midget with a felony rap sheet. I don't think we even got one colored resident within our borders. Not that I've seen, anyway."

"Just protecting your property values." As he spoke, the corners of Platt's mouth curled upward almost imperceptibly.

"I don't think I like that smile," the other cop said, fingering the handle of his baton.

I wiped perspiration from my upper lip. "We didn't come here looking for trouble, officers. We just wanted to see where a friend of ours died on the beach yesterday, so we could say our farewells."

"The junkie jazz guy," the taller cop said.

"Buddy Bixby," Platt said firmly.

"We feel his death may warrant an investigation," I said, trying to sound conciliatory. "You know, the usual detective work."

The two cops looked at each other and broke into laughter so raucous that a gull resting on a nearby railing took off crying into the night sky. I opened my mouth indignantly to ask why that was so funny, but Platt silenced me with a hand on my arm.

"We got a police chief here who's real tight with the purse strings," the taller cop said. "Very careful about how he spends our taxpayers' hard-earned dollars. He sure don't want to waste them looking into the overdose death of a junkie, even if he was a hot-shot horn player."

"That's what he gets for hanging around with colored musicians," the shorter cop said, looking straight at Platt and keeping his hand by his baton.

"We'll be gone by midnight," Platt repeated with steely calm, keeping his eyes steady until the other man finally looked away.

"I'll be watching my timepiece," the taller cop said, looking at me.

When they were gone, Platt turned away toward the railing where the gull had been.

"I'm sorry about that," I said, but he cut me off by raising a hand and waving me off, while keeping his back to me. He leaned on the railing, staring silently out at the dark water, while I left him alone to deal with things in his own way.

"PLATT."

He looked over as I pointed back across the beach toward a stairway at the foot of the pier. A hooded figure had just left the steps and was crossing the sand toward the water, angling in the direction of the shoreline where Buddy's body had been discovered. A minute later the figure was kneeling, placing a small bundle on the wet sand.

Platt was gone in a flash, running back down the pier on his muscular legs. He was roughly fifteen years my senior, and he'd had a bad back when I'd first met him in San Francisco. Just the same, he quickly left me behind.

As we rounded the top of the stairs and bounded down to the beach, the stranger looked up and started to rise. Platt called out but the figure took off running, away from us and into the darkness. By the time we reached the same spot, the stranger was gone, leaving behind a floral bouquet with a hand-printed message: *Buddy—Jam with Gabriel, sing with the angels, and be at peace forever. Pix.*

Platt scanned the dark beach but the stranger was nowhere to be seen.

Just then, a harsh light struck us from the direction of the strand. I shielded my eyes, squinting, and saw the two cops standing by their patrol car, aiming its spotlight across the wide beach in our direction. Behind them, a faded sign with sputtering lights advertised the Mermaid Restaurant. Nearby was a little bar called the Poop Deck, the kind with portholes and an anchor for decoration that you seem to find close to the water in every little beach town along the Southern California coast. Up in the hills, in the houses and apartments, most of the lights were out. Except for the soft splash of waves behind us, things were very quiet.

"We're in a small town," Platt said, "that probably has a big police chief who runs things his way. I can pretty much smell it." He took a last look around—at the texture of the sand, its contours, and the evidence of recent tide lines visible in the traces of seaweed and debris strewn in patterns along the shore. "If there's something fishy about Buddy Bixby's death, I doubt that it's going to be uncovered through the usual channels." His eyes came around to me. "Let's get out of here, while we can."

MINUTES later, at the stroke of midnight, I was driving north along Hermosa Avenue, careful to keep the speedometer precisely at the speed limit and braking cleanly at every stop sign. In my rearview mirror, I watched the two cops follow in their patrol car until we reached the city limits and finally left them behind, passing a sign that said, *Welcome to Manhattan Beach.*

Platt glanced at it as we went by. "I guess that depends on who you are and what you look like." He settled back in his seat, setting his jaw, while I could almost feel the steam coming off him. We drove all the way back to the Ambassador in silence. Platt went directly to his room, without so much as a simple good night.

Chapter 11

B Y LATE TUESDAY morning, I still hadn't heard from Sid
Zell about my overdue fee. I wanted to get Buddy
Bixby's share to his family as soon as possible, so I
called Zell directly at Premiere Alliance Pictures in the
Valley. When I got him on the phone, he sounded in fine
spirits, suggesting I drive out to the studio to join him for
lunch and pick up the check in person. He made no mention
of Buddy's passing, and neither did I.

While Platt began sniffing about privately for more details about Buddy's death, I drove down Lookout Mountain
Avenue from Beatrice's place and turned left onto Laurel
Canyon Boulevard. The narrow, two-lane road snaked up to
Mulholland Drive, then wound down through the canyon
into the arid San Fernando Valley, the vast, triangular-
shaped, northwest portion of the city. Bordered on three

sides by low mountains, the Valley—as it was known to locals—was customarily ten degrees hotter than the rest of L.A., which put the mercury several notches above one hundred as I reached the valley floor at Ventura Boulevard. With my windows down and the air conditioning off to avoid overheating the engine, it was like driving straight into a blast furnace.

Premiere Alliance was located further on, between Studio City and Burbank on more than two hundred acres in North Hollywood. The administrative building was near the front gate, looming above two dozen soundstages and various structures designated for wardrobe, props, editing, and the like. Beyond, to the northeast, was a vast backlot with outdoor sets designed to resemble a Midwestern Main Street, a modern metropolitan avenue, and an Old West town built on the edge of open land that had served as everything from frontier prairie to moonscapes in hundreds of flicks Premiere Alliance had ground out over the decades. Zell had founded the studio in the late '20s with two partners he'd later bought out, assuming the role of the studio's first and only production chief, one of the many Jews who'd pioneered the nascent movie industry when they found themselves excluded from the anti-Semitic culture of corporate America. Zell quickly developed a reputation as a man with a canny instinct for popular tastes and a reputation for hard bargaining and tight budgets. One apocryphal story had him on the set, watching over the snacks for the crew, cutting donuts in quarters to keep costs down. Anita Loos had kept me informed of such things since I was a small boy, when I'd first come to stay with her for the healthy climate in the years following my mother's death. "Sid Zell's a force of nature," she'd told me, "who always finds a way to survive."

It was through Anita that I'd met her friend Beatrice Gless. Neetsie and I had driven out one afternoon in her new '48 Buick Roadmaster to visit Beatrice in her office on the Premiere Alliance lot, where she was putting the finishing touches on the script for the original *Dead Aim*. I was seventeen then, just starting to shave, trying mightily to lose my virginity, and awed by this mythical place where Anita and other lucky souls somehow got paid to work, mingle, and party with the most glamorous and recognizable men and women in the world.

I remembered the studio gates as I passed through them now—tall, imposing, heavy with elaborate wrought iron, with the studio name arched in ostentatious gold plating overhead. To my surprise, I felt a rush of the old thrill sweep over me, an odd feeling that reverberated even more deeply when I spotted a two-sheet for the remake of *Dead Aim* on display, with Monica Rivers's incomparable face staring back at me pressing the barrel of a revolver to her lips.

I gave my name to the guard, who found it on his list, placed a guest pass on my dashboard, and told me politely to drive on in.

"AAAYYY, sweetie! How ya doin'?"

Sid Zell popped up from the big chair behind his enormous desk as his receptionist ushered me into his office. A large window looked down on soundstages and studio streets that didn't appear all that busy.

"Most of our projects are out on location," Zell said, as if reading my thoughts. "Studio's a little quiet." He winked. "Won't last. Premiere Alliance has big things on the horizon, one hell of a year coming up."

He came around the desk, pumping my hand with a ring

on one finger so big it pinched my flesh. "My personal chef is preparing lunch. We'll eat right here in the office, save some time, if that's OK. Something came up—meeting with Steve McQueen, couldn't get out of it, you know how it goes. The kid wants to do a picture with us; I've got him eating out of my hand. Sit down, sit down!"

He put me in a chair facing his desk and went back around and sat. On the wall behind him hung framed photographs of him with dozens of Hollywood stars and big shots. In the middle of it all, center stage, was a framed diploma from Harvard, dated 1917.

"So you're a Harvard man." I grinned. "I'm a Yalie myself."

"Class of '17, long before your time," Zell said. "There were maybe two Jews on the whole frigging campus, and the other one had changed his name to hide the fact that he was a Yid. You want to know what Uncle Sid learned at Harvard about running a business like this, a movie company?"

"What's that, Mr. Zell?"

"*Bopkes! Bopkes,* I tell you. You know why?" He leaned across the desk, as if letting me in on a priceless secret. "Because there *is* no other business like this. A man brings his smarts, he looks around, figures things out, meets the right people, makes the right deals, he's on top of the world. And the best part is, he gets to make up the rules as he goes. Because there are no rules in Hollywood, kid! That's how the Jews got in. You come out here, you can be whatever you want, and to hell with where you came from. We created this industry from the ground up, made up the rules as we went along, changed 'em when it suited us. Most exciting goddamn business in the world!"

He opened a humidor, offered me a cigar. When I turned

it down he clipped, moistened, and lit it for himself, inhaling deeply.

"Like right now," he went on, "I'm sitting here with this talented young man, this excellent musician, this beautiful boy, with a name that's ready-made for a marquee. Philip Damon, what a monicker! And what am I saying to myself? I'm saying he's going to score my next big picture."

I sat forward on my chair. "Me? Score the music for one of your films?"

"You got it, baby. Major production with Liz Taylor and Sean Connery that's a shoo-in come Oscar time. Taylor wants lush background music. Elegant, sophisticated—specifically the kind Archie Damon, your old man, used to play."

"Miss Taylor said that?"

"Her gorgeous *tush* was planted right in that chair you're sitting in now. So savor the moment, kid. Told me how much she'd loved dancing to your old man's orchestra, cheek to cheek with Nicky Hilton."

"Miss Taylor's my age, Mr. Zell. Born the same year."

"Yeah, so what?"

"My father died in '43, the year before *National Velvet* came out. Miss Taylor couldn't have been older than twelve. She didn't marry Nicky Hilton until—"

Zell's cigar hand flew up as if waving away a pesky bug. "So she was a prodigy, what do I know? So maybe it was Mickey Rooney, not Hilton she was dancing with. The point is the music's gotta be like another character in the movie, bringing back that great old sound from the thirties."

"It's a period piece?"

"Yeah, sure, period piece. And I'm listening to Liz and I'm saying to myself, who better than Philip Damon to score this picture? Who better than America's preeminent society bandleader? I'm practically *kvelling,* thinking about it! And Liz says, 'Sid, if you think he's right for the job, that's good enough for me.' I'm telling you, Damon, this broad thinks you're the cat's meow."

"I'm awfully flattered, Mr. Zell, but—"

"And that's not all. You know what else I'm thinking? We make a follow-up to *The Archie Damon Story,* the picture we did about your old man back in '52. This time, we do *The Philip Damon Story,* the way you lost your beloved wife, then all that *cockamamie* business up in San Francisco, the one that was all over the papers. Romance, music, murder, sex—it's got everything. And here's the beautiful part, sweetie—we don't hire anybody for the title role."

"We don't? How do we make the movie?"

"Because you'll be playing yourself!"

"Mr. Zell, really, I've had no experience—"

"You think Bob Evans had experience when they cast him in *Man of a Thousand Faces?* He'd done one picture, back in '52, *Lydia Bailey.* Pure dreck! Then a few years later Norma Shearer spots him beside the pool at the Beverly Hills Hotel and all of a sudden he's playing Irving Thalberg in a major motion picture. Irving Thalberg for chrissake! Philip, sweetheart, listen to me, you're a great-looking kid! *The Philip Damon Story*—this is a movie that was born to be made."

"I appreciate the offer, Mr. Zell, but I'm not sure I want to dredge up the past."

"There was that Negro detective who helped you solve the case—"

"Hercules Platt."

"Platt, Platt, that's the guy. It's good to put a black in a picture now and then; we should all try to do these things more often."

"He plays in my orchestra now, alto sax."

"This Platt plays in your band? This is beautiful! Listen, Poitier's perfect for the role, a little young, but that's sexy. I've already spoken to Sidney about it and he's ready to go, just as soon as we've got ourselves a solid script. A mensch, that Sidney."

"This is moving pretty fast," I said. "We haven't even discussed the rights to the story."

Zell stood and came around the desk, leaning down with his arm around my shoulder. "That's the beauty, don't you see? You'll be my coproducer. We'll keep our up-front costs down and make the big money at the back end. *Oy vey!* I'm telling you, Phillie, this could be one of the sweetest deals I ever made in all my years in this crazy business. And you know why I'm cutting you in on such a profitable venture? Because you got class. I like class in a partner."

"I'll need some time to think about it."

"Sure, of course, you take your time. It's important to think these things through, consider your options. You don't want to rush into anything, make a bad choice." He was back in his chair, facing me again, puffing on the cigar. "Take Monica Rivers, for example. I know she's caught your eye, kid. But just between us, man to man, I think it would be a serious mistake if you let yourself fall for this broad. There are thousands of beautiful girls in this town. A good-looking guy like you can have his pick. Listen to your Uncle Sid. Shop around. It's a big candy store."

I let out a sigh. "I appreciate the advice."

Zell looked at his watch. "*Oy vey!* Look at this. Am I a *schlemiel* or what? You mind grabbing lunch on your own? I got this meeting with McQueen. Very touchy, this guy. I don't want to piss him off."

I stood. "Of course not."

"You understand, business?"

"Sure."

Zell came around his desk, turning me toward the door. "Listen, I'm shooting a little picture out at Point Dume, north of Malibu. How about you come out to the set one day next week, see how movies get made, now that you're part of the industry."

"I'd enjoy that."

He walked me into his outer office, where he instructed his receptionist to put my name on a list of cleared visitors for the guard at the front gate. "Mr. Damon's going to be doing plenty of business with Premiere Alliance from now on. In fact, see if we can find an office for him right away, get him all set up."

She eyed his big cigar as he exhaled, and winced as he coughed and thumped his chest with his fist.

"Your wife's going to kill you, Mr. Zell, if she catches you smoking one of those."

Zell laughed through his cough. "Hell, the cigar'll probably kill me first!"

He shoved two of them into my jacket pocket and shook my hand again, which allowed me a closer look at his big ring. Not surprisingly, it was a Harvard class ring, an emerald set in gold. I'd seen plenty of them on friends who'd attended Harvard when I'd been at Yale. Something about this one struck me as odd, though. I just couldn't quite place what it was.

I had lunch alone at the Smokehouse over by Warner Bros., feeling overwhelmed by all the possibilities that had suddenly insinuated themselves into my life, if that's what they really were.

The more I let my imagination go, the more I started to
see a career move to Hollywood, playing occasional engagements at the Cocoanut Grove and lavish parties up in the
hills, learning to score films alongside the great Hollywood
composers, maybe even acting in a few, as far-fetched as that
seemed. It might be fun, playing myself before the cameras,
the way Dad had done. What did I have to lose? The movie
work would surely help my album sales, which had been
sluggish in recent years. Even more important, all of it
would nurture my relationship with Monica Rivers, which
would develop in spectacular fashion along with our enviable careers. It was a heady fantasy, but Sid Zell had made
it all seem possible. No matter how hard I tried to shake it
off, I couldn't.

As I drove back over the hill, my head still spinning, I
realized that amid all the fast talk, I'd never collected my
check.

Chapter 12

⟨ornament⟩

LATE THAT NIGHT, following our second show, Gloria, Platt,
and I trudged upstairs to Platt's room to pack up Buddy
Bixby's meager belongings. We could have done it earlier, but no one really had the heart for it.

Except for his trumpet, which had been found in its case
next to his body, Buddy had apparently owned little of
much value. The nicest item among his possessions was his
new tux from Sy Devore, which would now become his funeral suit.

"At least he'll go out in style," Gloria said, going through
the pockets. On the bed, she placed a few toothpicks, a near
empty pack of Chesterfields, a matchbook from the Tropicana Motel in West Hollywood, and an odd-looking piece
of soft sponge not much bigger than a man's thumb.

Platt picked up the matchbook, studied it for a moment,

then turned his attention to the swatch of sponge. I asked him what it was; he said he had no idea, which was why it intrigued him. He found an envelope in a drawer of the writing desk, placed the matchbook and piece of sponge inside, licked and sealed it, then scribbled a few notes on the outside before slipping it into an inside pocket of his tux. We were folding the last of Buddy's underwear and socks into his old suitcase when someone knocked on the door.

Gloria went to get it. "That's probably Peggy."

Gloria had told us that Buddy's sister would be dropping around for his things, but she'd apparently forgotten to tip Peggy Bixby that Platt and I would be there. As she stepped in, she reacted to us with obvious surprise, pulling back from the hug Gloria was giving her, looking suddenly shy. She was a plain but not unattractive woman in her early thirties, tallish and trim, with horn-rim glasses and her long, auburn hair pulled back into a ponytail. Her attire was economical and unstylish: an off-the-rack dress with simple belt, creamy in color, that hung a few inches below the knees; inexpensive flats that looked like they could use new heels; a simple pink scarf around her neck; and, for jewelry, one of those engraved, silver-plated ID bracelets that had become popular in the '50s, hanging loose on her left wrist. She eased herself into the room, with her eyes down and her shoulders protectively hunched.

"I didn't expect so many people." She tried to smile, while her eyes never quite found a place to settle.

"Only three," Gloria said, and introduced us all around.

Peggy shook our hands stiffly. "I meant to come hear Buddy play. I suppose I'll always regret that I didn't."

"I should have left a comp for his family," I said. "I'm sorry, somehow it never crossed my mind."

"Oh, no—I was busy grading papers Saturday night, anyway. I'd planned to come another night and bring Mom and Dad. It would have been nice to hear him play one last time. Especially here at the Ambassador, with such a fine orchestra. I never really enjoyed listening to Buddy in a lot of those clubs he played." She smiled, shrugging haplessly. "Jazz isn't really my thing. It's a little, I don't know— unstructured, I guess."

Her eyes went to Gloria as if looking for help. "I'm talking an awful lot. I'm sorry."

"I just cleaned out the pockets of Buddy's tuxedo," Gloria said. "It's there on the bed, in the garment bag. He only wore it that one day."

Peggy Bixby unzipped the garment bag to inspect the tux. Tears welled up in her eyes. "I didn't even know he owned something this nice."

"Philip purchased it for him."

Peggy turned to me urgently, almost pleading. "Did he look nice in it, Mr. Damon?"

"Very handsome, Peggy. A publicity person for the hotel had photos taken. I'll get you some copies."

"That would mean so much." She blinked back tears. "I hope he played well."

"He did a fine job. The audience loved him."

Platt raised his chin, regarding her keenly. "You didn't get a chance to catch him down at the Lighthouse late Saturday night?"

"Like I said, I'm not really a fan of jazz. And I live way out in Norwalk."

"Plus all those student papers to grade," Platt said.

"Teaching keeps me pretty busy."

"In the middle of summer?"

"Summer school."

"Of course." Platt's smile was perfunctory. "Never been out to Hermosa Beach, then?"

"It's quite a drive. My old Plymouth's not too reliable."

"I guess that means no." Peggy flinched, but Platt pushed on. "So when was the last time you saw Buddy?"

"I drove him to a few appointments when he was just out of jail. Probation officer, medical checkup, things like that. Just for a day or two, last week. Then he went to stay with friends, at some motel in West Hollywood."

"The Tropicana?"

"Yes, I think that was the name. Buddy called me a couple of times. We talked. But I never got to see him again before—before he left us."

"You two were close?"

"Buddy and Peggy were very close." Gloria fired her words at Platt like well-aimed bullets. "She probably doesn't need all these questions just now."

I indicated the garment bag and small suitcase on one of the beds. "I believe we've got everything packed up, except for a few items we cleaned out of Buddy's pockets. Cigarettes, things like that."

Peggy seemed to brighten. "I appreciate everything you've done. I just wish the police cared as much about Buddy as all of you do."

Platt raised his eyebrows. "Dragging their feet, are they?"

"They seem to be giving his case a low priority." Peggy walked over to the bed, picked up the garment bag and the old suitcase, and stared at them a moment as if she was looking at all that was left of her brother's life.

"His records will always be around," I said. "His trumpet and his voice will always be heard. People won't forget him, Peggy."

When she turned to face us, tears streamed from her eyes.

"I know Buddy made a mess of his life. But he was a decent guy for all that. Mom and Dad are devastated by what's happened. So am I. At least if we knew how he died, we could put it behind us. But the way the police are responding, I'm not sure we'll ever know."

Her words struck me with unexpected force, and resonated deeply. For two long, agonizing years after Diana's death, I'd had to endure not knowing who'd murdered my wife and unborn child. If it hadn't been for Hercules Platt and his dogged detective work, I might still not know. I felt a sudden connection to Peggy Bixby, forged by our shared knowledge of a special kind of grief. As much as I abhorred violence and all things murderous, and wanted to keep the safest distance possible from them, I also knew that if I could help Peggy Bixby in some way, I would.

She juggled the garment bag and small suitcase to shake hands first with me, then with Platt. As he took her hand, I noticed him turn her wrist just enough to get a look at the inscription on her silver-plated name bracelet: *Pix.*

"A gift from Buddy?" he asked.

"Yes—how did you know?"

Platt shrugged. "Sounds like a good nickname for a little sister."

Gloria asked Peggy if she wanted to go out for coffee and talk, but Peggy begged off, mentioning a half-day of classes, starting at 9 A.M.

"You like teaching?" It was Platt again, with one of his endless questions.

"It's challenging work," she said, "and it doesn't pay too well. But I love it just the same. Helping kids learn—there's nothing more I'd rather do with my life than that."

Gloria held her hand. "We'll be in touch?"

Peggy's eyes met Gloria's for a long moment without

faltering. "Sure, I'd like that." Then she glanced uneasily at Platt and me and was out the door.

PLATT waited for the door to close before he spoke, directing his words at Gloria. "You and Peggy are awfully close."

"Old friends." Gloria quickly busied herself, closing empty dresser drawers one by one.

"Back to around the time you got divorced eleven years ago?"

"Around then, yes." Gloria's back was to us as she replaced empty hangers in a closet and closed it up.

"That was how you happened to know Buddy Bixby— through his sister?"

Gloria turned and brushed past Platt to tidy up the bed. "Peggy knew I was a singer, looking for work. She thought he might be able to help."

"Was he?"

"Buddy was sweet, but he had enough trouble just taking care of himself."

"How long were you and Peggy romantically involved?"

Gloria swiveled, dark eyes flashing in a face set with hard lines.

"Platt," I protested, "for God's sake."

Platt stood facing Gloria, as if I weren't even in the room. "Unless I'm mistaken," he said, "you two were lovers, and it was rather serious."

Gloria held her ground, not backing down an inch. "I don't see how that's any of your business."

"Peggy Bixby lied to us, Gloria. About where she was Saturday night, about when she saw her brother last, about ever being in Hermosa Beach."

"You don't know that."

"I have my suspicions."

"I still don't see why my relationship with Peggy has anything—"

"It might, if it helps me find out why she's lying and what she doesn't want us to know."

They stared hard at each other for half a minute. When Gloria finally spoke, her tone was cutting, resentful. If nothing else came of this unpleasant confrontation, I thought, at least it sounded like Gloria was getting her voice back.

"Yes, Peggy and I were once romantically involved. It lasted two years, but the pressure was too much for her. All the hiding, the fear of being found out, because of her job as a schoolteacher. She broke it off. We both lost something good."

"I take it you still have feelings for her."

"Yes, Hercules, I still care about her." Gloria sneered smugly. "Have I answered your questions sufficiently, Inspector? Are you happy now?"

Platt's smile was pained, almost an apology. "I'm never happy when someone dies mysteriously, Gloria. Not until I know exactly how and why."

Chapter 13

I SLEPT LATE the next morning, dreaming in Technicolor of a glorious life in Hollywood with Monica Rivers.

In my dream, we floated from Malibu to Toluca Lake to Palm Springs on a magic carpet replete with champagne, fresh oranges, and Oscar statuettes that each of us had accepted the night before to standing ovations from our peers. Then Beatrice woke me and we drove to the Beverly Hills Hotel for lunch at the Polo Lounge, reminding me that in Lotus Land—if one has sufficient fame and money—it's possible to keep the fantasy intact and reality at bay, at least for a while.

Spindly palms, listless in the heat, towered over us as we ascended the drive in Beatrice's big Hudson, with a vintage Rolls-Royce ahead of us and a new Lamborghini just behind. As valets opened our doors and we stepped out, the Pink

Palace appeared virtually unchanged since I'd last seen it several years ago—pretty much the same, in fact, since its opening in 1912: a complex of suites, ballrooms, bars, cafés, and bungalows in the Mission Revival style, painted pink, with touches of green and white trim. It sprawled splendidly across twelve lushly landscaped acres, where carefully tended gardens of azaleas, camellias, roses, and magnolias burst into thousands of pink and white blooms, while the scent of orange blossoms floated in the air. This was where Marilyn Monroe had sipped milkshakes, Liz Taylor had cavorted with various husbands in bungalows that went for a thousand bucks a night, and, out on the verdant lawn, Douglas Fairbanks, Jr., had taught Freddie Bartholomew how to play croquet.

As we sauntered up the front walk, a few dozen beauties in tight swimsuits—male and female—lounged around the pool or frolicked in the water, drops sparkling on their evenly tanned skin. At one end, Troy Donahue—several years from *Parrish* and losing his shape—tested the spring on the diving board, while drawing surprisingly scant attention. Beatrice and I entered the hotel to the air-conditioned cool, passing under glittering chandeliers until we reached the fabled Polo Lounge. For more than thirty years, Beatrice had taken her lunch here every Wednesday, first with her husband, Bernie, also a writer, and now as a widow of not quite a decade.

"Gives me a sense of continuity," she explained as we were seated at her favorite table. "Especially now, when everything is changing faster than a dice game." She tapped her watch. "Your friend Mr. Platt seems to be tardy."

It was half past twelve and most of the tables were filled. We told the waitress we were expecting a third person and described him. When she was gone, Beatrice opened her purse and brought out the magnifying glass she always carried when dining, using it to scan the menu, even though she knew it by heart. All around us agents, producers, and actors were schmoozing, making deals or eye contact, or simply trying to impress. I marveled aloud at how everyone in Hollywood seemed so connected.

"Hollywood looks quite big to those on the outside," Beatrice said, barely looking up from the menu, "but it's actually a very small community."

Swifty Lazar spotted us and dropped over to our table, adjusting the big horn-rims on his nose and running a hand over his bald pate. "Sorry to hear about Buddy Bixby," Swifty said, sliding in next to Beatrice. "Good-looking boy—even had a shot at a movie career a few years back, when a pretty face could get you by a lot easier than it can these days. Although they say this kid Redford has a shot, so maybe I'm wrong."

Swifty was compulsively fastidious—he washed his hands dozens of times each day—and he began to systematically rearrange the condiments on the table, making sure each item was equidistant from the others. It reminded me of the famous story of Swifty and the equally phobic Howard Hughes, together in a men's room, having just washed their hands. Neither was willing to touch the doorknob on the way out, so they waited several minutes until someone finally came in.

"Buddy mentioned a film he'd appeared in," I said, "something for Sid Zell."

"One of those quickies Zell knocked off for the passion pits back in the '50s," Swifty replied. "Hot cars, pretty girls, and big tits in tight sweaters."

"Now Sid's trying to prop up Premiere Alliance with beach party flicks," Beatrice said. "Poor Sid—the man's flailing with both arms like a man about to go under for the last time."

"If he does, it's his own damn fault." Swifty began refolding our napkins in a precise configuration that seemed to please him. "The film business is on the brink of a new creative era, an opportunity to take some chances after decades of the morality code, a chance to do projects that TV wouldn't touch. And what's that schnook Zell putting his money into? *Dead Aim.*" He touched Beatrice's wrist. "Don't get me wrong, sweetie—I loved your script, back in '48. A film noir gem, destined to be a classic. But a *remake,* for crying out loud? What Sid Zell needs right now is something fresh, original, a hot flick that puts Premiere Alliance back on the map. I've got half a dozen brilliant books he could adapt, if he had the balls."

"He's talking about a follow-up to Dad's movie," I said, trying to sound optimistic.

Swifty peered up at me birdlike through his big glasses. "He's remaking *The Archie Damon Story*? No offense, kid, but it laid an egg the first time around."

"Not a remake—this one would be *The Philip Damon Story.*" I shrugged. "At least that's what he told me. He says he wants to do it as a top-quality production."

"A sequel to a flop. *Oy vey.*" Swifty stood. "All I can say is, get your money up front—and don't sign anything until you run it by me first."

Our waitress brought us cold drinks, which we sipped while watching Swifty work the tables. Along his route, he stopped to chat with the dapper publicist Hedley Pinkston, who was decked out in a nicely cut seersucker suit and saddle shoes, with silver cuff links and a white carnation. Next to Pinkston was Sal Mineo, the baby-faced actor with the puppy dog eyes, a fading career, and an underground reputation as a man's man—as opposed to a ladies' man.

Beatrice gazed thoughtfully across the sunny room. "One thing I've never understood is Hedley Pinkston's clout. Flacks are generally treated like doormats in this business, but Hedley's carved out his own special niche, established his own peculiar power base."

"What niche is that, Bea?"

"Protecting stars with problematic private lives." She shook her head in wonderment. "He's something of an enigma, that Hedley."

I was about to ask if that meant Monica Rivers had a problematic private life that needed protecting. Just then, however, Hercules Platt approached, carrying a large manila envelope and apologizing for being late.

Chapter 14

HERCULES PLATT WAS meeting Beatrice Gless for the first time and it went about as smoothly as the *Titanic*'s introduction to that iceberg.

Already irritable from waiting for her food, Beatrice urged Platt to look at his menu, puffing herself up and making it sound like a reproach for his tardiness. Platt was in an equally prickly mood, and apparently in no hurry to order. He glanced around the Polo Lounge, surveying the faces. "I've read about this place—making movie deals on cocktail napkins, that kind of thing. I don't imagine they get too many black folks in here."

"Before he died, I used to see Nat Cole fairly regularly," Beatrice said, sounding defensive, "if that means anything."

"Nat King Cole—America's favorite black man." Platt smiled tightly. "So soft-spoken and polite. Yes, I guess they'd like him here." It wasn't Platt's nature to talk this way, though I didn't blame him; I suspected his recent run-in with the two white cops out at the beach had something to do with it. His eyes fell on the large manila envelope in front of him. "I brought along some crime scene photos. They may not be the kind of thing you want to look at during lunch—especially not in a swank place like this."

"But you brought them just the same, didn't you?" Beatrice's voice was chilly. She raised herself up as she spoke, drawing in her double chin. "Do you think we might order first, Mr. Platt? I'm rather hungry."

"Sorry, Miss Gless. I didn't mean to hold you up."

"It's *Mrs.* Gless, Mr. Platt. And I strongly doubt that your tardiness was wholly unconscious. In truth, you made a choice between continuing what you were doing and showing us the courtesy of being punctual. Clearly, whatever you were doing was more important to you."

Thankfully, the waitress came around just then and jotted down our orders. As she left, I pushed the rolls and butter toward Beatrice and secretly prayed that our meals arrived quickly.

Platt picked up the big envelope, opening the flap. "You can look at them or not, Mrs. Gless. I wanted to prepare you, that's all." His smile was stiff. "No point in spoiling a pleasant lunch."

Beatrice laughed sharply. "I drove an ambulance in the war, Mr. Platt. Not your war—the Spanish Civil War. I don't imagine there's anything in that envelope more shocking than I've already seen firsthand."

I attempted a smile. "Now that we've got that settled, why don't we just look at the pictures? Anyway, I'm probably the one who'll throw up."

Platt pulled a stack of eight-by-tens from the envelope

and handed them to me. He informed us that they'd been shot by a county crime scene photographer on loan to the Hermosa Beach Police Department, then passed along through Platt's connections within the county sheriff's department. The photos showed Buddy on his back, one sleeve rolled up and a hypodermic needle protruding from the extended arm. His face was ashen—eyes open, jaw locked in a death grimace—with flies crawling near his open mouth, where a small crab was already investigating.

"I'm glad no one ordered the crab cakes," I said.

On one side of the body, near Buddy's head, his trumpet case rested a foot or two above the tide line. On the other side, near the extended arm, two distinct knee prints could be seen in the wet sand, as if someone had been kneeling beside him when he died, or possibly afterward. His pants were wet in front, where he'd apparently urinated as he died, or soon after death. Nothing gory, really, just morbid and unsettling.

As the photos made their way to Beatrice, Platt mentioned that he'd also uncovered something interesting in Buddy's hotel room charges—several phone calls to Sid Zell's office.

"The obvious question," Platt said, "is why Buddy Bixby would be trying to contact a big shot like Sid Zell."

"Maybe Buddy left something behind at Zell's house Saturday afternoon, after we performed there."

"These calls started Friday afternoon, the day before we went up to Bel-Air."

"The day *before?*" I thought about it a second. "Buddy once made a movie for Zell. Maybe he was trying to drum up more work."

"Maybe. But is that how it's done?" Platt's voice had an edge to it, almost like a rebuke. "Call the studio honcho directly, instead of having an agent or a manager do it?"

"I suppose not." I gave a little shrug. "I'm just trying to be helpful, Platt."

Beatrice, who'd been silent, held one of the photos close to her face, peering at it through her magnifying glass. "How closely have you examined these photos, Mr. Platt?"

"Not that closely, Mrs. Gless." His smile was patronizing. "I knew I was running late. I didn't want to be any later than I was already."

"No, I'm sure you didn't." She handed the photo and magnifying glass across the table to him. "You might want to inspect the sand for indentions, an inch or two beneath each knee print."

Platt reacted with curiosity, adjusting his seat for better window light, then lifting the magnifying glass to the photo and studying it keenly. When he passed them to me I did the same. Just below the knee prints next to Buddy Bixby's body were two smaller indentions in the wet sand, walnut-sized and so shallow they were barely visible. Because of the tide line that night, everything below the odd prints, including footprints, had been washed away. I handed everything back to Platt. He studied the photo again, more intently.

When he finally looked up, it was toward Beatrice. "You've got a sharp eye, Mrs. Gless."

"For years, I scrutinized the dailies of the films I wrote, looking for continuity problems and other small errors. Not normally a writer's function, but I'm the meticulous type. I'm afraid it became something of an obsession."

Platt smiled more openly, looking relaxed for the first time since arriving. "Obsessions can be useful, when constructively applied."

"I couldn't agree more, Mr. Platt. One certainly needs to

be obsessed to succeed in the writing trade. Ambition alone won't get you there, least of all in Hollywood."

"Given all those murder mysteries you've written, you must know a bit about detective work."

"I've always found the process of investigation and deduction interesting. And I've always admired a dedicated sleuth. From what Philip tells me, that description fits you quite aptly."

Platt handed back her magnifying glass. "Nice to have you on the team, Mrs. Gless."

"Nice to be included, Mr. Platt."

Just then, the food arrived. A minute or two later, her blood sugar restored, Beatrice was chatting with Hercules Platt as if he were a long lost friend.

WE spent the latter part of lunch stargazing, which managed to impress even Platt, especially when Lena Horne waltzed in between two agent types.

"My god, look at that woman," Platt said, losing his usual cool. "She's even more beautiful in the flesh."

Beatrice smiled with irony. "Too beautiful, I'm afraid."

She and Platt shared a knowing look that left me out. I raised my palms inquisitively. "Too beautiful, in this town? I don't get it."

"Hollywood defines female beauty in white terms," Beatrice said. "Black character actresses are welcome, especially if they're on the large or homely side. But when it comes to leading ladies, the studios restrict the choices to basically one shade."

"Come on—Lena Horne, Dorothy Dandridge?"

"Lena sings for a living," Beatrice pointed out. "And Dorothy, one of the most beautiful women to ever set foot on a studio lot? Look what's happened to poor Dorothy." Beatrice sighed heavily. "It's remarkable, the power this business has to create images and shape perceptions. And rather sad what we do with it."

Platt stared out the window at the fine homes nestled in the rising hills. "Pretty much what's going on out there in the rest of the world."

Beatrice gave him a moment to gaze at some of the most costly real estate in the world, then proffered a surprising question: "Did you know that Beverly Hills was first settled by a black woman, Mr. Platt?" His head swung around as Beatrice continued. "Her name was Maria Rita Valdez de la Villa, a Mexican woman of African descent. Early in the last century, she was granted a rancho of four thousand, five hundred acres to tend horses and cattle with her family. In 1854, she sold her land for three thousand dollars to two white men. They subdivided, and the rest is history—the only history most people seem interested in."

Platt cocked his head intently. "You're sure about this?"

"Several years ago, at my own expense, I did some research and wrote a film script based on her life. The only screenplay I ever wrote that wasn't a studio assignment. Not surprisingly, no one wanted to make it." Beatrice smiled ruefully. "It's somewhere in a box at the house, with dozens of other scripts I've written over the past thirty years. I suppose I'll have to sort through them all, now that I'm writing my memoirs. I can't even remember the plotlines of half of them."

"But most of the other scripts got made," I put in.

"Yes, thankfully." Beatrice rapped her knuckles for luck. "All but two, in fact. The one I just mentioned, and a horse race story Sid Zell assigned me back in the late thirties. I thought I did a good job with it, but he never put it into production. I've forgotten the plot details, I'm afraid. That's what happens to us *alte kockers*—the older we get, the more our memories turn to mush."

BY the time the plates were cleared, the talk had edged toward events at Sid Zell's anniversary party, both on and off the bandstand. Platt again brought up the fact that Buddy Bixby had been playing almost flawlessly until the unexpected sight of Nicky Pembrook had given him a jolt. I filled him in on the confrontation I'd witnessed later between Pembrook and Zell, which Monica Rivers had defused by shoving cash at the younger man before sending him away. I mentioned other details as well—the arrival of the surfer, Johnny Langley, and Nicky's girlfriend, Vicki Hart, who'd pleaded with Pembrook to hand over the gun he was carrying.

Platt placed his elbows on the table, using his folded hands as a cradle under his chin while he fixed me with his eyes. "You think you might see Miss Rivers again?"

I told him it was a possibility.

"Good. Do your best to gain her trust. See what you can find out about a possible connection between Buddy Bixby and Nicky Pembrook."

"I'm not sure I'm comfortable using Monica that way."

"In what way exactly do you feel comfortable using her?"

Beatrice chuckled but I wasn't amused. "That wasn't what I meant, Platt, and you know it."

Platt picked up the crime scene pictures and leafed through them again. "I'm not asking you to be comfortable, Damon. I'm asking you to get me some information."

He didn't say another word or take his eyes off the photos until the coffee and dessert arrived. Even then, he kept the pictures close by, ignoring his blueberries and cream as he studied the grim photographs like a man searching for a key lost in the sand.

Chapter 15

THE CHATEAU MARMONT sat overlooking the Sunset Strip like a Norman castle, stately but faded, decades of Hollywood history sealed within its solid walls.

It was nearing 1 A.M. when I turned off the boulevard and up the hotel's steep front drive. The night manager phoned Monica, who cleared me to come up. I crossed the comfortable, unpretentious lobby, pushed the button for the fifth floor, and felt my heart pump a little harder. I was carrying a dozen long-stemmed white roses, wondering if yellow would have been a better choice, then worried that I should have chosen red.

Having been to the Chateau Marmont on other occasions, I was accustomed to the many celebrities who'd dallied there—Greta Garbo, Boris Karloff, Paul Newman, countless others. Not long after my father died, the great director

Billy Wilder had let me come up to watch him shoot a scene from *Double Indemnity* in his room, which was doubling as Fred MacMurray's apartment in the film. I remember seeing Barbara Stanwyck that day—actually catching the scent of her cologne as she passed—and experiencing a distinctly male reaction that made me grateful that I was carrying a sweater. But never in my most hormonal adolescent fantasies had I imagined returning one day to the Marmont for a secret rendezvous with one of the most beautiful women in the movies, even if Monica Rivers hadn't yet made the A-list.

"PHILIP—come in, quickly!"

Monica Rivers drew me into her suite, double locking the door behind us. In the background, the new *Getz/Gilberto* album was playing on the hi-fi. Music for young lovers, I thought as I floated into the room.

"I'm sorry," Monica said, "but I believe someone's been following me." Then, breathlessly: "You brought me white roses. My favorite. How did you know?"

I shrugged haplessly.

"Never mind, they're perfect." She took them, found a vase in the kitchenette, and put them in water. "How are you, Philip?"

"Happy to see you—but are you sure you're OK? If someone's pestering you—"

"You're here now. I feel better." She came back into the room, set the roses on the coffee table, then fussed the flowers into place. She was wearing a simple one-piece gown of light chiffon, barely more substantial than a negligee, with nothing underneath. Her long dark hair was down and brushed back, setting off her remarkable face.

"Your hair's lovely that way, for what it's worth."

She turned from the flowers to face me. "You like it?"

I nodded and was about to kiss her when she offered me a drink. "Sure. Scotch if you've got it."

"Dewars?"

"How did you know?"

"It's what you ordered at lunch the other day."

"Nice of you to remember."

"Nice of you to meet me for lunch, under the circumstances. My life is rather complicated, as you've surely noticed."

I wanted very much to kiss her. Instead, while she poured the drinks, I made a half-hearted effort to follow Platt's dictate to do some probing. "That was quite an affair, up in Bel-Air at Sid Zell's place."

"Yes, he knows how to entertain, doesn't he?"

"Lots of famous faces," I said.

"Sid likes that, though he doesn't draw the names he once did. I guess he's burned some bridges along the way."

"There was a young man, arrived late. Looked familiar. Little guy, jug ears. I know I've seen him before."

Her hesitation was almost imperceptible. "You must mean Nicky Pembrook." She turned, handing me the Scotch. "Little Nicky Pembrook, as he was known in the early fifties, when Sid put him in the movies."

"Do you know him well?"

"Nicky? Just in passing. We were in a movie together once. I feel bad about what's happened to him. This business can be tough on anyone, but especially on the ones who find success too soon."

"I understand Zell's looking out for him, though. Got him a job working with horses, something like that."

"Yes, at the track." She paused, giving me an odd look. "So many questions. That's not like you."

"Maybe I'm getting star-struck."

"God, I hope not. I hate the wall that puts up."

I touched her arm. "No walls, then. I don't want anything between us, Monica. Not if we can help it."

Our eyes met and held. Then she said, "It's warm. Why don't we take our drinks out on the balcony, check out the view? Leave your jacket, why don't you." I slipped it off and she took hold of my tie. "Let's get rid of this as well. No point in being uncomfortable." She unbuttoned my collar, then two of the buttons below that. Her fingers lingered a moment, toying with a few chest hairs, before she smiled like a vixen and teased me with a fleeting glance. She grabbed my hand and led me through a draft of warm air to the balcony, where we set our drinks on the rail. A zillion lights were spread out before us like a sea of stars.

"This weather," she said. "It just won't let up."

"Seems to get under some people's skin."

She faced me, our lips inches apart. "And what is it that gets under your skin, Mr. Damon?"

"I think you know, Monica." I reached out and drew her closer, until our lips touched and our bodies pressed together. The feeling was sweet, erotic, electric, all at the same time. Our kisses were starting to sizzle when a flash of light illuminated the balcony, causing Monica to pull away, shrieking.

I looked across to the adjacent balcony, where the decrepit photographer Hudley Pinkston stood grinning malevolently. His camera hung from his neck, its spent flashbulb cooling, while he dug into a pocket of his cheap slacks for a fresh one. Monica raced inside to her phone while I made my way through the room and out into the hallway, where I pounded furiously on his door, getting no response.

A minute later, the manager arrived, apologizing profusely. "He must have signed in under a false name, wearing a disguise. I promise you, this won't happen again." He knocked on the door, threatening to use his key, until Hudley Pinkston finally opened it.

"Out," the manager said. "Now!"

Hudley looked much the same as I'd first seen him, up in the roadway at Sid Zell's place, when he'd ambushed Monica in her white Jag—the shabby clothes, the same drab hair in need of washing, the purple birthmark plainly visible on his neck. He retrieved his soiled jacket and stepped smugly past me, offering me a sneer. I grabbed his camera, breaking the strap as I ripped it from his neck. He wailed and clawed at me, attempting to get it back, but I was able to work the camera open just the same. When I had the film out, exposed to the light, I shoved everything back into his grubby hands.

"There you are, Hudley. I owe you for a roll of film."

He was screaming now, so enraged that his birthmark looked almost neon against his pallid skin. "She's a public figure! I have a right to shoot my pictures! I'll sue!"

"Sue to your heart's content, Hudley." I poked him in the chest. "But next time, maybe it's your heart I'll rip out, instead of your damned negatives."

The manager grabbed Hudley by the arm and started down the hall with him.

"Wait," Monica said. She approached Hudley, facing him directly. "You know, if you came to the premiere tomorrow night like the other photographers, you could shoot all the pictures you want. I'd be happy to get you a pass for the red carpet. Hedley could arrange it." She looked him over, making a face. "It might be nice if you cleaned up a little first."

Hudley puckered his unshaven face with contempt. "Come to an event arranged by Hedley? So I can get some stupid shots of you posing with someone Hedley personally

picked out? I don't think so, Miss Rivers. I take my photographs from real life."

"What is it you have against me, Mr. Pinkston?"

His eyes widened, gleeful, a little wild. "You don't
know?"

"No, I honestly don't."

"You're one of *them.*"

"One of them," she repeated.

"One of the rich, beautiful people who think you're so
much better than the rest of us, who live your lives as if the
rest of us are scum. Who think you're so special, so different.
But you're no different than the rest of us, are you, Miss
Rivers? You've made mistakes, haven't you? You've got se-
crets to hide, just like everybody else."

I saw her eyes falter, her jaw clench.

"Let's go," the manager said, dragging Hudley off again.

Hudley pulled up, jerking his arm free, screaming back
at us. "I'm after the truth. Tell my brother Hedley I said
that, will you? I'm after the truth that he and the rest of
the Hollywood publicity machine works so hard to conceal!"

The manager shoved him into the elevator. Monica, swallowing with effort and looking pale, turned quickly back
into her room.

"I feel badly about this." We were both inside, with the door
locked behind us and the curtains pulled shut. "I feel as if
I caused it."

"Forget it, Philip. Forget everything." Monica poured a
double Scotch without offering me one. "We just met, you
and I, just now."

She downed the Scotch, shut off the lights, grabbed me
with startling ferocity, and pulled me down onto the big

bed. Everything after that became frenzied and blurred, our nasty encounter with Hudley Pinkston receding quickly into the past. We very nearly tore the clothes off each other, making love with a kind of mutual desperation, our naked bodies bathed by the hot wind wafting through the pulled drapes. Monica's beauty and sensuality were overpowering, her passion boundless, her hunger insatiable. I'd finally become lost in my Hollywood dream, only for real, a dream that went on for hours and felt timeless, without beginning or end.

So entranced were we with each other, so utterly lost in discovery and pleasure, that we never heard the sirens screaming across the city as patrol cars raced in the direction of South Central L.A., also known as Watts.

Chapter 16

JUST BEFORE SUNUP, I kissed a sleeping Monica Rivers and slipped quietly out of the Chateau Marmont, feeling as if my life had forever changed.

Except for a coffeeshop or two the Sunset Strip was deserted, all the hip clubs and tony restaurants shuttered and their parking lots deathly still. Across the boulevard, the dawn cast its golden light over the upper pinnacle of the Sunset Tower Hotel, an Art Deco masterpiece so well used two decades earlier as a setting in *Murder, My Sweet*. In the distance, sirens continued to wail, but they seemed far away and in my afterglow I hardly noticed them. The heat no longer felt so enervating and oppressive; it seemed comforting now, almost sensual as it wrapped itself around me.

At least it felt that way until I got back to Beatrice's place up in Laurel Canyon and picked up the *Los Angeles*

Times from the front walk. The lead headline quickly brought me back down to earth: 1,000 RIOT IN L.A.

The article itself was brief—two columns and maybe twelve inches on the first page, a few more inches inside—stating the facts succinctly: Shortly after 7 P.M. the previous evening, two California Highway Patrol officers had stopped a car near Avalon Boulevard and 116th Street in Watts, a predominantly Negro neighborhood roughly seven miles south of downtown. When the officers attempted to detain two Negro brothers as part of a drunk driving investigation, their mother became involved. Angry words were spoken, tempers flared in the scorching heat. A crowd gathered and began throwing rocks. Matters escalated, though the violence was apparently being contained. At least that was the rather skimpy version in the *Times,* which had probably been forced to remake its front page to accommodate the late-breaking story, going with the minimal facts at hand.

The riot didn't seem likely to get out of hand, I thought. The LAPD had a reputation as one of the best organized and most disciplined and professional police forces in the world, unlike some of the other departments where racial riots had flared up and spread in recent years. Surely, I figured, the LAPD would handle matters firmly but with good sense, and have the city back to normal in short order. It was hard to imagine easygoing Los Angeles having much of a racial problem, certainly not the kind of tension needed to sustain a major social uprising.

I placed the open newspaper on the kitchen table for Beatrice, shed my tux, crawled into bed, and slept for hours.

LATE that afternoon, as Beatrice worked in her office sorting through papers related to her memoirs, I called Platt at the

Ambassador to remind him that she was taking me as her guest that night to the premiere of *Dead Aim*.

Premiere Alliance had scheduled the event early—7 P.M.—to accommodate a buffet and party afterward for invited guests, including the press. My plan was to race back to the Grove immediately following the screening, in time to take over for Jack Jones after he opened the split bill.

I asked Platt how his Buddy Bixby inquiry was going—nothing new to report, he said—and finally got around to mentioning the flare-up of violence in Watts.

His response was terse: "We've got our bags packed."

"From what I've seen on television," I said, "the situation seems to be under control."

"I wouldn't count on it. There are things white reporters just don't get, even if they like to think otherwise."

"You sound worried, Hercules."

"I've got relatives in South Central, and nearby. They tell me it's a powder keg, but I already knew that. They also tell me the fuse is lit. When you've got a police force that's almost all white, operating like military, it tends to happen sooner or later."

I knew almost nothing about South Central, except that it had long been regarded in Washington circles as one of the country's more manageable and successful minority neighborhoods. As we talked, though, I learned things from Platt that I'd never heard before. His relatives lived in an area of Watts once known as Mudtown, he said, where a number of distinguished black artists and political leaders had been born and raised, among them Ralph Bunche, the Nobel Prize–winning statesman who'd attended UCLA. Watts had become a vibrant center of Negro culture and politics until 1926, when the influential Ku Klux Klan had moved to annex the city to Los Angeles, thereby undercutting Negro voting power. By World War II, Platt said, restrictive homeowners' deeds in outlying areas had reinforced segregation and created a white wall around the ghetto, sealing out the better jobs and schools while sealing in the community's economic decline and growing social problems, not to mention its general despair.

"There's a lot of anger bottled up down there," Platt said. "More anger and frustration than most white folks can ever begin to understand."

I could hear how torn Platt was. As a retired cop with a distinguished record, he respected law and order above all else, even when the imperfect justice system sometimes failed. Yet I also knew that he lived with his own personal rage minute by minute, working mightily to keep it capped.

"Surely," I said, "the Ambassador's not in any danger."

"Like I said, we got our bags packed."

"Hercules, I—"

"You and Mrs. Gless enjoy your movie. Get here when you can. We'll be waiting for your downbeat."

BEATRICE appeared as I hung up, cats scurrying around her thick ankles.

"You look exasperated," she said, regarding me keenly.

"So do you."

"You first."

I offered a shrug. "Hercules, this riot business. I feel rather helpless."

"Understandable. There's not much any of us can do at the moment."

"OK, your turn."

She threw up her hands. "My life. It's all in that room in file cabinets and boxes that I haven't gone through for years and years. I come upon scripts I spent months writing that I've completely forgotten. I see the titles, but don't even know what they're about." She sighed heavily. "Pushing seventy can be very depressing, Philip. You realize how much there is behind you and how little lies ahead."

"Doesn't sound like you, Beatrice."

"I'm just worn out, that's all, trying to put things in some kind of order."

"Maybe it's a good night for a movie then."

She brightened. "Yes, maybe that will cheer us up. An escape to the cinema." She glanced at her watch. "Cocktail first?"

"I was just about to suggest it."

AS we sipped our drinks in the quiet of the living room, I related my encounter early that morning at the Chateau Marmont with the repulsive photographer, Hudley Pinkston.

"I understand the public's appetite for celebrity and glamour," I said. "It provides a bit of harmless fantasy, a chance to rise above one's humdrum life for a while. But what I've never quite figured out is what drives the bottom feeders, those wretches like Hudley Pinkston who spend their lives digging for dirt on anyone in the public eye."

"I do have some views on the subject." She glanced sideways at me, attempting modesty. "That is, if you'd care to hear them."

"By all means, Beatrice."

She shifted her considerable bulk to assume a more regal posture, then began speaking in the rather imperious manner she often adopted when discussing matters she found personally distasteful. "It strikes me," she said, "that people who wallow in celebrity gossip—either as the purveyors or the consumers—do it in direct proportion to the emptiness in their own lives. Invariably, they're people of limited spiritual and intellectual substance, and not much imagination. More often lonely than not, and lacking in self-esteem. Their strongest emotion seems to be envy—they seem compelled to tear others down, so they can boost themselves up, at least in their own eyes. I'm not a psychiatrist, but—"

"But you're certainly beginning to sound like one."

We both laughed.

"It's tawdry and shameful, that's all I'm saying, all this snooping into private lives. It speaks rather poorly of us as individuals, and as a society. What's most troubling is that it's a phenomenon that seems to be growing—this appetite for anything personal and sordid, picked from the bones of the famous by vultures like Hudley Pinkston."

I shuddered, thinking about him. "I don't know that I've ever encountered someone so capable of giving me the creeps."

"To be honest, very little is known about Hudley." Beatrice smiled with irony. "Isn't it interesting that the very people who take such delight in judging and exposing the foibles of others are often the least comfortable having their own lives looked into?"

"Monica invited him to bring his camera to her premiere tonight. Can you imagine?"

"Of course she did. Because she knew he'd never come. He's like a mole, hiding in the dark, where he feels safest."

I closed my eyes, shuddering again. "I just hope I never run into him again, that's all."

"And what about the Buddy Bixby business? Has Mr. Platt unearthed anything new that might interest a mystery buff like me?"

"I have a feeling he's preoccupied with the violence that's broken out."

"And rightfully so," Beatrice said. "Tsk, tsk, tsk. Such problems we humans create, with all our prejudice and fears." She reached over and patted my knee. "Drink up, Philip. It's a premiere, after all. We mustn't be late."

Chapter 17

THE WORLD PREMIERE of *Dead Aim* was scheduled in Westwood Village, a charming shopping and entertainment district adjacent to UCLA. It couldn't have been more than ten miles from South Central, yet it seemed a galaxy away.

Dating from the late '20s, the neighborhood was an appealing pastiche of sun-baked buildings in the Mediterranean and Spanish Revival style, replete with eye-catching domes, minarets, and fanciful spires, and the world's single densest collection of movie theaters. Two of the more ornate—the Fox Westwood Village and the Bruin—faced each other on opposite corners at the cozy intersection of Broxton and Weyburn. According to Beatrice, with the gradual decline of Hollywood Boulevard the studios increasingly used Westwood Village to open their movies. The remake of *Dead Aim* was having its splashy premiere at the Fox Westwood, a venerable structure that mixed Spanish Colonial Revival with a touch of Moderne, under a tapered tower sculpted with Art Deco designs that supported a vertical neon FOX sign at the top. When I first saw the theater, I found it perfect for the opening of a Monica Rivers movie, at least as I perceived her: showy and inviting, with a sense of stature and a touch of class.

Beatrice and I drove in separate vehicles, meeting at Mario's across the street to share a bottle of good Chianti and a platter of eggplant parmigiana for eleven bucks. I was wearing my usual tux with red carnation, while Beatrice looked resplendent in a flowing silvery blue silk gown and matching shawl, tastefully accessorized with silver; she'd done up her luxuriant white hair in a crowning bun, carrying herself, atop her pumps, in a manner that commanded attention and respect. When we arrived at the theater, we found hundreds of fans crowded against the red velvet ropes, gushing or squealing each time they glimpsed someone famous. The press was penned up like a herd of sheep near a special section of the red carpet. Compliant celebrities, under the watchful eye of publicists, paused briefly on their way in to smile for the cameras and give the reporters an inane quote or two. Beatrice and I, being unimportant, were directed to the other side of the crimson carpet that bypassed all the folderol.

As we were about to step into the big lobby, a wave of screams erupted, dwarfing the adulation that had gone before. I looked back to see Hedley Pinkston at the curb, dressed sharply in evening wear, holding open the door of a long white limousine. Monica Rivers presented herself in spectacular fashion, extending one of the magnificent legs I'd stroked with such carnal joy barely half a day past. From the other side, Rock Hudson emerged, a trim, towering, broad-shouldered man who looked chiseled from granite yet oddly soft at the same time. As the screams rose to greet them, the two stars sauntered up the carpet arm in arm, so physically flawless before the flashing cameras that they seemed, for a moment, as unreal as their fixed smiles.

"We need to get inside," Beatrice said. "They'll only hold the reserved seats for another minute or two."

A uniformed usher took our passes, led us to our seats, and ripped off the tape that protected them from the less well connected. Seated, Beatrice found her eyeglasses and put them on, while I took in the cavernous theater. It was plush and ornate in the style of the finest movie houses of the Depression era, with a high, decorative ceiling hung with elaborate chandeliers and a wide stage and screen down front. Hundreds of people buzzed about the aisles and seats, all of whom seemed intent on seeing or being seen.

"Industry crowd," Beatrice said, with a hint of distaste.

Lorna Draper stood out prominently, looking anxious as her eyes darted about, never resting any one place too long. From time to time, she waved and smiled but when I followed the trajectory of her eyes, I never saw anyone waving back, or even paying attention. Pint-sized Nicky Pembrook was also there, holding hands with Vicki Hart, who smiled dutifully while Nicky tried to shake hands and chat up people who didn't seem terribly interested in talking to him. Nearby, watching like a hawk, was Johnny Langley, the muscular surfer who seemed to be Nicky's hired keeper; he was outfitted in a faded Hawaiian shirt, tattered jeans, and a pair of Chuck Taylor low-cuts, the perfect complement to his bronzed skin and sun-bleached mop. I'd done far more socializing in my thirty-four years than anyone my age had good reason to, and perhaps I sometimes used it as a buffer against loneliness. Yet I also took great joy in many of the people I knew; in a sense, because of my unusual childhood, my friends had always been my closest family. Yet here, in this bustling theater, there seemed to be a desperate, artificial quality to all the social energy, and I commented on it to Beatrice.

"Everybody's working an angle," she said, "looking for a deal, trying to make a new connection. You survive in this town by who you know, or who your agent knows, although you rarely trust any of them. Fred Allen said it best: 'You can take all the sincerity in Hollywood, stuff it up an ant's ass, and still have room for an agent's heart.'"

I craned my neck, hoping to catch sight of Monica Rivers, but instead found myself rising to shake Sid Zell's outstretched hand.

"Philip, sweetie! So what's your decision? Are we going to make a movie or not?"

"Mr. Zell, I—"

"Just kidding! Take another day or two to think about it." He swiveled on his polished loafers, looking past me. "Beatrice, sweetheart! My favorite screenwriter in the world. Come here, baby, give Sid a hug."

She stepped to the aisle, towering half a foot above him, and he stretched to get his arms around her wide girth.

"So just how badly did you butcher my script, Sid?"

"Go on, your script was a masterpiece, we barely changed a word." Zell glanced around as he spoke, waving, shouting out the occasional greeting before picking up the conversation again. "Maybe a line here or there, a little piece of action, nothing more. One thing I learned a long time ago, Beatrice—you don't mess with perfection."

"As long as I get my check for the rewrite, Sid. Which, by the way, my agent tells me is overdue."

He threw up his small hands. "Aaayyy, such a small thing to worry about on such a big night. Sit back, enjoy, I'll make a call first thing tomorrow." Then, as if a lightbulb had popped on in his head: "So I hear you're working on your memoirs."

"I expect to start writing in another week or two."

"You want to tell me what you're going to say about me? Or do I have to wait until the damn book comes out?" He laughed unconvincingly. "You probably want me to buy a copy, am I right?"

"How can you be so sure you'll be mentioned?"

Zell glanced at me. "She loves to make the jokes, this *bubee.*" Then, back to Beatrice: "You want an interview? Photos? A filmography?"

"There is one anecdote I want to use, Sid, if I can get the details right."

"*One?* What am I, chopped liver? We work together for nearly thirty years, I get one piddling mention in your book?" He turned and threw a kiss to a statuesque beauty taking her seat across the aisle. "Claudia Cardinale. Italy's greatest work of art since the Sistine Chapel. Geez, what a piece of tail." His eyes came back around to Beatrice. "So what's this anecdote you want to use?"

"Happened at a story meeting, back in the late thirties," Beatrice said. "As usual, you were taking credit for an idea that someone else had thought up. I must have been in a combative mood, because I challenged you to come up with an original idea of your own for once. When I backed it up with a twenty-dollar wager, you took me on."

"*Meshugge*! Why would I make a bet like that?"

"Because, Sid, you're an inveterate gambler who never

walked away from a chance to win some money."

Zell shook his head defiantly. "I'm sorry, I don't remember this. I don't think this happened. This was when?"

"Just before the war. To my surprise, at the next story meeting, you actually brought a fresh idea to the table, a premise good enough to hang a story on."

Zell brightened. "Yeah? And I got my twenty clams?" When Beatrice nodded, he gleefully clapped his hands. "Hah! So which picture was it?"

"It was a racetrack movie, something about a father, a con man, fixing races but finally bonding with his kid. That's about all that sticks. And the title, that I remember—*Sure Bet*. Short, punchy. I came up with that."

Zell's busy eyes suddenly settled. "You're going to mention that cockamamie project in your book?"

"Like I said, the anecdote, about the bet—"

Zell snapped like a turtle. "It never got made, it was piffle!"

"Perhaps to you, Sid. But I thought I did a decent job with the script. I was always mystified why you failed to put it into production. Horse race plotlines were quite popular back then. You could have borrowed Mickey Rooney from MGM, had yourself a winner."

"MGM would have wanted an arm and a leg!"

The more upset Zell became, the more Beatrice's eyes took on a special twinkle. "I'm really very keen to take a look at the script again after all these years. Glean some of the plot details I've forgotten."

He leaned in, lowering his voice. "Trust me, Beatrice, you don't want this in your book. For chrissake, all the great movies Sid Zell produced? You want anecdotes, I'll give you anecdotes coming out your ears. But, please, not some cockamamie movie that never got made."

"No, I like it." Beatrice smiled placidly. "It may just be the only original story premise ever to come out of the mouth of the great Sid Zell. I just have to find my notes, put the details together."

Zell smiled tightly, speaking crisply. "Sure, Beatrice. It's your book. You write whatever you want." He stared at her a moment longer until the lights dimmed, then turned away, looking vaguely distracted.

Beatrice settled her big body comfortably in her seat, looking pleased. "Always fun to stick a burr under Sid's saddle."

I glanced around one last time, hoping for another glimpse of Monica Rivers. There she was, coming down the aisle with Rock Hudson, surely the single most beautiful woman in the place, Claudia Cardinale notwithstanding. Hedley Pinkston was with them, directing them to their reserved seats a few rows behind us.

I proffered a small wave, but if Monica saw it, she gave no sign.

THE remake of *Dead Aim* was a disappointment, with leaden dialogue, implausible plot twists, and a plethora of self-conscious sex scenes, including a steamy shower sequence that seemed sure to stir controversy. Yet I sat transfixed through the film's ninety-two minutes, unable to take my eyes off Monica Rivers, or waiting with growing anticipation for the next frame in which she might reappear. As the credits rolled at the end and the lights came up, the applause was predictably enthusiastic. Beatrice wanted to make a speedy exit, to avoid facing anyone else associated with the movie.

"The rule is, you tell them you loved it or you do a fast

disappearing act. At my age, I no longer have the stomach to lie so baldly."

"I didn't think the movie was that bad."

"Oh, Philip!" We pushed our way into the crowded aisle, heading upward. "They butchered my rewrite, changed most of the dialogue, gutted all the subtlety and subtext. Stuck in enough silly plot twists to fill a daytime soap opera. And all that gratuitous sex! I'm no prude but how many showers did Monica's character really need? What is she, an obsessive-compulsive?"

"Swifty should appreciate that part, anyway."

As we made our way up the aisle, I saw Monica Rivers and Rock Hudson rising from their seats, surrounded by hovering sycophants.

"Monica was quite good," Beatrice whispered, "and I thought Richard Widmark acquitted himself very well, as usual. The movie may open decently because of the more exploitive elements. But the film looks like the last gasp of a studio trying desperately to survive. Poor Sid—I hear he gambled the farm on it."

Suddenly, I was face-to-face with Monica.

I felt a charge of excitement, and opened my mouth to say hello. Our eyes met for half a second before her mother stepped forcefully between us, looking as hard as steel. Hedley Pinkston turned Monica quickly up the aisle with Rock Hudson on his other side, pushing them through the crowd like an autocratic father herding two obedient children away from temptation and misadventure.

Chapter 18

THE NEXT DAY was Friday the 13th and luck didn't seem to be in the air.

The Los Angeles newspapers reported that mobs were looting stores and destroying cars in Watts. Seventy-five people had been injured, several fires had been started, and the governor had put the National Guard on standby alert. The *L.A. Times* ran a photograph of one of its white reporters standing in his jacket, tie, and horn-rim glasses, interviewing Negroes about their views on the lawlessness shocking the city.

"It's been coming for a long, long time," Beatrice said, while I worked my way through one of her incomparable Belgian waffles, which was drenched in butter and warm maple syrup. Beatrice and Bernard Gless had been involved in the Civil Rights movement as far back as the forties;

Beatrice had continued her activism after his death, travel-
ing south several times in recent years for protest actions,
despite the danger. "The only thing shocking to me is that
everyone's acting so surprised."

I sought escape from the news pages in the entertainment
section, where Hedda Hopper reported that Rock Hudson
would soon have to tear himself away from Monica Rivers
to shoot scenes in New York for *Seconds*. Below that was a
report by an Associated Press writer named James Bacon,
who declared that $100,000 was the new standard of re-
spectability for a movie star's home. Sinatra's hilltop lair in
Coldwater Canyon had just sold for an astonishing
$200,000. Someone else had paid $225,000 for Judy Gar-
land's twenty-two-room mansion, only to tear it down for
the lot. For a kicker, Bacon declared that any movie star
who lived in a house costing under $100,000 was "either a
has-been or a penny-pinching oddball."

"Everything's bigger than life out here, Philip. You know
that." Beatrice filled her coffee cup and sat down opposite
me, fixing me with her thoughtful eyes. "Our perception of
reality can become seriously distorted. That covers a lot of
territory, of course." Her pause sounded pregnant. "Rela-
tionships, even."

"If you're referring to Monica, Bea, I'm not ready to call
it quits."

Beatrice reached over, pinched my cheek. "All I'm saying,
dear one, is go in with your eyes wide open."

I drove to the Ambassador that evening turning the dial for
the latest news on the expanding riot.

KFWB provided ongoing coverage, but also announced
that it intended to bring listeners "continuous reports of the

Beatles' U.S. tour," "news of every Beatles appearance and press conference," "exclusive KFWBeatles interviews," and "every exciting highlight of the Beatles' American tour every hour," all of it available only on the "KFWBeatles Line."

I pulled into the Ambassador trying to concentrate on the evening's show, asking myself if there were any numbers that should come out. Songs like "Heat Wave," for example, that might not have the same crowd appeal anymore. As I strode into the Cocoanut Grove, Gloria Velez sat on a stool near the piano, plunking a guitar.

"What's that for?"

"I'm practicing," she said.

"For what?"

"For the inevitable day when we add some rock numbers to our play list."

"Are you doing this to upset me?"

She just smiled and continued picking at the guitar. I sat down at the piano, drowning her out with a furious version of Johnny Mercer's "Something's Gotta Give."

FOR the first time since we'd opened at the Grove the previous weekend, we failed to sell out the house. Even those who showed up seemed uneasy, particularly when we finished a number and sirens could be heard wailing in the distance.

It's always a challenge playing to a half-filled dance floor and empty tables scattered about the room. Yet I also found myself preoccupied by thoughts of Monica Rivers and my need to be with her again as soon as possible. Gloria, who was back on vocals, had picked up on my romantic drift, and inserted a song on the playlist that she sang especially

for me: "I Fall in Love Too Easily." But I never really heard
the words that night; all I could think about was getting
through our two shows and over to the Chateau Marmont
for another rapturous night with the woman who literally
occupied my dreams.

THE manager behind the front desk recognized me and I used
a house phone to call up to Monica's fifth-floor suite. When
she picked up, she didn't sound all that happy to hear my
voice. I told her I was downstairs, but she said she was too
upset by the negative reviews of *Dead Aim* to see me, even
though she'd gotten decent notices herself.

"I'll cheer you up," I said, "make you forget all about
those silly reviews. You know what they call critics—people
who go into the street after the battle's over to shoot the
wounded."

"I'm sorry, Philip, but I have a splitting headache."

"I'll give you a nice massage, rub your tension away."

"I'm just not up to seeing anyone. Call me in a day or
two, will you, when I'm feeling better? I really need to be
alone tonight."

She hung up, and I did the same, dispirited. I was on my
way out when I bumped into the novelist Terry Southern,
who was on his way in. I'd heard he was in town—his script
for *Dr. Strangelove* had made him a hot commodity in Hollywood—and I'd expected to run into him sooner or later.
He always dropped by if he was around and I was playing,
and we usually went looking for good jazz afterward, often
finding it in hip, back alley clubs where we stayed until the
wee hours. Terry had tons of friends, whom he called by pet
nicknames—mine was P.D.—although he moved through
life always observing from a wry distance. That night, as

usual, he was unkempt and slightly stoned, wearing a sear-sucker jacket that needed pressing.

"Hey, P.D., my man!" A Texan, his twang had long ago been lost to hip jive and slang. "What a gas, running into you like this."

He pumped my hand, using his other hand to push back his mop of unruly brown hair. I told him I'd stopped by the Marmont to visit a friend but was on my way home.

"At one A.M.? The day's only an hour old!"

I tried to beg off but he wouldn't hear of it, promising a party upstairs that would knock my socks off. He turned me around, slung an arm over my shoulders, and headed me toward the elevator.

"Great group of cats, P.D., and some very fine birds. Hollywood crowd, counterculture cats, destined for big things. Very hip, very groovy. Listen, I heard about Buddy Bixby, man. What a drag. The cat was very cool."

A minute later, I was in an upstairs suite with a drink in my hand, in the midst of a gregarious group, a few of whom I knew or recognized. Candice Bergen, Edgar's daughter, was there, whom I'd met once or twice before. Peter Fonda, Angelica Huston, a couple of other familiar faces, whom I knew through their famous fathers. Terry introduced me around to a blur of names: Dean Stockwell, Karen Black, Michael J. Pollard, Teri Garr, Warren Oates, others I quickly forgot. A young actor named Devin Hooper, bug-eyed and manic with energy, took one look at my sharp tux and carnation and insisted I pose for a photograph in the kitchen. He placed me on a chair between Angelica and a handsome young actor named Jack Nicholson, who had the most devilish eyebrows and grin I'd ever seen. In the background, a Bob Dylan LP was playing on a turntable and laughter erupted every so often like bursts of machine-gun fire. I'd never been to a party quite so loose and without pretension.

"I dig the contrast, man, the whole Yin and Yang thing," Hooper said, snapping his Nikon from various angles while a half-smoked joint dangled from his lips. "This is frigging fantastic, man—the old style, on its way out, and the new wave, on its way in. I love this, man!"

The old style. That was what I'd suddenly become, at age thirty-four, but I wasn't in the mood to contemplate it just then. When Hooper had his pictures, and I'd had another drink, I made my polite excuses and began working my way toward the door. The sweet smell of burning cannabis drifted in from the big balcony outside, where a group had gathered to stare off across the city, watching fires sprout up in South Central. I kept hearing two terms copped from the beat drug culture—*groovy* and *far-out*—as I bid Terry Southern good-bye, suggesting archly that he stop by the Grove one night if he still had a taste for some old-fashioned ballad and swing.

"Don't take it like that, P.D.," he said, chasing after me. "Devin didn't mean anything with that 'old style' remark. He's high as a kite, that's all."

Terry blocked my path to the elevator so I made my escape via the stairwell, my mood growing darker by the second. I was a little drunk, a little lonely, and probably feeling a little lost. There was only one thing just then that could set me right—to hold Monica Rivers again, if only for a moment. As I reached her floor, I paused in the stairwell landing, unable to continue down without at least putting an ear to her door. If I heard nothing, and saw no light beneath the door, I'd continue on my way, leaving her undisturbed. If she was still up, I'd knock.

I opened the stairwell door, about to step out. That's

when I saw Nicky Pembrook down the hall. He stood outside Monica's suite, tapping lightly, looking anxious. I receded a step, deeper into the stairwell, closing the door to just a crack. The longer Nicky waited, the more agitated he seemed to get, clenching and unclenching his small fists and rocking on the balls of his little feet. Monica opened her door, looked around, kissed Nicky quickly, and pulled him inside.

I stood there for several minutes, trying to digest what I'd just seen. Then I left the Marmont feeling disconsolate and betrayed, telling myself cynically that I should be happy for Monica, since she'd apparently gotten over her splitting headache, and her need to be alone.

Chapter 19

I NEVER WENT home that night.

Instead, I parked across the boulevard with a take-out cup of coffee, staring up at the windows of Monica's suite and humming "Blues in the Night" like a lovesick college kid. From time to time, I glimpsed Monica and Nicky in silhouette. They touched several times and one embrace lasted several minutes, his head against her shoulder. In between the embraces, their silhouettes disappeared, leaving the rest to my imagination.

Pembrook finally emerged from the hotel around 5 A.M. and drove off, but still I didn't leave. I sat in the Chrysler, watching her windows, while the hours passed and a series of other melancholy Sinatra tunes wafted through my head—"Sleep Warm," "It's a Lonesome Old Town," "I Guess I'll Hang My Tears Out to Dry." Just as "Ebb Tide" was fading

I was hearing the opening strains of "Good-Bye" I saw Monica pulling out from the hotel garage in her white Jag. She was wearing a strapless summer dress, a wide-brimmed hat, and dark glasses, looking every bit the stylish Hollywood actress.

It was twelve noon, straight up. I switched on the ignition and followed her, without the slightest notion of what I was doing, or why. All I knew was I couldn't let her go, not yet, not so easily. I had to know what was going on. I had to have some answers.

Vaguely, in the back of my mind, was the queer notion that Buddy Bixby might somehow be involved in all this. But Bixby—and his recent death—came under the purview of Hercules Platt. I had no idea where Platt was at that moment, or what he'd been up to since last night. So I tailed Monica, trying to sort things out the way Platt would have, and only getting more confused.

SHE drove south along various streets for roughly thirty-five minutes until she was into the city of Rosewood, a community with a sizable Negro population several miles west of Watts. Patrol cars were out in force, cruising the streets or parked watchfully at the larger intersections. Columns of dark smoke could be seen in the distance, toward South Central, and the sound of sirens never let up.

As Monica turned into the vast parking lot of the Rosewood Gardens Race Track, I followed at a safe distance. She left her Jag with a valet at the VIP section, while I parked where I could. I jumped out and tried to catch up, but by the time I reached the turnstiles, I'd lost her among the thousands of gamblers streaming into the big stadium.

I doubled back, found the valet who'd taken her car, told him I was late for a date with Monica Rivers—the owner of the white Jag—and wondered how I might find her. He told me she usually emerged to pick up her car with Mr. Zell, the movie producer. He suggested I should look for them among the private boxes in the lower deck.

I entered the stadium to the crowd's escalating roar, followed by shouts of jubilation or groans of disappointment. In the unfamiliar labyrinth of tunnels and stairwells, I lost my sense of direction and emerged out a tunnel at the west end of the track, not far from the paddocks and stables. A race had obviously just ended: patrons were tearing up tickets, studying racing sheets, or heading toward the windows to collect their winnings or place new bets. Spread out before me was a wide, clean dirt track running around a lovely infield of lakes and gardens, complete with floating swans, like a set borrowed from Frank Capra's *Lost Horizon*.

I leaned back against the railing, scanning the lower boxes toward the middle of the track for Monica Rivers and Sid Zell. Several minutes passed this way, to no avail—too many boxes, too many faces, at least from this far off. At the risk of being spotted, I was about to move closer, when I noticed a number of young men riding or walking the spent horses back toward the stable area behind me.

Among them was Little Nicky Pembrook. He was on foot, leading a sleek black mare with shiny, sinewy flanks, and thick froth at her mouth. Even now, several minutes after the race had ended, her breathing was unusually labored, and the wild look in her eyes suggested confusion, possibly fear. Pembrook stroked her muzzle gently as he walked beside her. He'd always seemed on edge but today he looked more troubled than usual.

A moment later, he disappeared into the stables with the weary mount, reaching up toward her flaring nostrils while she whinnied and jerked her head.

It took me the better part of an hour to locate Monica Rivers and Sid Zell. By then, I'd found a restroom, cleaned up the best I could, and grabbed a hot dog and a Coke to sustain me in my search. I also picked up a racing form in the lounge and placed two five-dollar bets on the next race, one on the 4-to-1 favorite, another on the 15-to-1 long shot, to give me a reason for being there in case I got discovered.

Monica and Zell were in a private box with a choice location, several rows above track level for a good view and dead even with the finish line. When I spotted them, as I came down the aisle behind them to their right, a high-stakes race of three-year-olds was in progress. Zell was on his feet, jumping up and down and hollering, as the horses rounded the far turn. Monica rose to his side, though she seemed less interested in the dramatic race developing out on the track than in trying to get his attention, to engage him in a serious conversation. I scanned my racing form, following the numbers on the jockeys and the call by the track announcer. As the horses charged the finish line, the long shot surged ahead to win, while the top three favorites lagged behind, seemingly out of gas.

Zell raised a triumphant fist in the air, looking like he'd just won an Academy Award. He and Monica left their box, climbing an aisle in the direction of the payoff windows, while I discreetly followed. Zell exchanged his ticket for a

huge roll of cash, thumbing eagerly through it as he and
Monica walked away. She looked frustrated to the point of
anger, but seemed resigned to the fact that whatever she'd
wanted to discuss with him would have to wait until another
day.

I slipped up to the same window, turned in my winning
ticket to the cashier.

"I guess I should have bet more heavily," I said. "Like
that guy ahead of me."

The cashier looked up from counting out my winnings.
"Mr. Zell? Definitely a high roller. Sure knows how to pick
'em too. Walked away with a bundle just now."

The cashier counted off seventy-five dollars, which he
shoved at me under the bars of his window.

"He plays the horses a lot?"

"Mr. Zell? He's been here almost every day since the
season opened."

"What's his secret?"

"Beats me, but he sure has a knack for knowing when
the big horses are going to have an off day."

"Does he always come with the same lady?"

The cashier looked beyond me at Monica and Zell as they
headed toward an exit.

"Usually younger," he said, and followed it with a wink.

BY the time I reached the parking lot, Monica Rivers and
Sid Zell were driving off in their separate vehicles. I jumped
in my car and tried to chase after her, thinking maybe I
could flag her down, suggest we get a drink somewhere, talk
over some things. But as she pulled out into street traffic,
it became quickly apparent that the best thing to do was
get out of Rosewood as fast as possible.

The cops were in a frenzy of activity, erecting barricades at intersections, sealing off side streets with their patrol cars, checking their shotguns for ammunition. All around, sirens wailed—not just patrol cars but ambulances and fire engines and paddy wagons speeding past. With great urgency, uniformed officers were directing traffic out of the stadium parking lot, pointing every car west, away from Watts. Tension was palpable in the air.

As I drove out of Rosewood, I saw sheets of plywood going up over store windows, the words *Black Owned* spray-painted across the front. A convoy of military trucks streamed past me, filled with anxious-looking National Guardsmen, each one armed with a heavy rifle. I hit the gas pedal and quickly put Rosewood behind me.

It wasn't until I got back to Laurel Canyon that I saw the morning *L.A. Times,* with its two-deck, banner headline:

EIGHT MEN SLAIN,
GUARD MOVES IN

Fires raged unchecked, according to the report, while another front-page headline suggested a cause for all the trouble: RACIAL UNREST LAID TO NEGRO FAMILY FAILURE. Another piece ran below this chilling summation: "GET WHITEY," SCREAM BLOOD-HUNGRY MOBS. More riot articles were sprinkled on the inside pages, amid endless department store ads showing pretty white models wearing the latest fashions.

By nightfall, the authorities were enforcing a curfew over a fifty-square-mile area, with Watts at the epicenter. The Ambassador Hotel temporarily shuttered the Cocoanut Grove for security reasons and members of the orchestra scattered to various locations to put some distance between themselves and the growing violence.

All but one checked in to let me know they were OK and where they were. I kept waiting, but after nearly twenty-four hours, I still hadn't heard from Hercules Platt.

Chapter 20

"AS LONG AS we can see the Hollywood Sign," Gloria said, "we know we're in the general vicinity."

I was driving and Gloria Velez was giving directions, reading from a set of instructions Claudette Colbert had personally dictated to Gloria over the phone.

"It seems a little strange," I said, "heading for a party in the Hollywood Hills while half the city burns."

"It's a Saturday night," Gloria said. "The Grove's shut down. We might as well get out, get our minds off all the trouble."

"Who exactly is going to be at this party?"

"An interesting mix." Gloria's tone was cryptic, playful. She checked street numbers as we approached the open gates of a steep drive. "Turn in here and go all the way to the top."

*   *   *

CLAUDETTE Colbert resided in a grandly spacious, two-story home that was Beaux Arts in style, with a hint of French about it. The striking exterior feature was a Palladian-like porch; inside, a wide, sweeping staircase dominated the opulent living room. A number of the rooms displayed the work of French impressionists, although several eighteenth-century English paintings—including originals by Gainsborough, Lawrence, and Reynolds—hung from various walls.

"Holy moly," Gloria said, looking around at the big rooms and the fine furnishings. "I'm glad I made myself respectable."

"More than respectable," I said, looking her over. "Smashing would be more like it." Her dark hair was pulled back off her heart-shaped face, showing to full effect her wide brown eyes and feathery lashes; a sheathlike dress of red satin hugged her compact but curvaceous body; her gold accessories, tastefully understated, complemented her dark, sultry looks. I leaned close, whispering in her ear. "Be truthful, Gloria. Did you dress for someone in particular? Miss Colbert perhaps?"

Before she could respond, Claudette Colbert found us, greeting us hospitably and offering drinks.

"Music to my ears," I said.

"Speaking of music, Mr. Damon, my grand piano has just been tuned. Feel free to try it out, if you'd like."

"A drink or two, and I just might." I glanced at Gloria with a wink. "Especially if we can find a vocalist willing to fill the bill."

Miss Colbert saw to our cocktails, then left us to meet

Robert Taylor and Barbara Stanwyck coming in the entry hall. Gloria raised her glass of sherry, indicating the next room. "Shall we find a corner and do some stargazing?"

We settled near a draped window between the grand piano and a magestic Kentia palm, where we could take in a couple of dozen guests at once. Off to the side, Randolph Scott and Vincent Price were hobnobbing, both accompanied by their wives. Near the big fireplace, Edward Everett Horton carried on with Clifton Webb and Ramón Novarro, the three of them bursting suddenly into high-pitched laughter. Across the room, Dan Dailey huddled with Janet Gaynor, chatting over cocktails and cigarettes. Cary Grant, who'd lived with Randolph Scott for a time in pleasant domesticity, stood across the room chatting up a buxom young blonde who seemed to have Grant's full attention. Gloria had been right—an interesting mix indeed.

"You must be the singer Gloria Velez." William Haines approached with a tall martini in one hand and a slender gentleman on his other arm. They were both in their sixties, dapper and suave. Haines separated from his companion and, with a bow, kissed Gloria's hand. "Claudette described you in the most flattering terms. She told me I should make a point of meeting you."

Gloria may not have recognized Haines, but I did. He'd been a well-known film actor until Louis B. Mayer had given him an ultimatum in 1933 to choose between his career and living unapologetically as a homosexual. Haines had chosen the latter; he quit acting and became a top Hollywood decorator, charging exorbitant fees for designing the homes of some of the same studio executives who'd blackballed him—thanks to their wives, who hired him.

His eyes moved from Gloria to me, making a quick appraisal. "And this fine-looking young man, so tall, dark, and handsome. This one I recognize from his album covers. Philip Damon, if I'm not mistaken."

I raised my glass to him and he introduced his friend, Jimmie Shields. "We've just begun our fifth decade together, Jimmie and I. Joan Crawford insists we have the best marriage in Hollywood." Haines cast his mischievous eyes across the room. "You know the saying about Hollywood men, don't you, Mr. Damon?"

"I'm not sure I do."

"Half of them are queer and the other half can't seem to decide." He winked broadly. "Kind of like the navy." His eyes slid appreciatively toward the lanky, handsome Randolph Scott. "*Follow the Fleet*, indeed."

Haines asked Gloria if he might introduce her around, in particular to Marlene Dietrich, who was having a smoke on an upstairs veranda with Cesar Romero and the director Dorothy Arzner. "I think Marlene's in one of her moods," Haines said. "You're just the fresh young flower to bring her down to earth."

I excused myself to refresh my drink and step outside for some air. On my way out, I found a telephone and used it to call Beatrice, to check on any phone messages that might have come in. She told me there were none.

It was nearing midnight, and I still hadn't heard from Hercules Platt.

I stepped across the brick patio behind Claudette Colbert's manse, passed through an elaborate garden of hedges and blooming rose bushes, and strode over a broad lawn toward the sparkle of city lights. As I neared the edge of the property, I noticed a tall, broad-shouldered figure leaning on the waist-high wall. His back was to me as he stared out at the vast metropolis that Dorothy Parker had dubbed "seventy-two suburbs in search of a city." To the south, buildings could be seen blazing away in Watts and surrounding neighborhoods.

The man turned at my approach, a spent cigarette in one hand, a leather-and-chrome pocket flask in the other. His tie was askew, his hair mussed, his demeanor drunk and morose. Despite the flaws, he was still unmistakably Rock Hudson.

"Evening," I said.

He glanced at his watch. "Two minutes past midnight. Officially, another day. Tick, tick, tick."

He faced the city again, looking out.

"I'd read that you were in New York," I said, "shooting scenes for a new movie."

He shifted his eyes, studied my face. "Do we know each other?"

"Philip." I extended my hand. He set aside his flask to shake it.

"I'm flying to New York tomorrow," he said, "unless they shut down the airport. Hell of a mess, this racial situation." He glanced at the ashy stub in his fingers, flicked it over the wall. "You wouldn't happen to have a cigarette, would you?"

"Sorry, don't smoke." I realized he didn't have a clue who I was, which was just as well, given my feelings for Monica.

"I should quit, anyway." He stared out again, sounding weary. "At my age, I'd better start taking care of myself. It's not like I'm Spencer Tracy, is it—hired for my acting skills."

"You're still a young actor, and you've done some fine work."

Hudson glanced over, laughing harshly. "I'm turning forty, pal—*forty.*"

"Like I said—"

"Everything's about to change, I can feel it. Music, the movies, all of it. Hell, it's happening already. You wonder what you'll be doing five years from now. I don't see the masses lining up for too many more Rock Hudson–Doris Day flicks." He shuddered. "There's always TV, I guess."

"Whatever happens, you've had an enviable career."

"You know how long it's been since *Giant*? Almost a decade. The year after it was released, the exhibitors voted me the country's top box-office star. And what happened?"

"You've made a lot of movies since."

"A lot of crap, for the most part." He put the flask to his lips. His Adam's apple bobbed as the liquor rolled down. "My work in *Pillow Talk* wasn't exactly Oscar caliber, was it?"

"For what it's worth," I said, "I always felt you had a natural, easygoing quality. You definitely have a presence."

He looked at me keenly as if trying to gauge how much to trust me, or what I might want. "I've never had an acting lesson, you know." He took another drink, sagging a little, looking more vulnerable. "You develop certain skills when you're forced to grow up hiding the truth. You become a consummate liar, a great pretender." He laughed, but it sounded bitter. "Valuable assets, especially in this town."

An awkward silence followed. Finally, I said what I'd been building up to from the moment I'd first engaged him: "I'm surprised you're not with Monica Rivers tonight."

Hudson snorted a laugh. "Hedley Pinkston let us have the night off." Hudson glanced my way. "You know Hedley?"

"Not well. We've been introduced."

Suddenly, he reeled off the names of several actors of less prominence whose careers had been destroyed by scandal in recent years—a vice arrest, a drug habit, statutory rape. Hudson's speech was slurred, his tongue loosened by the alcohol. The words were coming so fast I was having trouble sorting them out. "*Confidential* ruined all of them," he said, "thanks to Hudley Pinkston's photographs and grubbing around. I wonder how many others his brother will barter away to keep me safe, how many other lives Hedley judges my career to be worth." From his lips came an exhalation of disgust. "Hedley, Hudley—sometimes I wonder which one is the true evil twin."

He mumbled something about *Rio Bravo*, a film released in 1959, and *El Dorado*, currently in production, both directed by Howard Hawks. "Different titles and names for the characters," Hudson said knowingly, "but that's about all that's different."

He tipped the flask again but found it empty. When he wobbled I put a hand on his back to prop him up. He looked me over with his drunken eyes.

"I hate to disappoint you, pal, but I'm a gentleman." He grinned, causing the corners of his eyes to crinkle. "And, as everyone knows, gentlemen prefer blondes."

Before I could correct his misperception, he told me it was time to find a cigarette. He tucked away his spent flask, collected himself, and strode back across the wide lawn, while I tried to make sense of his odd allusions to the Pinkston twins, and to movies with overlapping plot elements.

Chapter 21

THE NEXT MORNING, Beatrice and I sat glued to the television set, absorbing the latest riot news: looting, sniping, Molotov cocktails, fire damage approaching $20 million and the death toll at twenty-five.

The phone rang. I grabbed it. It was Hercules Platt.

"Where the hell have you been, Platt?"

"I'm with family, over in West Adams. As a P.I., I've got a permit to carry a gun. I thought I might be useful to them. We're all OK. Thanks for asking."

I apologized, told him I'd been concerned, and asked him what part of town he was talking about. West Adams, he explained, was an architecturally historic district near downtown that had once been home to some of Hollywood's elite, including Hattie McDaniel, Ethel Waters, and Butterfly McQueen. Caucasian residents, however, had taken umbrage to Negroes moving in. White flight in the '40s had turned West Adams into a ghetto headed for serious decline.

"So I'm staying in a fine old Victorian once owned by Busby Berkeley," Platt said, "in need of a new roof and front porch. That is, if we don't get burned out first."

I asked if he could get away to attend the memorial for Buddy Bixby, scheduled that afternoon in Hollywood. He told me he'd meet me there, if he could get past the police barricades in between.

THE memorial for Buddy Bixby was held at Shelly's Manne Hole on Cahuenga Boulevard, a popular club operated by the jazz drummer Shelly Manne. When I arrived at three with Gloria Velez and other members of the band, Platt was waiting out front, saxophone case in hand.

Inside, the cigarette smoke was thick and the booze was flowing. Shelly was up on the stage with his sticks and a makeshift band of remarkable talent: Hampton Hawes on piano, Shorty Rogers on trumpet, Charlie Mingus on bass, and Art Pepper playing alto sax. Dozens more musicians filled the room, many of them older black players, the elder statesmen who'd been forced to form their own union in the forties, when the music business was segregated and Jim Crow laws forbade them from working in the movie industry, where so much of the work was. In the fifties, it was the great influx of white musicians to the West Coast scene who played a cooler, more technical brand of jazz that kept many of the gifted black artists from making a living, one reason so many of them had taken off to Europe for so many years. Most had finally come back, only to find soul music and R&B luring young black audiences away, and the struggle continued. Still, they'd managed to make fantastic music in the jazz clubs along Central Avenue, the legendary street that gave South Central its name, and in outlying joints like the Lighthouse and Birdland West, where many classic jazz recordings had been put to vinyl. It was great to see so many of them here today, under one roof, celebrating America's one truly indigenous art form.

Platt had coffee while I drank Scotch and we took turns jamming until Peggy Bixby showed up around four. She took the stage shyly, thanked everyone for coming and Shelly for lending the space. She'd let her hair down, literally if not figuratively, and lost the eyeglasses for a while; her face was surprisingly pretty for someone who seemed determined to play down her looks. She said a few words about her brother, not much, but enough to let us know that Buddy had always thought of his fellow musicians as his second family. We'd been passing the hat and Gloria turned over a nice pile of cash to help with funeral expenses. Then Peggy stepped from the stage, joining Platt and me at our table down front, while Gloria picked up the microphone.

Dave Brubeck was at the piano now and he cued the other guys. A moment later, Gloria was singing Buddy's signature song, "Good Morning, Heartache," slowly and deeply felt, in a way that would have made him proud. As she sang, she kept her eyes right on Peggy Bixby, who finally let her guard down, dissolving into tears.

A couple of tunes later, Gloria put the mike aside and joined us. I asked Peggy if she wanted something to drink, and she requested a Virgin Mary. Gloria took a chair beside her, pulling it close.

Peggy thanked her for the special song, began crying again and opened her handbag, fumbling for a tissue. By accident, she dumped her purse in the process, spilling the contents beneath the table. Platt and I were quickly on all fours, gathering up the scattered items. Among them was a business card for a life insurance agency that I picked up and started to tuck back into Peggy's purse. Platt snatched it, along with the handbag, studying the card intently for a half a minute as if committing it to memory. As I looked on, mortified, he opened Peggy's wallet and systematically inspected what he found inside, before handing everything back to her with an innocent smile.

Peggy got her Virgin Mary but seemed more interested in Gloria. The two women bent their heads low, talking in murmurs neither Platt nor I could hear above the sound of the musicians jamming passionately in the background. When Gloria and Peggy left together an hour later, I had no doubt that their old feelings for each other had been rekindled. Less clear was just what Hercules Platt was up to. As usual, he wasn't saying much. A few musicians drifted out over the next couple of hours but the guys were really into the jam session and most of us stayed on. Then, rather suddenly around seven, many of the black players were on their feet almost en masse, grabbing their hats and instruments, hollering good-byes, heading for the door. Platt was among them.

I suggested we drive over to El Cholo in Silverlake for some choice Mexican food. Platt just tapped his watch, smiled ruefully, and shuffled out with the others. Afterward, as I realized why, I could have kicked myself: He was headed back to the Negro neighborhoods and an 8 P.M. curfew that didn't apply to the rest of us.

I picked up some Chinese for dinner and headed home. A note was waiting for me on the kitchen counter: Beatrice was out with Rabbi Kaminsky, dancing to Louis Armstrong at the Royal Tahitian, their way of coping with all the madness. I finally got around to opening the *L.A. Times*, which carried a front-page article under an ominous headline:

"BURN, BABY, BURN" SLOGAN USED AS FIREBUGS PUT AREA TO TORCH

According to a bio credit, the writer was a Negro salesman from the advertising department who'd been recruited as a reporter, apparently because the paper had no blacks on its news staff. The slogan, he wrote, had been the innocent, on-air signature of a local deejay, KGFJ's Magnificent Montague. Rioters had co-opted the phrase as their inflammatory war cry, as well as a password for safe passage on the street. *Burn, Baby, Burn*. I had to admit, it had a nice ring to it. Someone would probably turn it into a lyric, I thought, one of those screaming rock groups that could plaster it as a title on an album cover and sell a million copies to tone-deaf kids.

At that moment, the world felt like it was literally going to hell. I poured a Dewars straight and deep, flipped through Beatrice's collection of old 45s, selected a few, and slipped a stack onto her turntable: "Haunted Heart" by Jo Stafford, "Ev'ry Time We Say Goodbye" by Jeri Southern, "Deep Song" by Billie Holiday, a few others. They reminded me of the great film noir classics of the '40s, especially those from Raymond Chandler but also a few originals written by

Beatrice herself. The kind of movies Toots Shor had lamented, that never got made anymore, or at least not very well.

I stretched out on the sofa, letting the alcohol do its job, losing myself in the music, trying to hold off the future just a little longer.

Chapter 22

SID ZELL HAD invited me to visit the location of a movie he was shooting out in Point Dume, and I decided to take him up on it. On Monday, shortly after lunch, I was cruising north along Pacific Coast Highway through Malibu, while the ocean sparkled like a Panavision dream.

The picture was *Zombie Surfers from Mars*. Zell's assistant had advised me to look for a hand-painted sign along PCH indicating where to turn off.

"Don't make the mistake of turning at the first movie location you come to," she'd warned me. "That would be *How to Stuff a Wild Bikini*, the new Frankie and Annette flick. Our shoot is two miles further on."

"I thought that one was already out."

"You're probably thinking of *Beach Blanket Bingo*, Mr.

Damon. They shot that last year. Just watch for the *Zombie Surfers* sign."

I spotted it as I careened down a sweeping curve with a wide sandy beach spread out below me, bordered by cliffs and picturesque outcroppings of rocks. Camera trucks, catering vans, and honey wagons were lined up in a long parking lot like a circus caravan. Out on the beach, a crew was filming a group of attractive young actors and extras in swimsuits. They were gyrating like puppets, performing some kind of go-go dance to a recording of the most godawful music, while in the deep background surfers rode their big boards in the frothy waves.

As I made my way across the sand, most of the surfers were trotting out of the water to guzzle soda while they got their instructions for the next scene. A few kneeled in the sand above their long surfboards, working hard with walletsized bars of wax, layering the upper middle portion to provide more traction for their footwork. Only one surfer had stayed out on the water—a bronzed, muscular fellow with sun-bleached hair, cutting up a wave in a style that somehow combined a feeling of glorious abandon with consummate skill, not unlike fine jazz.

"Langley! Johnny Langley!" An assistant director stood at shoreline, bellowing through a bullhorn. "Langley, we need to clear the water for the next setup."

Johnny Langley ignored the A.D.'s instructions long enough to catch one more wave, riding in with all the grace and freedom of a bird in flight, as if the ocean were the sky and belonged to him alone. Watching from shore was Nicky Pembrook, a look of awe on his boyish face.

Sid Zell approached, laying a hand on my shoulder, welcoming me to the set. Over the next half hour, he gave me a crash course in moviemaking, spinning out such terms as *blocking the scene, diffusion, dolly shot, walk-through,* and *zoom.* I glanced around at a couple of dozen crew members scurrying to move cameras, lay track, check light meters, and dab actors with makeup.

"I guess I never realized how complicated shooting a movie could be."

"Piece of cake," Zell said, "once you've cranked out a few hundred." He handed me a sheaf of papers he'd been carrying, rolled up in one hand. "Here are your lines for Wednesday. I've booked you for a screen test in the evening. I'd shoot it earlier but I got business that day."

I started to protest; he cut me off.

"Not to worry. It's just a short scene to see how you feel in front of the camera. Look it over tonight, get a feel for the basic emotion. That's all it's for."

"But Mr. Zell, a screen test—"

He turned away from me, beckoning to a voluptuous chlorine blonde who'd been standing around in the skimpiest bikini I'd seen this side of St. Tropez.

"Cherry, honey, I want you to meet Philip Damon. Philip, Cherry Topping, up-and-coming star of stage, screen, and television. Cherry's here to film a little cameo as a favor to her Uncle Sid. She'll be at the studio on Wednesday, shooting your screen test with you." Zell leaned in, winking. "It's a romantic scene, kid—heavy on the lip lock."

Cherry Topping extended her hand, speaking in a low, breathy voice. "Pleased to meet you, Mr. Damon. I'm a big fan of your music."

Zell made his apologies and left us to attend to some business. As he trudged across the sand, Cherry Topping praised him as a man of great artistic vision who was incredibly generous in giving new talent a chance. As she talked, I watched Zell pause among a group of extras in two-piece swimsuits, teenage girls with budding breasts, flat tummies, and nicely rounded derrieres. Within moments, he had them giggling and blushing, while his hand strayed to one girl's lower back, following its curve to rest on the crest of her perky bottom. Without turning her head, she reached back and removed his hand. When it returned a moment later, she stepped abruptly away from him, turning to face the ocean as her eyes scanned the beach. It was then that I recognized Nicky Pembrook's girlfriend, Vicki Hart.

She walked directly toward the water, where she snatched up Nicky's hand, kissing him affectionately on the cheek. He turned to smile fondly at her for a moment, but his eyes were quickly back on Johnny Langley, who came trotting up from the tide, dripping wet. He dumped his surfboard off on Nicky, who accepted it gratefully, struggling to hold up the big board with his spindly arms.

"YOU and Nicky seem quite close."

I'd discovered Vicki Hart alone in the shade of a large umbrella close to shore, and introduced myself. Nicky was down by the water again, out of camera range, watching Johnny Langley paddle out on his knees to catch a wave, doubling for the star in the current shot.

"I love Nicky more than anything." Vicki seemed sweet and unassuming, without a trace of pretension. She'd been born and raised in Ohio, she said, by parents who were still together after thirty years. "Corn fed, right on the farm." She laughed, lowering her eyes. "I saw Natalie Wood in *West Side Story*, and that was it—I knew I had to get to Hollywood somehow and become an actress."

She acknowledged that Nicky had problems, but said he

was working hard to straighten out his life. He had the job at the racetrack and was only on the location today because Rosewood Gardens had been shut down by the riots. "He's awfully worried about those horses—if they're getting fed and exercised properly. For now, we're staying at a motel in West Hollywood, but we're hoping to put together enough money to rent an apartment and start a real home."

"The Tropicana Motel, by any chance?" I recalled the matchbook Gloria Velez had discovered in a pocket of Buddy Bixby's tuxedo, following his death.

"How did you know?"

I didn't, so I winged it. "Everything else around there is on the pricey side, isn't it?"

"It's not the greatest place," Vicki conceded. "A lot of rock 'n' roll people stay there, the ones who really haven't made it yet. I think that's why Nicky likes it—if he couldn't be a surfer, like Johnny, he'd probably want to be in a rock band. He wants to make it big again. You know, like when he was in the movies as a boy."

"They say rock and roll is what every kid dreams of these days."

She laughed, embarrassed. "Not me. I'm determined to be a serious actress. I'm just an extra now, but I'm taking classes."

"I guess Mr. Zell helps out—keeping you working as an extra."

"You noticed." Her smile tightened. "Yes, Mr. Zell gives me a 'hand' every chance he gets."

"Why do you put up with it?"

"With the problems Nicky's had, we both need the work, so we can build a nest egg, get a decent start."

"Zell apparently expects something extra in return."

She set her jaw firmly. "The more Mr. Zell can't have

something, the more he wants it." She smiled tartly. "That can be useful, if you're pretty enough."

So Vicki Hart wasn't the sweet young innocent she'd at first appeared to be.

"I'm surprised Zell doesn't get Nicky some extra work, on some of these movies. You'd think that would be easy enough."

"Nicky never wants to work in front of the camera again, Mr. Damon. Not even as an extra, in the background. He says it was too painful. Do you know how Mr. Zell got Nicky to cry for certain scenes? He'd whisper in Nicky's ear that he had no father or mother, that they gave him away because they didn't want him. Nicky was a little kid, raised by aunts. It always worked. He'd break down crying, Mr. Zell would step out of camera range, and they'd get their shot."

"It can be an ugly business, I guess."

"Nicky wants to produce movies now—that's where the money is."

"I thought he wanted to be a rock star."

"He's keeping his options open, just in case. Mr. Zell promised him that if he straightens out, he'll bring him into the company, let him work his way up."

"That job at Rosewood Gardens, working with horses. That must be a test, then—to see if Nicky can handle responsibility."

"That's exactly what Mr. Zell told Nicky. It's the second chance Nicky needs so badly." She held up one hand, showing me two crossed fingers. "He can do it, Mr. Damon, I know he can. Even if nobody else believes in him, I do."

We watched the cameras roll as Johnny Langley switched from his knees to a straddling position, sighted a swell building on the horizon, pulled his surfboard around so the nose pointed toward shore, fell to a prone position, and began paddling with his powerful shoulders and arms. As the swell overtook him, he let it pick up his board, propelling it forward with increasing speed. With perfect timing, Langley jumped to his feet, planted them in the center of the big board, then worked his stance backward and forward like the nimblest of dancers. He rode the cresting wave like that for nearly a minute until he was out on the very edge of the nose, "hanging ten" as he somehow kept his balance, shifting his supple body to accommodate the mass and motion of the water.

Finally, the A.D. yelled, "Cut!" Then Langley was hunched on both knees again, paddling back out to do it all over again, while Nicky watched in adulation.

"Nicky apparently holds Johnny Langley in high regard."

Vicki laughed. "I think he'd *be* Johnny if it were somehow possible. Johnny's OK. He takes care of Nicky when he gets out of control, usually when Mr. Zell asks him to."

Cherry Topping sauntered past, making eyes at me before moving on. I wondered aloud if she had any scenes left to shoot that day. Vicki Hart giggled.

"What's so funny?"

"You won't find her name on the call sheet, Mr. Damon."

"Zell told me she has a small part in the movie."

"Cherry Topping's not an actress, Mr. Damon. She works at the Body Shop on the Sunset Strip. That's the only place she gets any billing."

"You're saying she's a stripper."

"I think they call themselves exotic dancers now."

I scratched my head. "Is anybody in this business what they claim to be?"

"I like to think I am, Mr. Damon." Vicki Hart laughed but it didn't sound very happy. "Maybe that's why I'm not very successful yet. Nicky says that's the key, to just be yourself in front of the camera. But I don't know if I can do that."

"Why not, Vicki?"

She pursed her lips, looking brave but doubtful. "Because that's how you get hurt, the way Nicky did. I want to be an actress, I guess, but I'm not sure I'm willing to let them use me like that. Sometimes, I think maybe I'd be happier back in Ohio, away from all this."

"A minute ago, you said—"

"I know—that I was determined to be a serious actress. I guess I'm confused. You probably think I'm silly, don't you? Just a silly kid, who doesn't know what she wants. I guess you think Nicky and I are both pretty silly."

"If it makes you feel any better, Vicki, I'm confused myself sometimes." I was thinking of Monica Rivers, of course, and how badly I wanted to see her again, if only to confront her about her clandestine rendezvous with Nicky Pembrook at the Chateau Marmont. I'm not sure any woman had ever confused me quite as much.

BY late afternoon, *Zombie Surfers from Mars* had only one shot left to film, but the director was having trouble getting the take he needed. Clouds had gathered and the lighting crew was scrambling to adjust. It only proved that even in Southern California—where the beautiful light and temperate climate had attracted the early movie pioneers—shooting conditions weren't always perfect.

The long waits between shots were getting tedious, and I decided it was time to go. That's when Cherry Topping found me again, to ask if she might catch a ride with me back into town. I lied, telling her I was meeting friends for dinner in the Palisades. She placed a hand on my chest and rubbed her knee against the inside of my leg.

"Maybe you could change your plans, Mr. Damon. Maybe *we* could have dinner instead." She pouted seductively beneath her chlorine curls and teased her impressive cleavage with a painted nail. "Or something just as good."

I attempted to gently disengage myself, but Cherry was draped on me like a strand of wet seaweed. Just then, the director called for quiet and readied the cameras to roll. Before he could signal for action—while I was still trying to extricate myself from Cherry's determined embrace—a brazen voice cracked across the beach, shouting expletives at Sid Zell. All heads turned to see Monica Rivers storming across the sand in our direction, carrying her high heels like weapons. As she zeroed in on Cherry, Zell rushed to head Monica off. It looked as if she was about to inflict serious damage on Cherry's voluptuous anatomy when the stripper peeled herself away from me and Zell stepped between them.

"Monica, sweetie, what a surprise."

"Don't 'sweetie' me, Sid! Every time a man looks sideways at me, you send in this bimbo to distract him."

"I am not a bimbo," Cherry Topping said. "I'm an *actress*."

"You couldn't act your way out of a speeding ticket with a horny cop."

Tears sprang to Cherry's eyes. "Mr. Zell, are you going to let her speak to me that way, in front of so many of my colleagues?"

"Cherry, get lost." Zell snapped his fingers, causing a production assistant to step forward. "Take her home, now."

Monica let loose with a foul-mouthed diatribe, lambasting Zell for everything from the fine print of his contracts to the low quality of the food his catering trucks served on location. Several times, Zell alternately tried to get a word in and looked at his watch. Finally, he glanced up at the changing light in the sky, throwing up his hands.

"Are you happy, Monica? You ruined the last shot of the day. You know what this is going to cost me?"

Behind him, the beleaguered A.D. used his bullhorn to call the surfers in from the water.

Monica stepped forward, right into Zell's face. "Happy, Sid? I'll tell you what's going to make me happy." She stepped to my side, taking my arm. "Philip is going to drive me out to Palm Springs this evening, where I'm going to have a meeting with Mr. George Cukor."

"I am?"

Monica ignored me, staying on Zell. "You do know who George Cukor is, don't you, Sid? Director, sensitive to actresses, makes great pictures. *Little Women. The Philadelphia Story. My Fair Lady.*"

Zell looked skeptical. "You're going to see George Cukor?"

"Yes, Sid, all on my own. About a plum role in a wonderful film he intends to direct, instead of the kind of garbage you keep foisting on me. I heard about it through Swifty Lazar." She turned to me, her eyes blazing. "We'll take my car, Philip. You can pick yours up in the morning."

I looked around, taking in the faces. Almost every set of eyes was on us. The only disinterested party seemed to be Johnny Langley. I watched him toss a bar of wax to Nicky Pembrook and order him to put a fresh layer on his surfboard, to provide better footing. Nicky kneeled devotedly over the board, eagerly waxing every inch, even the rails along the sides, which didn't seem necessary.

"Philip?" Monica lowered her Ray-Bans on her nose, peering at me above the rims. "I'd like to leave now, while we still have some daylight left."

I glanced at Sid Zell, smiled weakly, offered him an apologetic shrug. "Sure, Monica, I'll drive you out to the desert. It'll give us time to talk."

Zell raised his voice, giving it an edge. "Do I need to remind you, Monica, that you have an interview with Rona Barrett in the morning?"

Monica pushed her dark glasses back up, raising her shaped eyebrows at the same time. "Maybe I'll make my interview with Rona, and maybe I won't."

As we trudged back up the beach, I heard Zell behind us, screaming at some poor lackey, "Find Hedley Pinkston and get him on the goddamn phone!"

MONICA had the top down on her Jag. As I sat behind the wheel, acquainting myself with the unfamiliar gearbox positions, I took a last look at Sid Zell's picturesque location.

Out on the beach, the crew was packing up its equipment. Nicky Pembrook and Vicki Hart stood hand in hand at the edge of the water, sharing a tender kiss. Johnny Langley was out on the water again, riding the waves he seemed to love more than anything. Behind him, pelicans and gulls glided low, looking for dinner.

Monica laid a hand on my thigh and smiled the way only certain women can. I shifted the Jag into gear and we took off for the Springs.

Chapter 23

MONICA AND I sped across the desert east of Los Angeles with the sun fading and the warm air blowing through our hair.

We talked, laughed, and leaned close from time to time to share a kiss, while I did my best to keep my eyes on the highway ahead, relishing the time I had alone with her. I still had serious questions for Monica, starting with the night she'd shared with Nicky Pembrook at the Marmont, and the silhouette embraces I'd seen. For now, though, she seemed interested in nothing more than being with me— *close* to me—and I didn't want to spoil it.

It might have been a perfect drive if I hadn't noticed a yellow '56 Mercury in the rearview mirror, following at a fixed distance, mile after mile.

* * *

ACCORDING to Monica, George Cukor kept a Palm Springs house for getaways and socializing, tucked privately along a quiet side street off Gene Autry Trail.

As we turned off Palm Canyon Drive, away from the hubbub of hotels and restaurants, the distant mountains were deep purple in the twilight. Shaggy fronds of towering palm trees trembled all around us in a gentle breeze that barely tempered the arid heat. When we found the house, Monica got out without a word and marched on her high heels straight up the front walk and rang the bell. The house was a one-story white stucco, tasteful with clean lines in a modern design, landscaped naturally with rock and cactus. I caught up to her but stayed on the walkway, off the step, not sure what role I was supposed to play. From over a high wall, I could hear the splash of bodies in a swimming pool and lots of laughter that sounded male.

George Cukor came to the door in a light terrycloth robe and open-toed sandals. As Monica spoke to him, it was clear he wasn't expecting her. He was a small, slightly built gentleman with white hair and wire-rimmed spectacles, pleasant looking in a grandfatherly way and surprisingly gracious despite the awkward situation. Monica explained that she only wanted a few minutes of his time, that she felt so strongly about working with him that she'd come all the way from Los Angeles, risking his displeasure, just to speak with him. He glanced over his shoulder, into the house, then back again.

"A minute, Mr. Cukor, that's all I ask." Monica clasped her hands in front of her, fingers intertwined, as if praying. "It would mean so much."

He explained that he was entertaining friends, but agreed to see her briefly. He escorted us into his living room, asked his Filipino houseboy to bring me something cold to drink, then left me there and disappeared with Monica into another room.

Through the big windows across a dining area I saw an expansive patio and kidney-shaped swimming pool, where fifteen or twenty men lounged, dived, or splashed. They seemed almost evenly divided by age: half in their twenties or thereabouts, uniformly tan, trim, and attractive; the rest past fifty, with well-maintained faces and bodies that nonetheless gave away their advancing years. It was an extremely friendly gathering, with a good deal of laughter and affectionate touching, and the occasional stolen kiss.

Within minutes, Mr. Cukor reappeared with Monica, thanking her for taking such an interest in his film but sounding relieved to be getting rid of her.

"FOR someone known as a woman's director," I said, "he doesn't seem to have too many females in his immediate social circle. Odd not to see one girl in the bunch."

We stood on the front walk, while laughter and splashing water mingled over the wall behind us.

"I don't know," Monica said. "It's not much different than Errol Flynn's old place, on certain occasions. Merely a matter of gender."

"You knew Flynn?"

"It's where I met Sid Zell. Poolside at Flynn's house up in Montecito. I went up with my mother, around the time Sid was casting *Dangerous Beauty*."

"Zell and Flynn were pals?"

"Like a lot of powerful men in Hollywood, they shared a special affection for budding beauties between the ages of fifteen and twenty." A hard edge came into her voice. "And, believe me, there were plenty of us like that around Hollywood. Still are, of course. Always will be."

"You sound bitter. What's that about?"

"I don't know a pretty woman in the movie business who doesn't feel at least a little bitter, Philip. Marilyn Monroe may have been smiling when she remarked that in Hollywood, a girl's virtue is much less important than her hairdo. But she's not smiling now, is she?"

I'd known Marilyn, through my father's old friend Joe DiMaggio. "No, Marilyn's dead and gone, rest her soul."

Monica nibbled at her lip, her voice tough. "Then there's that famous line about Hollywood by Frances Marion—'I feel like I've spent my life searching for a man I can look up to without lying down.' Sometimes, I feel the same."

I put my hands on her shoulders. "At the moment, you're looking up to me. Is that so terrible?"

A smile softened her face. "No. Looking up into your eyes is altogether different, Philip. Because *you're* different— different from any man I've ever known."

"Different in a good way?"

"Different in the best way."

"And what about other men, Monica? Plenty of them desire you. They must throw themselves at you right and left. I'll bet your suite at the Marmont has its share of male visitors."

She looked genuinely hurt. "Why would you say that, Philip?"

"I don't know. Maybe I'm turning into a cynic, losing my ability to trust. Maybe Tinseltown's getting to me."

"There's no one but you, Philip. You have to believe that."

"I'd like to believe you, Monica. I really would."

"Maybe this will help convince you."

She grabbed me and pressed her lips to mine. There was real passion in the kiss, yet a certain tenderness as well. You can tell when a woman's kissing you for real, when there's deep feeling behind it, and that's the way Monica kissed me at that moment. I pulled her closer— gently, to let her know I was giving, not demanding. I felt her arms wrap around me, smelled her hair and her cologne, sensed her relax as she abandoned whatever history with men troubled her so, and forged a new history with me. It was so easy between us, once she allowed herself to let go and we found each other, each of us surrendering at our melting point. She could be unpredictable, mercurial, contradictory as hell. But when she was like this, being with her was heavenly, one of those moments you wished you could freeze forever in time.

Which is exactly what happened next, though not the way I would have wished. Instead, the moment was both shattered and recorded in the glare of an unexpected flashbulb—Hudley Pinkston again, tripping his camera's shutter from a few feet away, where he'd stepped from the shadow of a massive saguaro cactus.

I separated from Monica and started after him with my fists clenched. She grabbed me and held me back, telling me to let him go, that violence would just make matters worse. We stood at the edge of the street, watching him dash down and across to his yellow Mercury. He leaped in and took off with his tires burning rubber, coming back toward us. He accelerated suddenly, careening nearly out of control, until his big car sideswiped the passenger door of Monica's white Jag, leaving an ugly swath of damage and transferred paint that looked almost deliberate.

"Hey!"

I ran into the middle of the street, shouting for him to

stop, but he never slowed. A quick turn at the end of the street and he was gone.

When I reached the Jag, Monica was already there, but the damage to her convertible didn't seem all that important to her. I suggested we call the police and report the incident immediately.

"Absolutely not," she said. "It would just blow things up bigger." Her voice sounded distant, a bit tremulous. "He's got his picture now. He can do whatever he wants with it. No point in aggravating him. Maybe if I play nice, and make a generous offer, he'll let me buy it back from him."

"For God sake's, Monica, it's just a photo of two people kissing—two people who care about each other."

She looked at me like I was hopelessly naïve. "The *wrong* people, Philip. He'll use that photo to expose my relationship with Rock as a fraud. I'll look foolish; Rock, possibly worse. It could raise uncomfortable questions for him, cause the scum at the gossip rags to start digging around. We could both be hurt, Rock and I, unless I can find some way to contain it."

"What about me, Monica? Where do I fit in?" She dropped her eyes, said nothing. "Frankly, I think you're overreacting."

Her voice suddenly became chill, accusatory. "Do you, Philip? Is that why you suddenly kissed me, with no regard for who might be watching?"

"As I recall, you kissed me. We *shared* that kiss, Monica. Two adults, falling in love."

"You wouldn't understand."

"Try me."

She raised her hands toward the night sky, her voice shaking. "This is my career, Philip—my livelihood, everything I've worked for. There's much more at stake for me than for you." She held out her hand. "Give me the keys. I'll drive us back."

"Maybe we should take a room for the night. So you can relax, get some perspective on this. It'll give us a chance to talk, to steal some private time together."

"I have to be up early—that Rona Barrett interview. Rona's someone you don't stand up. Anyway, I'm not in much of a mood for romance, if it's all the same."

A minute later, Monica and I were back on Palm Canyon Drive, heading west through a landscape of shimmering motel pools and bright neon, toward the dark stretch of road that would take us back to Interstate 10.

HALFWAY to the interstate, surrounded by shadowy dunes and canyons, I asked Monica to ease up on the accelerator. She was pushing eighty and I didn't like it, even though we hadn't passed another vehicle for several minutes. Instead of slowing, though, she pressed her foot defiantly down on the gas pedal, as if to punish me for what had happened back in Palm Springs. A moment after that her foot eased and the needle on the speedometer began to drop. She craned for a better look up the road.

"What's that?"

"I'm not sure," I said.

We coasted in, staring at Hudley Pinkston's yellow Mercury off to the side. It was over the embankment at an angle, headlights and taillights still burning, its two upraised wheels spinning slowly to a stop. Monica pulled to the shoulder while I rummaged in the glove compartment for a flashlight she said I'd find there. When I had it, I climbed out, telling her to flag down the next approaching vehicle by flashing her headlights, in case we needed help.

I managed to get the driver's door open on the Mercury and the flashlight quickly showed me that Hudley Pinkston was no longer inside. There was blood on the dashboard and the top of the steering wheel—not much, really—but the windshield glass was intact, with no cracks. A Rolleiflex camera lay on the floor in front of the passenger seat, amid a clutter of old parking tickets, crumpled food wrappers, and empty Nehi soda bottles.

I crawled back out and walked around the car, casting my beam about but seeing nothing but sand and sagebrush. When I climbed back up to the Jag, Monica was looking anxiously up and down the deserted road.

"We need to get out of here, Philip."

I ignored her, crossed the road, made a quick inspection of the other side. The only life I glimpsed was a long-tailed lizard darting between rocks. If Pinkston had been injured, I figured, he must have gotten himself up to the road and caught a ride back into town, just before we'd arrived.

"Philip, let's go!"

I walked back to her. "What's the problem, Monica?"

"You don't see?" She glanced first at the passenger side of her Jaguar, crumpled and streaked with yellow paint, then at the driver's side of Pinkston's upended Mercury, with its matching damage. "Look at this scene, at the evidence! To anyone else, it's going to look like I ran him off the road."

She was right. That was exactly how it would look.

"Philip, please, let's go. Now!"

I looked west, up the highway, but saw no headlights. Behind us, however, in the direction of the Springs, were two distant headlight beams slowly approaching like a pair of unblinking eyes. I remembered the camera, felt the sickening tug of temptation, made a split-second decision. I handed Monica the flashlight, told her to take the passenger side, then leaped over the embankment and scrambled back inside Hudley Pinkston's wrecked car.

Half a minute later, I was behind the wheel of the Jag, handing his camera to Monica. I pulled back out on the road, watching the approaching headlights getting closer in the rearview mirror. Steadily, fighting my nerves, I pressed down on the accelerator until the needle hit the hundred mark, hoping I'd put enough distance between us and the other driver to obscure at least our license plate.

I'D stopped shaking by the time I made my next decision, fifteen or twenty miles up the highway. As we cruised through the dark desert, I told Monica to open the camera and remove the film. She did, wordlessly. I saw a ravine ahead and heaved the camera as hard as I could as we raced by, then tossed the exposed film after it. After that, we relaxed a little, but not much. We passed a sign that read: *Don't Be a Litterbug!* Our laughter was a wonderful release.

"I promise not to turn you in, Philip."

"For destroying Hudley's precious photograph?"

"For littering." She kept a straight face for half a second more, then we were both laughing again. She took my hand, looking serious. "It means a lot, the risk you just took for me."

"It's behind us now. That's what's important."

"Look, I'm sorry for the way I acted back there, sorry for a lot of my behavior recently. I've been under a lot of pressure. I'm afraid I've let it get to me."

"It's OK, I understand."

"No, it's not OK. I have no right to take it out on you." She reached up, ran her fingers through my hair. "You're special, Philip. Guys like you don't come along all that often. I don't want anything to come between us, to spoil it for us. From now on, I'm putting you first—*us*—first."

She kissed my cheek, drenched me with a wonderful smile, then turned her attention to the radio. She fiddled with the dial until she landed on KFI, an L.A. station with a powerful signal that played oldies. A new selection was just starting—Jerome Kern's "All the Things You Are." I chuckled to myself, hearing it. Monica asked me what was so funny.

"Nothing, really. Just—it's my favorite song, that's all."

She perked up in surprise. " 'All the Things You Are'—really?"

"Really, truly, Monica. My favorite song of all time." She was looking at me oddly. "What?"

"It's my favorite song, too, Philip." Her voice was lilting, filled with astonishment. "Has been since I first heard it years ago."

I grinned. "How about that?"

"Yes," she said, "how about that."

She slipped her arm through mine and laid her head on my shoulder. We listened to our favorite song that way, speeding through the comforting darkness and the desert calm, our troubles fast receding behind us. Everything felt OK again. OK—except for those nagging questions about Nicky Pembrook that I lacked the heart to ask just yet.

Chapter 24

I WAS A few minutes past midnight when I parked along Mulholland Drive in front of the house Monica shared with her mother. Lights were on, inside and out.

Monica didn't climb from the Jag right away. "I'm surprised Mother's still up. She usually takes a sedative after dinner and turns in early."

"Maybe we should see if she's OK."

"Yes, let's go in."

"She'll throw a fit when she sees me," I said.

"I'm a big girl, I can handle it. It's time she realizes she can't control my life forever. Especially now that you're a part of it."

"If she takes a poke at me, will you protect me?"

Monica smiled, kissed me, and promised that she would. We climbed from the car, Monica fumbling in her handbag

for her key. Before she had it out of the lock, Lorna Draper
pulled the door open, startling us both. Her eyes were red-
rimmed and filled with emotion—not the fury I'd expected,
but something closer to anguish.

Monica saw it too. "Mother, what is it?"

"Come inside, sweetie." Lorna's voice was shaky. "You,
too, Mr. Damon. Something's happened."

We stepped into a house that was more like a museum
of Lorna Draper's failed dreams. Adorning the walls were
movie posters from B pictures she'd appeared in, even those
in which her billing was so low the lettering was barely
large enough to read. Framed photographs were everywhere
about the place, dozens of them—glossy publicity stills in
which she aged from a smoldering young beauty to a woman
of a certain age with hard lines beginning to shape her face,
or pictures of her with celebrities large and small, living or
dead, always with a glorious smile.

She stood in the middle of the cluttered living room,
facing her daughter. "Sit down, darling." Her hands were
trembling; she pressed them together but it didn't help.

Monica sat, pulling me by the hand down beside her.
"Mother, you're scaring me."

Lorna Draper took a deep breath, composing herself. Very
quickly, she crossed herself, muttering something in Spanish. Then she blurted out what was troubling her: "I'm
afraid Nicky's dead."

Monica gasped, put a hand to her mouth.

"It was the riots," Lorna said. "Apparently, last night, he
tried to get to Rosewood Gardens to be with the horses, to
be sure they were cared for. It's the only possible explanation. The authorities found his body in an alley near the
racetrack. He'd been badly beaten and they'd carved something into his stomach—*Burn, Baby, Burn.*"

Monica's chin trembled. "No, not Nicky."

Lorna sat beside Monica, taking the other side. "I'm sorry, baby. But I'm afraid it's true." Monica looked up at me, tears falling, eyes filled with shock. I slipped an arm around her, rubbing her shoulder but feeling perplexed and useless.

"A mob," Lorna went on, "that's what the police figure. They found other victims, all Negroes. Nicky just happened to get caught up in it, I guess—wrong place at the wrong time." Lorna's composure finally cracked and her tears spilled over. "He should never have been down there. But you know how Nicky felt about horses. He couldn't bear to see them suffer."

Monica drew in a deep breath, sagging pitifully. Lorna took her other hand. "I'm so sorry that you had to find out like this. He's with God now, baby. Little Nicky Pembrook's finally at peace."

Then, as if suddenly remembering I was there, Lorna said awkwardly, "Monica and Nicky worked together on a movie once. They weren't terribly close but she was fond of him, just the same." She squeezed her daughter's hand. "My baby has such a big heart, don't you, honey?"

My head spun with questions: Why had Monica given cash to Nicky up at Sid Zell's place the day my combo had played there? Why had Nicky been in her hotel suite in the wee, small hours, as they'd shared their intimate embraces? Why did she continue to be so secretive about him, hiding her true feelings? So many questions, but this wasn't the time to ask them.

I told Lorna and Monica that I was sorry to hear the news, and asked if there was anything I could do. They thanked me but told me no, so I suggested I should probably go.

*   *   *

I waited alone outside for a taxi. Just as one appeared up the road, I heard the gate open behind me.

Monica rushed out, throwing her arms around me, burying her face against my shoulder, sobbing. As the taxi pulled up, she got control of herself and kissed me with a need that seemed aching and raw, completely trusting, with nothing held back.

"You mean so much to me, Philip. More than I can ever say."

She dashed back in, leaving me more in love with her than ever, if just as confused.

Chapter 25

THE NEXT DAY, Tuesday, I called Hercules Platt and told him what had happened to Nicky Pembrook. Also, that a good deal more had transpired that I thought he should know about, but not over the phone. He told me to sit tight, that he'd get to Beatrice's house as soon as he could borrow a car from one of his relatives.

The Watts riot—some were calling it a rebellion—had just been declared officially over. Before it was contained, the violence had spread over eleven square miles, with flare-ups as far away as Venice and Long Beach. The death toll was set at thirty-five, including one white police officer and twenty-eight Negroes; more than 20,000 law enforcement officers and nearly 15,000 troops had been called in to regain control; property damage was estimated at $40 million. It seemed inconceivable that anything like it would ever occur again.

Platt arrived a little after ten, looking haggard and grim, and asked if he might have a cup of coffee. I brought it to him black, the way he always drank it.

"I feel a little guilty," I said, "asking you to come over like this, in light of what you and your family just went through."

We sat facing each other in the living room. Beatrice was out, the cats were napping, and the house was still.

"We all went through it, each in his own way," Platt said tersely. "What bothers me most is that next time, after nothing changes, it will just be worse."

"Surely we'll never see anything like this again."

Platt smiled, as if to himself. "What is it you want to tell me, Damon?"

I related the events of the previous day, while he encouraged me to go over every detail, no matter how insignificant it might seem. After that, we scanned the morning *L.A. Times,* hoping to learn more about Nicky Pembrook's death. Platt seemed more than willing to focus on the smaller picture, taking his mind off the greater horror that hovered around us like the acrid smoke that still hung over the city. He fired off endless questions with the same zeal he'd shown toward the Buddy Bixby homicide, slipping into the role of detective that allowed his remarkable mind to roam and sift and examine.

To our surprise, the newspaper carried no mention of Pembrook's passing. Beatrice had picked up the two Hollywood trade papers—*Daily Variety* and the *Hollywood Reporter*—down at the Laurel Canyon market, and she laid them on the table in front of us.

"Not a word about Nicky in either one," she said. "Maybe

the *Herald-Examiner* will have something this afternoon."

She had found two items in the trade papers that were of nominal interest. First, *Dead Aim* had managed a decent weekend opening across the country, taking in $220,000 at the box office. Second, Hedley Pinkston was to be honored with a Lifetime Achievement Award at the annual Movie Publicists Association luncheon on Friday. But not one word about Nicky Pembrook.

"Is it possible," I asked Platt, "that Lorna Draper was somehow misinformed last night, when she told Monica and me that Pembrook had been found dead?"

Before he could reply, the doorbell sounded and Beatrice went to answer it. Rabbi Kaminsky appeared, big and bearded, waving us back to our seats. He'd dropped by, he said, to enlist Beatrice's support in a synagogue fund-raising drive to help the victims of the riots. She told him she'd do whatever she could, and suggested I might perform at some kind of benefit, which seemed a fine idea to me. The phone rang. Beatrice took it, then told me Sid Zell was on the line, asking for me.

I spoke to him standing up. "Mr. Zell, good morning. I apologize for that unfortunate business at the beach yesterday. I'm not sure I handled it very well."

"Such a bunch of nonsense! I'm just sorry you had to schlep all the way out and then have to deal with that bitch Monica. Listen, I'm taking you and Beatrice out for a nice dinner tonight—to celebrate the boffo opening of *Dead Aim*. We'll go to Chasen's, have ourselves a real meal."

"Tonight, Mr. Zell? I don't know—after what's just happened."

"You're speaking of Nicky Pembrook?"

"You've heard then."

"Bob Thomas of the AP woke me this morning to get a

quote for his story. He got wind of it a few hours ago, when it made the police blotter. Terrible thing, terrible."

"I know that Monica and her mother are quite upset."

"I was like an uncle to the kid. I did everything I could to help the boy get straightened out. I feel awful about what happened. But life goes on, yes? Chasen's, eight P.M.? I got some business I want to discuss. You'll be there?"

I covered the phone and asked Beatrice if she could make it. She rolled her eyes but said she could.

"Sure, Mr. Zell. We'll see you at eight sharp."

At Platt's request, I did my best to relate my conversation with Sid Zell verbatim.

"If the official notice of Pembrook's death didn't hit the police blotter until this morning," Platt said, "that explains why the morning papers didn't carry it." He sipped his coffee thoughtfully. "But it doesn't explain how Lorna Draper learned of it late last night—before any of the news outlets, even the wire services. They've got reporters working out of the cop shop round the clock who should have gotten word from their police sources, or seen the first police report as soon as it was filed."

"Maybe it was overlooked, with all that's been going on."

"Sure, that's possible." But Platt didn't sound convinced. "This kid was famous once. If he died in the riots, you'd think they'd jump on an angle like that. Unless there's some reason she knew about it before anybody else."

Beatrice flicked on the television to images of looters running from stores with their arms filled with merchandise, footage replayed from previous days. I studied Platt from the side, saw how conflicted he was watching it. The coverage became more intense, with scenes of rampaging and violence, Molotov cocktails being heaved at police vehicles, men beating other men senseless.

"Chaos like this," Rabbi Kaminsky said sadly, "it can so easily be used as a cover for more common crimes that have nothing to do with the black man's justifiable rage."

"Amen," Platt said.

Finally, a report came on detailing the discovery of Nicky Pembrook's body amid the destruction near the Rosewood Gardens Race Track. It stated the likely cause of death as blunt force trauma to the head and recounted the grim fact that the words "Burn, Baby, Burn" had been carved into his stomach. A brief profile followed, chronicling Little Nicky Pembrook's brief career, with clips from a few of his films as he danced, sang, and rode ponies across the purple sage as a child.

"Vicki Hart must be in terrible shape over this," I said.

Platt watched the newscast transfixed, not even blinking, as if he never heard me.

SHORTLY before noon, Rabbi Kaminsky left to do more fund-raising, sharing a tender kiss with Beatrice at the door. Platt had asked to use the phone, saying he had to call a man about an insurance policy. As he hung up, jotting in his notebook, he told us he was on his way downtown to the county records center to do some digging, and was gone a moment later.

"I like this Hercules Platt," Beatrice said as we made a lunch of tuna sandwiches while the cats sniffed the air and waited to lick the can. "He's a man of few words, which can sometimes be worrisome. Just the same, I think quite highly of him."

"He doesn't miss much, that's for sure."

"I sensed that," Beatrice said. "Mind like a steel trap, that one."

Afterward, with the dishes dried and put away, she asked me if I'd join her for "a special little research trip" of our own, down in Beverly Hills. I told her I'd be happy to tag along, playing Nick to her Nora.

THE Academy of Motion Picture Arts and Sciences—the organization responsible for the Oscars—was housed in a modern three-story building on Wilshire Boulevard, a mile or two east of Rodeo Drive. Beatrice, who'd donated her screenwriting Oscar to the Academy for permanent display, had been using the organization's research library in preparation for writing her memoirs. By half past one, we were signed in, pouring over an endless set of documents—vintage Hollywood publications, resource books, press kits, publicity stills, production credits—while Beatrice jotted notes in her lovely, looping handwriting.

"As a writer," Beatrice said, "I always like to establish a timeline for each of my characters. Helps me to find some order, to see a structure start to emerge. Then I look for ways that these subplots might weave together, forming and supporting the main story. That's the key to a well-crafted plot, you know—the subplots, what they reveal about the characters and their possible motivations."

"I'm not sure how I can help, Bea. But I'll do what I can."

"Let's start with *The Filmgoer's Companion,* with its alphabetical entries. Open to the D listings, Philip, see if Lorna Draper's in there. The author, Leslie Halliwell tends to be inclusive, even of the less successful and less talented."

*   *   *

BY closing time, Beatrice had filled a yellow legal pad with notes that meant relatively little to me. As we drove home, she sat silently on the passenger side, looking pensive and marking certain items in code that I didn't understand. She continued that way at home, in her office, while I fed the cats and fixed cocktails for the two of us. By the time we took our drinks out to the veranda, she'd copied and organized certain facts into ten distinct groupings that she read to me aloud:

1) *According to* The Filmgoer's Companion, *Lorna Draper's birth name was Consuelo Montero, which she later changed, along with her look, to compete for mainstream roles in American movies.*

2) *In 1926, at age 18, Lorna landed a showy part in a Sid Zell silent feature,* Damsel in Distress. *Her career foundered when talkies came in and she never rose above supporting roles in B pictures.*

3) *Her daughter was born in 1929 but did not make her feature film debut—as Monica Rivers—until she was an experienced stage actress of 27.*

4) *One of Lorna Draper's supporting roles was in Sid Zell's* Dangerous Beauty. *It was shot in 1946, when Monica would have been 17.*

5) *Under Sid Zell's stewardship, Premiere Alliance Pictures introduced Little Nicky Pembrook in 1953, at age 6, and developed him into "the Jackie Cooper of the '50s," as an old copy of* Photoplay *dubbed him.*

6)   *The publicist assigned to Nicky Pembrook was Hedley Pinkston, who made much of the boy's background as an orphan raised by two aunts who wished to remain anonymous and out of the limelight.*

7)   *At various times, Hedley Pinkston also represented Sid Zell, Lorna Draper, and Monica Rivers, among many Hollywood luminaries.*

8)   *A biography of Hedley in a recent* Who's Who in Hollywood *mentioned him coming west in the early thirties from Kentucky, where he'd worked as a young newspaper reporter, "before rising to the top as Hollywood's most influential personal publicist."*

9)   *In 1961, Nicky Pembrook, Buddy Bixby, and Johnny Langley appeared together in the same hot rod movie,* Wheels on Fire. *It was Nicky's last and Buddy's only film appearance, in which Johnny Langley was listed as a stunt driver.*

10) *The next year, at 16, Nicky Pembrook was arrested for heroin possession and sentenced to six months in juvenile detention, effectively ending his movie career.*

"It's a lot to digest," I said. "Although I'm not sure what any of it means."

"If nothing else, Philip, it links all these people, doesn't it?"

"Links them to what, other than each other?"

"An interesting question, that one."

I reached for her list. Beatrice handed it over, and I scanned her ten points on my own. "Monica Rivers seems to be right in the middle of all your research."

Using her pinkie, Beatrice swirled the lime wedge in her

gin and tonic. "Smack dab in the middle, I'm afraid."

"But why, Bea? What's the connection?"

"An even more interesting question, Philip." Beatrice extended her glass to mine, uniting the rims. "Here's to some productive sleuthing with your friend Hercules Platt. I believe he may turn you into an amateur detective yet."

"I'm not sure that's a direction I'd like to take."

"I'm afraid that life sometimes takes us in its own direction, Philip, regardless of our trepidations. And thank goodness, I say. What would life be without its surprises and challenges?" She raised her glass. "Cheers, *bubeleh.*"

Chapter 26

THE CURFEW CONTINUED in the riot area that night and the Cocoanut Grove remained closed as a precaution, so meeting Sid Zell at Chasen's presented no problem for me schedule-wise.

Beatrice and I arrived a few minutes before eight. After its humble beginnings in a cornfield in 1936, the vaunted Beverly Hills restaurant had quickly caught on as a favorite haunt of Hollywood's greatest stars. Over the decades, it had grown into a sprawling, two-story, French Colonial complex surrounded by an expansive parking lot, and served by the most efficient valets in the business. So popular was its famous chili that Elizabeth Taylor had reportedly ordered containers of it flown to her by commercial jet while she was shooting *Cleopatra* overseas. If you had to pick a restaurant that would never go out of business, no matter what the shifting trends, it was Chasen's.

Sid Zell was waiting for us in a booth in the main dining room, waving us over with an unlit cigar while he talked into a telephone plugged into an outlet behind him. As we crossed the room, we passed Jimmy Stewart and his wife, Gloria, Bob and Dolores Hope, and a dozen others who were nearly as famous as God.

"Remember what we discussed on the drive over," Beatrice said. "Seven names, a certain order. Let's see what kind of response it gets."

"I have no idea where you're going with this, Bea."

"Fishing, Philip. Remember, until midnight, you're Nick and I'm Nora, even if I am old enough to be your grandmother."

"Why midnight?"

"Because that's when the magic spell wears off for ordinary folks like us." She gave me a sideways glance that looked cautionary. "It's only the actors who get to go on being other people."

Sid Zell got off the phone before we reached him, schmoozed for a minute, then barked orders at the waiter for drinks and food that indicated he still wasn't heeding his doctor's warnings about coronary disease.

While we sipped cocktails, Zell reduced my life story to the elements he considered essential for translation to the big screen: My unusual childhood as the son of musician Archie Damon, which would be handled quickly in a prologue. My brief, blissful marriage to my wife, Diana, before her murder in 1961, which would provide a short first act. For the long second act, my trip to San Francisco two years later for an engagement at the Fairmont Hotel, where a murder on the dance floor thrust me into one of the most complicated homicide cases in the city's history; also, into an ill-fated romance with Lenore Ashley, a local poet who bore a striking resemblance to my late wife. For the final act, my dangerous pursuit of a cold-blooded killer, assisted by the brilliant detective work of Inspector Hercules Platt, who would end up solving several linked murders—including Diana's—before saving my life in a thrilling conclusion.

"It's got all the elements," Zell said as the Caesar salads arrived. "This movie I got to make."

Beatrice lifted her fork but left it poised in midair. "So what's in it for us, Sid? Philip said you wanted to talk business."

Zell grinned at me, while waving a hand at Beatrice. "That's what I love about this dame. She gets straight to the heart of the narrative. An Oscar, dozens of credits, a legacy that will live forever. This woman's a genius, and I say this without a shred of insincerity."

"Sid," Beatrice said. "Save the butter for your roll."

"OK, so here's what I'm thinking. You, me, Philip— equal partners in *The Philip Damon Story*. Is it brilliant, or what?"

"Equal partners," Beatrice said.

"Coproducers. You write the script. Philip stars and scores the music. Everybody waves their fees up front, takes their cut at the back end. We keep the costs down, maximize the returns, split the profits three ways. Win-win all the way around."

"How about a wager, Sid?" Beatrice opened her purse, found a hundred-dollar bill, placed it on the table. "I'm willing to bet that Premiere Alliance Pictures has never paid a dime in profit participation in its forty-year history. By the time you've done your creative accounting, cooked the books, added everything from pedicures to toilet paper to the overhead, there will be no profits to share."

"Beatrice, baby, why do you talk to me like this?"

"Because I've known you for nearly thirty years." She went to work on her salad but kept talking. "By the way, you still owe me my fee for the *Dead Aim* rewrite, even though almost none of it ended up on-screen."

"Put your money away, sweetheart. We're three close friends breaking bread. We leave it at that, OK? But I'm warning you, sweetie, I'm going to make this picture, with you or without you." Zell swung his head in my direction. "Did I tell you who I have in mind to play Lenore Ashley, this poet chick you fell in love with up in Frisco?"

I took a wild guess. "Julie Christie?"

"Like we could afford her." Zell smiled slyly, then hit me with his thunderbolt: "Somebody I already got under contract—Monica Rivers."

I sat forward. "Monica?"

"Did I say Shelley Winters? Of course Monica. Close your eyes. Picture you and Monica, up there on the big screen together."

"I haven't even taken my screen test yet."

Beatrice shot me a look. "You're taking a screen test?"

"I'm thinking about it."

"Oh, Philip, for God's sake."

Zell sat back, the picture of nonchalance. "Unless you think I should get Troy Donahue to play your part. I'm sure he's available, after that piece of crap he just made with Joey Heatherton."

"*My Blood Runs Cold,*" Beatrice said.

"Exactly my reaction when I saw the rough cut," Zell said.

Beatrice raised her chin, fixing Zell with her mischievous

eyes. "What about Rock Hudson, Sid? I thought he was the man in Monica's life."

"By the time we start shooting *The Philip Damon Story,* we will have milked the Rock Hudson bit for all it's worth. Philip and Monica will be Hollywood's hot new couple." He swung his eyes back to me. "Only for real."

"Imagine that," Beatrice said, "a publicity ploy with a grain of truth to it."

"It's brilliant, a natural," Zell said. "I'm telling you, this is genius!"

"You're willing to take a chance on a complete novice like Philip?"

"What can I say? I've got a big heart."

"Come to think of it, Sid, you have given a few people their big breaks."

"It's my nature." Zell shrugged modestly. "Some would say my weakness."

"Lorna Draper, for example," Beatrice said. "Back in '26, in *Damsel in Distress.*"

"For an old broad, Beatrice, your memory's pretty sharp."

"And Little Nicky Pembrook, he made his first picture for you, didn't he, Sid? Monica Rivers, too, if I'm not mistaken."

"I'm blessed, the talent I've discovered, the wonderful friends I've made. You're nice to people, it comes back to you."

Under the table, Beatrice nudged me with her knee.

"And Buddy Bixby," I said. "You gave him a shot back in '61, in that hot rod movie, *Wheels on Fire.*"

"It was a small part. He was a nice-looking kid."

Beatrice laid her fork aside. "Wasn't that Nicky's last movie?"

"Could have been. Sure, I guess it was."

"Didn't that surfer work on that one as well?" she asked. "What's his name—Johnny Langley. Didn't he do some stunt driving?"

"I don't know, Beatrice. How am I supposed to remember these things? He might have worked on the picture. Who cares? It was a nothing movie, a quickie for the hardtops."

"I'm surprised you haven't found a leading role for Johnny Langley," Beatrice said. "Blond, blue-eyed, good features, all those muscles. Maybe he deserves a shot."

"Muscles, but no brains. I doubt he could learn his lines, that kid's so dumb."

"Cue cards, Sid. It wouldn't be the first time."

"You got some story ideas, Beatrice? Because I'm always open."

"*Goy on a Dolphin?*"

Zell burst out laughing. "Beatrice, you kidder. Eat your food! I'm paying good money for this spread." He shook his head, grinning. "*Goy on a Dolphin.* This I have to pass along to Esther."

Zell dug into his plate, but Beatrice barely moved. "Funny, isn't it, how all those people we just spoke of are connected in some way. Lorna, Nicky, Monica, Buddy Bixby, Johnny Langley. And you, Sid. Six people, so closely linked."

"Don't forget Hedley Pinkston," I said. "He was a publicist at just about every turn. That makes seven."

Zell's eyes roved the restaurant. "Half the people in this room have worked together, Beatrice. And the other half have probably shared the same sheets. Everybody's connected in this frigging town, you know that. Eat your food, for chrissake."

"But not quite like this, do you think?"

"What's with the questions, Beatrice? You got a few people who happened to work for Sid Zell, who's made hundreds of pictures. This is something to get your knickers in a twist, that these people have some cockamamie connection?"

"You don't find it curious?"

"What's to be curious?"

"That two of them have recently turned up dead, under odd circumstances, only days apart."

Zell stared at her, eyes unblinking, like two windows whose shades have suddenly snapped open. "Two people suddenly buying the farm like that, who once worked together on a film? A coincidence, maybe. Curious? No, I don't see it so curious."

"Unless there's a further connection," Beatrice said.

"Like what kind of further connection?"

"That their murders are related in some way. That would certainly be curious, wouldn't it, Sid?"

"Related? You got a junkie musician dead on the beach of an overdose. And a washed-up kid actor stupid enough to get caught up in a race riot, with tragic results. No, I don't see a connection, sorry."

"A kid actor who was also an addict," I said.

"Who once worked on a movie with the other dead addict," Beatrice said, "both of them connected to all the others we've already mentioned."

"This is nonsense." Zell dug into his food but chewed mechanically, as if his mind were somewhere else entirely.

"You're probably right, Sid—nonsense." Beatrice smiled blandly and turned her attention to her food, while Zell continued to chew, staring at the tablecloth between them.

I could almost hear the machinery behind his fixed eyes, clanking at full speed, as his mind raced to process what we'd just suggested, even though I wasn't quite sure myself just what that was. Whatever it was, it had Sid Zell spooked, which Beatrice confirmed to me with a knowing, sideways glance.

IT was nearing ten when Beatrice placed her napkin on the table and thanked Sid Zell for dinner. Zell glanced at his Rolex. "But you're not leaving yet? It's early. We haven't even seen the dessert tray."

Beatrice began sliding out. "Late enough for this senior citizen. Besides, I want to be up early, working on my book. Shall we go, Philip?"

"I've never known you to pass up dessert, Beatrice." Zell sounded genuinely affronted. "Am I such bad company, you suddenly leave me like this?"

"You're always interesting company, Sid." She patted his wrist. "Be sure to cut me a check for *Dead Aim*, before I have to sic my lawyer and the Writers Guild on you."

"At least stay for an after," Sid pleaded. "A nice cognac, for the drive home."

"Give my best to Esther," Beatrice said.

"Sure, sure." Zell glanced irritably at his watch, sounding distracted. "Of course, I'll pass along your regards to the wife."

I thanked him for the meal and told him I'd see him tomorrow evening. He looked up as if drawing a blank.

"The screen test," I reminded him.

"Right, sure, the screen test."

Beatrice was ahead of me, almost to the foyer. I caught up and slipped my arm through hers, while Dave and Maude Chasen bid us a cordial good night. When I looked back, Sid Zell was already reaching for the phone, all business.

Chapter 27

"I DON'T REMEMBER leaving a lamp on in my office."

Beatrice moved beside me up the front walk, glancing around the east side of the house, where light from her study window softly penetrated the trees. She found her keys, opened the front door, and waited for the cats to come scurrying, as they always did. When they failed to show, she placed a hand on my wrist.

"Something's not right, Philip."

She grabbed an umbrella and a heavy cane from the stand near the door, handing the umbrella to me.

"Maybe we should call the police," I whispered.

But she was already stepping through the dark house ahead of me, toward the distant light. It appeared as a sliver through a crack in the door at the end of a long hallway, which we entered together.

"Beatrice, let me check. You go to the phone, call the cops."

"I'd feel foolish if they came all the way up here and it was nothing."

Our whispers seemed to boom in the darkness.

"Go to the phone and wait, then. I'll take a look. Then we'll decide what to do."

"If someone's broken in," she hissed, "I'm sure he's gone by now—out the back, probably. Burglars don't stay around to discuss inventory, I don't imagine."

"Wait by the phone. That's an order."

I rotated her big shoulders, pointing her back toward the middle of the house, watching until she disappeared into the blackness. When I turned back around, the light at the end of the hallway had gone out. I proceeded halfway down before stopping, realizing someone had to be in that room, waiting.

"Make the phone call!" I shouted.

I turned quickly, ready to dash back to Beatrice and get her out of the house—but not quickly enough. Something hard and heavy crashed down on my skull from behind. The reality of getting knocked on the head like that is quite different from the way it's shown in the movies. One doesn't just go down in a convenient heap, out cold until it's time to wake up for the next scene. That night, I learned that it's quite difficult to pound a person into unconsciousness—think of a hard-fought boxing match, how many blows it often takes. I threw up my hands to defend against an assailant I couldn't quite see, flailing my arms and bouncing against walls, feeling disoriented and panicked. The intruder got in another thump or two to my head and things became fuzzy, though I managed to keep my feet until he landed a fist sharply to the side of my jaw. At that point, I felt my legs go out from under me as if they'd been poleaxed.

After that I was floating in Never-Never Land for a while.

"PHILIP? Philip, can you hear me?"

Beatrice's voice grew increasingly clear as my brain circuitry gradually reconnected. I opened my eyes, blinking slowly. She stood over me with a uniformed police officer on either side. They'd picked me up and laid me on the living room couch, unbuttoned my collar, taken off my shoes.

The look on Beatrice's face was strained, stricken. "An ambulance is coming. Just lie quietly, Philip." Tears spilled over, making rivulets on her soft, wrinkled cheeks.

Against her orders, I sat up slowly, groaning, rubbing my head. There was no blood, just a lump or two. "You're all right, then?" I asked. "He left you alone?"

She told me the intruder had escaped from the house unseen, moments before she'd ventured back down the hallway to find me slumped unconscious on the floor. "He ransacked my office. Went through everything—file cabinets, desk drawers, boxes of old scripts and other papers. Turned it upside down, made a terrible mess."

"What did he get?"

"I have no idea. There's more than three decades of material in there and none of it's been indexed or catalogued."

One of the cats jumped up to be scratched. They'd all returned, apparently from various hiding places they'd sought when the stranger had broken in.

"He came in through a side window," one of the cops said. "I've suggested Mrs. Gless start locking up. Wouldn't be a bad idea to get a dog, either."

"Oh, my, no," Beatrice said. "The cats would never put up with that."

"So you don't know what was taken?"

"I've made a quick survey of the rooms, Philip. Nothing seems to be missing, not even my silver setting. The burglar only seemed interested in my office. What on earth could he have wanted in there?"

"Whatever it was, he was willing to hurt someone to get it."

THE ambulance arrived within minutes. I was embarrassed and didn't want to go to the hospital, but Beatrice insisted, if only as a precaution. As they wheeled me out on a stretcher, I asked her to call Hercules Platt at the Ambassador and tell him what had happened.

"I've already spoken with Mr. Platt. He's on his way over now. I have a few things I'd like to discuss with him while you're being attended to down at Cedars-Sinai."

"Perhaps he could swing by the hospital afterward. I'll need a ride home. And if anyone can help us make sense of this, it's Platt."

"I've been thinking exactly the same thing, dear one."

The attendants hoisted the stretcher up into the rear of the ambulance. Beatrice shook a finger at me. "Now don't be stubborn, Philip—do as the doctors say."

I promised I would. They closed the doors and the ambulance pulled away. I watched Beatrice out the back window, standing by the road, waving bravely. She was trying not to look too concerned, but not really pulling it off.

It was after midnight, I reminded myself. No more Nick and Nora, playing harmlessly at being detectives. The magic spell had passed.

Chapter 28

HERCULES PLATT ARRIVED at the Cedars-Sinai Medical Center emergency room just as a physician was signing me out. He was a young Jewish guy out of UCLA and possibly a frustrated comic, because he laughed rather too hard after telling me the X rays of my head showed nothing.

"You'll have a sore noggin for a couple of days," he said. "Aspirin should help the headache. Stay off your feet for a while."

I was still a little wobbly as Platt led me down to the street, where Gloria Velez waited with a rental car. I repeated what the doctor had told me and said I felt OK, but also that I was craving some soup, my favorite elixir.

Fifteen minutes later, we were sitting in a booth at Canter's on Fairfax, just up the street from CBS Television City.

"You spoke to Beatrice, I guess," I said to Platt.

He nodded. "She filled me in on what the two of you discovered at the Academy library."

"Mean anything to you?"

"Might. I learned something from the preliminary autopsy on Nicky Pembrook that's more concrete." He gave Gloria a brief summation on Nicky's death—the crushed skull, the riot slogan carved into his stomach, the location where the body was found, near the Rosewood Gardens Race Track. Then Platt looked my way. "The coroner discovered traces of paraffin in Nicky's hair and flesh near the base of the skull, where the fatal blow was delivered."

"Paraffin?"

Platt nodded. "Another odd note—Nicky's wallet was still on him, apparently untouched. Inside the wallet was a card for notification in case of emergency. The name on the card was Lorna Draper."

"Lorna Draper?" Gloria leaned forward on her elbows. "Isn't that Monica Rivers's mother?"

Platt nodded. "Her name on that card explains why she learned about Nicky's death before anyone else, even the newspeople."

"But why would he be carrying her name in his wallet?"

Platt glanced my way for the explanation. I made my best effort. "She must be one of the aunts Beatrice and I read about in our research—one of the anonymous aunts who raised him after he was orphaned as a boy. Is that how you see it, Platt?"

"Seems possible, given everything you and Beatrice have told me."

Gloria sat back, picking up the thread. "Is it possible Monica Rivers is the other aunt? That they raised him together?"

208   Peter Duchin and John Morgan Wilson

"It would certainly explain why they were both so upset to learn of his death," I said. Inside, I was feeling enormous relief, because it also explained the clandestine kiss I saw Monica give Nicky Pembrook at the Chateau Marmont, and the intimate hours he spent with her afterward. He must have gone to her for counsel, troubled by something. Or maybe he'd wanted more money, for his drug habit. The next day, I figured, she'd met Zell at the racetrack, hoping to discuss it with him, if she could only get his mind off the horses long enough. At least that was my theory, which I proffered to Platt.

He dug into a jacket pocket, came up with a folded envelope, opened it, and withdrew three thumb-sized pieces of sponge, which he laid on the table. "The coroner removed these from a pocket of Nicky Pembrook's pants. Because of the riots, they've got bodies stacked up like cordwood down there. They aren't paying much attention to items like this. A medical examiner who owes me a favor let me borrow them for a while."

The pieces of sponge looked similar to the one Gloria had found the previous week in a pocket of Buddy Bixby's tuxedo, and she said so. Platt reached into his jacket again, came up with another envelope, opened it, removed the piece of sponge she was speaking of, and placed it on the table near the others.

"Quite similar," he said.

"It clearly links Nicky Pembrook and Buddy Bixby in some way," I said. "But how? I'm baffled."

"That makes two of us," Gloria said.

"Given some time, I suspect we'll sort it out." Platt regarded Gloria keenly. "But you may be able to help us with something else, Gloria."

"In what way?"

"By telling us a little more about Peggy Bixby."

Gloria bristled. "What about Peggy?"

"I contacted an insurance broker Peggy's been doing business with, used my considerable charm to wring some information out of him."

Gloria's voice grew sharp. "You've been snooping around Peggy's private business? Why?"

"While Buddy was in jail, Peggy took out a fifty-thousand-dollar insurance policy on his life, naming herself as the sole beneficiary."

"What right do you have to—?"

"Within days of his passing," Platt went on, "before her tears were even dry, she was filling out the paperwork to claim the death benefit."

"She had burial expenses, in case you've forgotten."

"I recall that we gave her quite a bit of cash from the memorial at Shelly's Manne Hole. Peggy's also gainfully employed, collecting a regular paycheck."

"She's a public schoolteacher, Hercules."

"A noble profession," Platt said. "I have a sister up in Oakland in the same line of work."

"Then you know how badly they get paid. You also know that, as a woman, Peggy earns less than her male counterparts who do the same work. There should be laws against that, but there aren't."

"So you're saying she has plenty of motivation to want that insurance money."

"Don't twist my words, Hercules."

"With fifty grand, she could bury her brother in style and have enough left over to pay cash for a nice little house in the suburbs, with a new Ford in the garage, bought and paid for, and a nest egg put away for retirement. Something a single schoolteacher can only dream about. Especially one who's female, as you've pointed out."

Gloria sneered. "You love playing the tough guy, don't you?"

Platt pushed on, unfazed. "Peggy told us she hadn't seen her brother since he got out of jail, that she'd never been to Hermosa Beach, that she stays away from jazz clubs. Yet she fits to a T the description of the woman who was with Buddy at the Lighthouse the night he died. Her nickname, Pix, was on that floral bouquet left on the beach the night Philip and I were out there, when a stranger took off in the dark."

Gloria's eyes flashed. "What are you suggesting?"

"I'm simply asking questions, Gloria. If that was Peggy at the Lighthouse, what was it she slipped Buddy that he hid away in his pocket so quickly? Was it a dose of smack he'd begged her to bring to him? Did she see an opportunity to give him a hot shot, a lethal dose? Was she taking a shortcut to that little house and nice retirement in the suburbs?"

"Philip, are you going to sit here and listen to this?"

"He's just raising questions, Gloria." I shrugged. "That's how Platt works. You know that."

"I don't like his questions." Her eyes gave off sparks. "And I don't think I like him very much, either. Not at the moment, anyway."

Platt eyed her evenly. "I'm not asking you to like me, Gloria, just to help me find out how Buddy Bixby died."

"Peggy Bixby's a gentle person, incapable of what you're suggesting. I know her, remember? What do you know about her, except for your nasty insinuations?"

"I know that each time I've seen her, she's been secretive and guarded, and almost certainly telling lies."

"He's got a point, Gloria."

"If she's secretive and guarded, it's by necessity." Gloria stood, tossing cash on the table to cover her end of the check.

"Don't you myopic, insensitive, self-centered, heterosexual males understand *anything?*"

She stormed out of Canter's, turning heads and scattering waitresses to a chorus of Yiddish exclamations. Platt glanced at me across the table, looking regretful. "I'm afraid we just lost our ride." He studied the four pieces of sponge on the table, then carefully put them back in their respective envelopes, which he tucked away again.

"You're on to something, Platt. How about letting me in on it?"

Platt waved to our waitress, asking her to bring me the check.

"I'd better catch a cab," Platt said. "It's a long walk back to the Ambassador and not the best time for a black man to be out at this hour."

NOTHING more was said that night about where Platt may or may not have been heading with his investigation. As usual, he was biding his time, putting all his cards in order, waiting for just the right moment to show his hand. It may have come from having been the only black inspector in the San Francisco Police Department, a man who'd learned to nail down every aspect of his case before he presented it to his superiors, especially if the suspect happened to be white.

I rode home in the back of a taxi, thinking about the deaths of Buddy Bixby and Nicky Pembrook, and how deeply they'd affected various people. Then I remembered another name that had once concerned me: Angel Vargas. The stable hand who'd been found dead at Rosewood Gardens some time back, and pretty much forgotten in all the ensuing trouble. Somewhere, down in Mexico, Vargas had a family that was mourning him as well, while his murder went unsolved. Where did Angel Vargas fit into all this, I wondered. Angel Vargas, the forgotten man.

Chapter 29

B EATRICE WAS UP early next morning, first to check on me, then to sort through papers in her office, determined to figure out what the burglar had been after the previous night.

I slept until noon, woke to a throbbing headache, and took two aspirin with my coffee. When I felt better, I went over the script pages Sid Zell had given me to study for my screen test that night. Beatrice emerged from her office in the early afternoon to tell me she'd placed all her screenplays in chronological order, something she should have done years ago. The problem was, she said, that she'd sometimes worked on several scripts at once, writing scenes for different movies on the same day, as Zell had his actors running from stage to stage, shooting three or four pictures simultaneously. She could barely remember in which decades she'd penned certain scripts, she said, let alone the premises and plot details of each project. Thankfully, the cover page of every draft was dated in the lower right-hand corner. In the end, when she finally had all her scripts together, sorting and logging them hadn't been that difficult.

"So now I've got a chronological record of my work," she said, "first script to last. Whew! What a relief."

"Is everything there? All the scripts?"

"As far as I can tell, Philip, there's just one script missing, along with a set of notes that went with it." She pursed her lips, looking perplexed. "It's that racetrack yarn that I wrote for Sid Zell nearly thirty years ago, *Sure Bet*."

"How is it you remember that one, with everything else so hazy?"

"Like I said before, it was the only original idea Sid ever had. I recall that much, even if the rest escapes me. And that wager we had—the twenty dollars. I haven't forgotten that." She laughed. "It still rankles, losing a bet to the likes of Sid Zell."

"You must have misplaced it over the years, Beatrice. I can't imagine why anyone would break in just to get his hands on an old movie script. Especially one that never went into production."

"Neither can I, Philip. Neither can I."

MY screen test was set for 7 P.M., a late hour that would allow Zell to complete his business and his production crew to finish up their day's work on *Zombie Surfers from Mars*. Beatrice and I arrived at Premiere Alliance Pictures at half past five, to give me time to get into makeup and Beatrice a chance to sneak over to the story department to see what she might learn about her missing script.

"If I could find a synopsis of it," she said, "then at least I'd know how the story worked itself out. *Sure Bet.* Racetrack drama. Father-son con game. That's about all I remember."

"Maybe if you try not to think about it—"

"It's been almost three decades, Philip. When you get to be my age, you'll understand."

We parted ways and Beatrice headed toward a group of older buildings that did double duty, like so many structures on the lot: first, as the Premiere Alliance story department and script storage facility; second, as a Main Street façade for period films set in the first half of the century.

Makeup wasn't ready for me so I killed some time strolling the streets, dodging messenger boys on heavy-duty Schwinns who pedaled furiously among the buildings, the baskets of their bicycles stacked with film canisters. I poked my nose into soundstages, watched grips building sets, and ogled pretty girls in miniskirts dashing around with scripts in their arms and pens clenched in their teeth.

I was about to head back to the makeup department when I stumbled upon some editing rooms and a hand-drawn sign with a familiar movie title: *Zombie Surfers from Mars.* In one of the small editing bays, a slim young man with unruly hair and wire-rimmed spectacles sat slumped over a Movieola, cutting and splicing film that he spooled through with a hand crank. He looked up as I looked in. I introduced myself, mentioned my connection to Sid Zell, and asked if I could watch him work. He was bright and intense, a recent graduate from NYU named Doug Waterman. He was just out from New York, he said, and assigned to assemble the second unit footage from Zell's latest beach party movie.

"What a headache." He showed me the section of film that was giving him so much trouble—a glaring continuity problem involving the primary surfing stand-in, Johnny Langley.

"They shot this footage yesterday," Waterman said. "The problem is, Langley's riding a different surfboard than the one he used during the rest of the shoot. It wouldn't be so bad if the two surfboards were a reasonably close match. But you can see how unalike they are."

He ran footage of Langley carving up the waves, shot during the early weeks of the production. Then he showed me the new footage again, the film shot yesterday.

"This new surfboard is at least a foot shorter. It's narrower, with a sharper nose and a smaller fin, and the colors are off. Even the surf shop logo is different. This is just a work print, so it's no big deal now. But at some point I'm going have to match this footage with the old stuff. I guess we'll just have to cut away to long shots and hope the audience doesn't notice."

"Or care," I said. "It's not like they're paying to see *Citizen Kane*."

Waterman gave me a sharp look. "*I* care, Mr. Damon."

I smiled weakly. "Sorry."

He sighed deeply. "That's the problem with these schlock productions. Things like continuity are almost an afterthought."

I thanked him for his time and expertise. Making movies was new to me, I said, and I still wasn't convinced it was a career direction I wanted to pursue.

"Come back tomorrow if you want to see some truly great filmmaking," Waterman said. "We're cutting in the scene when the spaceship lands in the middle of the beach party and the zombie surfers learn to go-go dance. The producer spent about twelve dollars on the spaceship." He smiled with effort. "It's a living, I guess."

* * *

A male makeup artist with flighty hands and a pronounced lisp was waiting for me upon my return. "We have to hurry, Mr. Damon, if we want you on that soundstage at seven."

He led me down a hallway and into a room filled with mirrors and makeup lights and more jars of creams, foundations, and blushes than the cosmetics department at Bergdorf's. As we entered, a trim, silver-haired man in a vanilla suit straightened suddenly from his reflection in the glass, swinging around in our direction.

It was Hedley Pinkston. He held a small container of makeup in his right hand and a cotton swab in his left.

"Damon, what a surprise."

"Didn't mean to startle you, Pinkston. Touching up, are you?"

He raised the back of his hand, showing me some mottled skin, looking chagrined. "Liver spots, I'm afraid. Vanity's got the best of me. I try to keep them covered."

The makeup artist paused to swipe at Pinkston with a towel. "Got a bit on your collar, Mr. Pinkston. Such fine fabric, too. You'll want to get that to the cleaners as soon as you can."

He put me in a chair, turned me toward a mirror, studied my face in the glass. "Very nice cheekbones, Mr. Damon. Excellent chin, fine nose. Good skin, too—it's nice to work on a man who takes care of himself." He picked up a brush. "Let's start with the hair, shall we?"

I warned him to go easy, explaining that I'd taken a couple of lumps the night before, when I'd run into a burglar on his way out.

"He sounds like a brute! You're lucky he didn't do some real damage." The makeup artist threw a glance behind him.

"Did you hear that, Mr. Pinkston? Mr. Damon was assaulted last night by a violent thug. Can you imagine?"

But his words went unheeded, because Hedley Pinkston was no longer in the room. He'd slipped out with remarkable stealth, completely unnoticed.

Chapter 30

"PHILIP, I THINK we should leave immediately."

Beatrice found me as I emerged from the bungalow that served as the makeup department, on my way to my screen test on Stage 12. She clutched my forearm tightly, her eyes anxious.

"What is it, Bea? What's happened?"

"It isn't so much what's happened as what's missing. I'm not sure we're safe here on the lot. Especially after the violent events of last night."

"Philip, there you are!"

We turned at the sound of Sid Zell's voice. He stood several yards away, wearing a white linen suit and lots of gold, reminding me of a small show dog groomed and turned out to make him look as worthy and important as the larger breeds. Hedley Pinkston stood beside him, not quite half a foot taller, scrutinizing Beatrice and me.

"I've got camera and lighting crews waiting, Philip." Zell glanced at his watch. "It's after seven. Time is money."

"Beatrice was thinking maybe I shouldn't."

Zell tilted his head imploringly. "Beatrice, sweetie—still trying to talk Philip out of this screen test? What's the harm? We're talking half an hour out of the boy's life, for crying out loud."

Beatrice loosened her grip on my arm.

"Go ahead, Philip. If it's what you really want to do."

I lowered my voice. "You'll be all right?"

"Just get it done and come find me. We need to talk."

"Come with me, Bea."

She glanced at Zell, who waited impatiently. "No, if you're going to do this, you don't want any distractions. Screen tests can be nerve-wracking enough."

"Hedley," Zell said, "why don't you take Beatrice over to my office? There's a nice bottle of champagne cooling behind the bar. You two can sip the bubbly and catch up on old times."

Beatrice straightened my tie, fussed a couple of hairs into place. "Break a leg, sweetheart."

ZELL and I arrived on Stage 12 to find an assistant director dispensing instructions to a small crew. Cherry Topping was also there, dressed in a skintight black skirt with a split up the thigh and a hot pink cashmere sweater that strained at the seams. When she saw me, she lit up like a Sunset Strip marquee.

"There's my costar!"

"Hello, Cherry. You're looking well."

"Thank you, Mr. Damon. I can't wait to get started. This

is what I live for, you know—cinema. Even if I am just developing."

I stole a peek at her impressive cleavage. "You appear to be developing very nicely."

"The crew was just telling me the same thing!"

The scene Zell had chosen cast Cherry Topping and me as a pair of star-crossed lovers who bump into each other at a train station and share a final minute together. It called for some breathless declarations of hopeless love, culminating in a kiss that would have to last forever. The A.D. positioned Cherry and me under the warm lamps, giving us specific directions about hitting our marks, finding our key light, and managing certain angles for the camera. I tried to concentrate on what the man was saying but found myself increasingly distracted by Cherry's magnificent breasts. They thrust so far ahead of the rest of her that I wasn't sure how I was going to manage the kiss without some skillful maneuvering. At the same time, I was trying desperately to remember the lines I'd studied that morning. I suddenly had a headache and my body felt ridiculously lumpish and unresponsive. Instead of my lines, an oft-quoted Oscar Wilde remark came into my head: *Actresses are more than women and actors a little less than men.*

Cherry might very well have been thinking the same thing. To my surprise, she seemed utterly at ease and eager to get on with it. Her smile was warm and supportive, her eyes bright with anticipation, even a kind of native intelligence, as if this tiny role had liberated and transformed her. It was those monumental breasts that bothered me. Not that I didn't like large breasts, quite the contrary; it's just that as they swelled to occupy so much space between us, I had no idea where to direct my eyes or hands. I suddenly had no clear sense of distance and proportion, of where or how to move. When the A.D. called for quiet on the set, he might just as well have been my executioner asking for the black hood. Instantly, my mind went blank—every scripted line forgotten. At the same time, I experienced something I'd only heard about from actors and stand-up comics who'd experienced sudden and extreme stage fright. Flop sweat, they called it. Every pore in my body opened at once, lathering me from head to toe in perspiration, while my skin burned and my head grew light.

I stepped away from Cherry, out of camera range. "I'm sorry. I can't do this."

"Jesus Christ." Zell jumped down from his tall chair, urging me to take a minute, collect myself. "Somebody get the kid some water! Makeup! Pat him down!"

"No, Mr. Zell. There's no need. This isn't who I am." I turned to Cherry, offered my apologies, told her I was sure she would have been great in the scene if only I hadn't mucked it up.

"I understand, Mr. Damon. Not everyone has the calling."

"Hold it," Zell said. "We came here to shoot a screen test, we'll damn well shoot a screen test." He barked at the crew. "Give him five minutes to relax, then relight the set."

"Mr. Zell, the screen test is over." Zell's head came around fast, his jaw tighter than a stage grip's vise clamp. I shrugged. "I'm sorry, I feel like an idiot for causing such a mess."

He came over, reaching up to put a paternal arm around my shoulders. "Listen, kid. I know these things can be a pain. But you'll get through it, you'll see. Did you know that I gave your old man his first screen test?"

"I knew he'd made a few movies in the thirties, but—"

"Right here, on Soundstage 12. Directed it myself, got

him through it just fine. Your father would want you to do this, Philip. You wouldn't want to let him down, would you?"

"Of course not."

"So take a minute, get yourself together, and we'll shoot the damn screen test."

"I'm not sure why it's so important to you."

"Because when I set my mind on something, I don't back down, I don't give up. That's why your father wanted to work with me. Because Sid Zell gets movies made." He grinned. "He was a mensch, your old man. Like a brother to me. Like I said, he'd want you to see this through."

Zell turned away, snapping his fingers at the A.D. His Harvard class ring caught my attention as it glinted under the lights. I took a deep breath before I spoke.

"You're a liar, Mr. Zell, and I resent you using Dad's memory like that."

An instant hush fell over the set. Zell's shoulders bunched like an angry fist and his protruding ears turned crimson. Every eye was on the two of us.

"Dad shot his screen test at MGM," I said. "I know, because it happened on my seventh birthday, and I was there. Rouben Mamoulian was the director. He had a big cake brought in afterward. Ruby Keeler lit the candles. Zasu Pitts cut the cake. Deanna Durbin handed me my slice and gave me a great big kiss."

Zell swiveled to face me. His voice was low, like a growl. "No one has ever called Sid Zell a liar. Not to his face."

"Actually, your back was to me."

"Am I supposed to laugh at that, Damon?"

"The point is, I don't want to do this screen test and I don't want to do business with you. I guess my pride matters more than I thought it did."

"Let me tell you what matters, you little punk. What matters is what's real, tangible. This stage is real. These cameras are real. The movies I make, and the money, they're real."

"So's that Harvard diploma on your office wall, Mr. Zell—and that Harvard class ring you're wearing."

He rubbed the big ring without looking at it. "Damn right they are."

"I went to Yale, but some of my closest pals from my college days were Harvard guys—Porcelians, as a matter of fact. Were you a Porcelian, Mr. Zell?"

Zell began to fidget. "I don't have time for this crap!"

"You don't know what a Porcelian is, do you? Because you never attended Harvard a day in your life. Your diploma and your class ring—they're from different eras, decades apart. It took me a while to figure out what seemed odd about them. You bought them, the way you buy a lot of things—including people."

Zell set his jaw, silent for a moment. "I could have made you as big as your old man, Damon. I still can."

"I'm not for sale, Mr. Zell."

He kept his furious eyes fixed on me while his voice cracked like a whip across the stage. "Kill the sound, kill the damn lights, sign the overtime sheets. We're finished here."

I headed for the nearest exit, not sure where it would take me, except out.

Chapter 31

⌒

I STEPPED FROM Stage 12 onto a narrow, unfamiliar street. The lot was dark and largely deserted now—no more messenger boys on bikes or miniskirted assistants running errands. I started up the empty street, intent on finding Beatrice as soon as possible, thinking about what she'd said not half an hour earlier: *I think we should leave immediately. I'm not sure we're safe here on the lot, you and I.* And after that: *Come find me. We need to talk.*

In my haste, I became disoriented in the grid of intersecting streets and looming sets. I found myself on Main Street, which should have felt comforting and innocent with its quaint Victorian and Midwestern façades, a nostalgic backdrop for movies set in an earlier time. Instead, it struck me as lonely and intimidating, a place of false fronts, recessed doorways, and deep shadows where anyone might be concealed. A minute later I was on New York Street, which was lined with sets suggesting Manhattan street corners and the lower floors of massive skyscrapers. I stopped to look and listen, hoping to get my bearings, or see someone who might give me directions to the executive building where Beatrice was presumably waiting in Sid Zell's office.

Instead, I heard footsteps somewhere in the darkness behind me, coming in my direction.

Funny how your imagination can exaggerate the portent of human footsteps when you've got a lump or two on your head and troubling questions about recent homicides on your mind. I took off down New York Street, cut around the corner, and raced down a long block past a faux city square. I stopped again, heard the footfalls coming faster, and decided not to wait around. I cut through the make-believe park toward another fake street corner, intending to get around it and find some dark alleyway, to see who might be following me.

Just as I reached and turned the corner, I was nearly flattened by someone walking briskly toward me—Monica.

"Philip! There you are."

"Monica—you scared the stuffing out of me." I grinned. "A pleasant scare, I have to admit."

She grabbed my hand. "Come, quickly."

"What's going on?"

She pulled me around the corner and across the street to an old building that looked like a warehouse. She tried a door, found it unlocked, made it creak as she pulled it open.

"Wardrobe," she whispered, closing the door behind us. Inside, the lighting was dim, cast by faint bulbs high up in the rafters. The air was pungent with the odor of musty clothing. "Not the most romantic place—but it's private."

"How did you find me?"

"I heard about your screen test, so I came out."

"I completely screwed it up, by the way. I'm not at all cut out for your line of work."

"I know. I was there."

"You were in the studio when I suffered my bout of stage fright?"

She nodded and grabbed my hand again, then led me down row after row of bins, shelves, and crude closets, all of which seemed to be overflowing with old movie costumes. "I stayed back in the shadows," she said, "watching and listening. I didn't want to get in your way or distract you."

"You were OK with me and Cherry Topping together?"

"I've calmed down about that. Sid's just using her to try to keep us apart—hoping you'll fall for that Jayne Mansfield body. I have more faith in you than that."

"It takes a lot more than looks to make me fall for a woman, Monica."

"You realize Sid's all about control," she said. "But it's not going to work, because he doesn't own me anymore. Two more pictures on my contract, then I'm free."

"I guess we won't be making *The Philip Damon Story* together, not after the way I made such a fool of myself back there."

She faced me, our lips close. "I didn't see a man make a fool of himself, Philip. I saw a man who knows who he is, a man who makes his own decisions." Her eyes grew bright, excited. "A man who's not afraid to stand up to Sid Zell and tell him the truth."

I kissed her hard and our hands started roving, but I pulled away.

"Monica, there's something I have to tell you."

She found my eyes, her smile fading. "What is it? You sound so serious."

"I know about your relationship with Nicky Pembrook."

She stiffened, shifting her eyes. "You do?"

"Beatrice and I did some research. Then we put our heads together with Hercules Platt, figured things out."

"I see."

"I know that your mother raised Nicky after he was orphaned. Which means you helped raise him, too. You and Lorna are the two 'aunts' who stayed anonymously in the background, while Sid Zell turned him into a child star."

Monica shuddered noticeably, as if relieved to finally have the truth out. "I suppose it doesn't matter if you know, now that Nicky's gone." Her eyes grew soft, vulnerable. "Do you hate me for deceiving you, Philip?"

"Of course not. You'd been protecting Nicky since he was a baby, close to twenty years. There was no reason to suddenly change that."

"It's decent of you to see it that way."

"It must have been difficult, keeping it secret for so long. Especially with the three of you in the public eye."

"It was rough at times, sure. Mother and I thought it was for the best, though. For Nicky's sake."

"When I realized the truth, I suddenly understood why his death was such a blow to you—after you'd tried so hard to convince me you barely knew him."

Tears welled up in her eyes. "That's why you're so important to me, Philip, why I had to come find you tonight. The way you were there for me when I learned that Nicky was gone. Nobody's ever been so good to me, Philip, like you have. I won't ever forget it."

We melded into each other, two souls suddenly in touch, kissing like there was no tomorrow. Together, we fell onto a table piled with folded clothes that smelled as if they'd just come back from laundering. Hanging all around us on racks were costumes from movies going back decades. The cuff of a black trench coat at eye level was stapled with a hand-printed tag: DANE CLARK, *WEB OF LIES*, 1948. I barely glimpsed at it as Monica pulled me down on top of her.

"Make love to me, Philip. Right here, right now."

Maybe it was that maddening mix of need and passion, mystery and vulnerability, that had me in Monica's thrall. I was always off-balance, trying to figure her out—off-balance, and falling hard.

IT was nearly eight as Monica and I adjusted our clothes, stole a final kiss, and stepped from the wardrobe facility back onto the studio lot. My thought was to find Beatrice as quickly as possible, after keeping her waiting for so long. But first I had to deal with Hedley Pinkston.

He was waiting for Monica and me just outside the door, rocking on his Florsheims with his hands clasped behind his back.

"Finished with our little love scene, are we?"

Monica faced him squarely, a fist planted on each hip. "How long have you been out here?"

"I chased after Philip when he left Stage 12, to take him to Beatrice. For some reason, he chose to elude me. I saw the two of you sneak in here, so I stuck my head in the door. It wasn't difficult, figuring out what was going on. You project spectacularly, Monica. Must be all that vocal training."

"Bastard," she said.

I asked where Beatrice was.

"In your car, near the security kiosk. She seemed more comfortable waiting for you near the guards. Struck me as a bit on edge. You, too, Damon, as a matter of fact."

"We encountered a burglar last night, up in Laurel Canyon. You wouldn't know anything about that, would you, Hedley?"

"Afraid I can't help you there." His narrow eyes shifted to Monica, then back to me. "However, there is another matter that warrants discussion, which concerns you both."

"I'm listening, Pinkston. Make it quick."

He smiled like the Cheshire cat. "I'm referring to your little trip to Palm Springs the other night. That, and the roadside wreck you were foolish enough to become involved with after my imbecilic twin ran his Mercury off the road."

Monica drew her hands together, wringing them anxiously. "How did you know about that?"

"A witness has come forward—someone who saw Philip take something from Hudley's car before jumping back into your Jaguar and racing off."

"Oh, my god." Monica turned away, pacing. "I knew this would happen. I knew it!"

Pinkston bore down on her. "It's a felony, you know, to leave the scene of a collision that involves injury, without reporting it. Hit-and-run they call it. Tsk, tsk, tsk. They could give you jail time for this, Monica. Look what they did to Bob Mitchum, for a single marijuana cigarette."

"Listen," I said, "we came upon that wreck after the fact."

"That's what you say, Damon."

"It's the truth, damn it."

"Still, it looks bad, doesn't it? According to the police, there was blood in the car. From what I understand, Monica's Jag has some damage that matches up exactly to the damage on Hudley's Mercury, as if she deliberately forced him off the road."

Monica stopped pacing to face him. "How would you know that?"

"The next day, you left your Jag towed at a body shop. I made a personal inspection myself."

"You've been having me watched!"

"For your own good, Monica, since you seem bent on self-destruction."

I stepped between them. "You're blowing this all out of proportion, Pinkston."

"Am I? Hudley's still missing, along with his camera. You both have argued publicly with him. Frankly, it doesn't look good for either of you."

"It was my idea to take the camera. I'll take the heat on this, the whole thing. Just keep Monica out of it."

"Don't be naïve, Damon. Monica's a star. There's no way to keep her out of it. Unless, of course—" He broke off, letting his thought float like a toxic cloud.

Monica seized his wrist, panic rising in her voice. "What, Hedley? What can we do?"

"I've managed to put a lid on it for now, Monica. But from now on, you're going to have to do exactly as I tell you."

She laughed a little, sadly and without much resolve, as if this moment had been inevitable all along, as if destiny had been leading her to it.

"For the immediate future," Pinkston went on, "you'll appear publicly only with Rock, until I say otherwise. You're not to see Damon again, not even privately. Tomorrow, you'll sign an exclusive, long-term contract with me for personal publicity, and renew your contract with Premiere Alliance Pictures for another five years. You're going to be a good little girl, Monica, or risk a terrible scandal. You know what that can mean, don't you?" She hung her head, saying nothing but nodding pathetically. "Look what happened to Ingrid Bergman, after her affair with Rossellini.

For years, she barely worked, and then only in Europe. And she was a major star, Monica, not a B actress like you. They'll toss you aside like yesterday's garbage. I'm sure Suzanne Pleshette or a dozen other good-looking girls would be happy to step in and replace you. Besides, Suzanne's younger, isn't she?"

Monica flinched, as if his words were lashes from a whip. I faced her, taking her by the shoulders, trying to see her eyes.

"Don't listen to him, Monica. We'll tell the truth, explain what happened, why we acted the way we did. What have we done that's so terrible?"

Finally, she looked up. "No, Philip. I can't risk it." Her fragile smile was etched in surrender. "We had some good times, didn't we?"

"Don't do this, Monica. Don't give up this kind of power to him."

"I don't really have a choice, Philip." She fought back tears. "Take away my career and what am I? Just another pretty face, getting older fast."

"You're an actress, and a good one."

"This town is filled with good actresses who never get anywhere."

"Then forget about Hollywood. You can return to the stage. We'll get married, grow old together. It's what two people do who are crazy about each other. We'll get out of this insane city, raise some kids, have a real life somewhere else. Would that be so bad?"

She touched my face, looked into my eyes. "No, that wouldn't be so bad. If I thought it was possible. If I thought dreams like that really came true."

"It is possible, damn it."

She drew away from me. "Take care of yourself, Philip.

Every time I hear 'All the Things You Are,' I'll be thinking of you."

I reached for her but she turned and ran, around a corner toward the façade of Main Street. I stood watching long after she was gone. Pinkston laid a hand on my shoulder, like we were buddies. I stared hard at it, and he removed it.

"Look at it this way, Damon. Monica's pushing forty. The fact is, her days as a leading lady are numbered. In a few years, she'll be doing TV, happy for the work. You're a young guy, with all kinds of chicks out there to choose from."

I slugged him hard in the gut, doubling him over, leaving him on his knees, gasping for air. It didn't make me feel better but I was glad I did it just the same.

AS Beatrice and I drove through the wrought-iron gates, leaving Premiere Alliance Pictures behind, I asked her what it was that had her so jumpy.

"I went through all the old script files at the studio," she said, "looking for some kind of coverage on *Sure Bet.* The woman who runs the story department is very organized. She's got every script catalogued and indexed, alphabetically, by year, cross-referenced every which way. So if something was there, I would have found it."

I glanced over as I drove. "Nothing?"

"Not a trace, Philip—no drafts, no synopsis, not so much as an office memo."

"Seems like someone's gone to a lot of trouble to make that script disappear."

"Doesn't it, though? It's as if *Sure Bet* never existed— except perhaps in the imagination of a foolish old lady."

Chapter 32

THE NEXT MORNING, riding to Rosewood, I filled Hercules Platt in on the events of the previous day. As he drove, he drew the tiniest details from me one by one and with the utmost care, like a mother extracting splinters from a child's finger.

Platt had borrowed his daughter's car, an old Ford that chugged along, needing a valve job. We drove through streets where riot cleanup was in progress and businesses were attempting to reopen, those that hadn't been too severely damaged. Nicky's body had been found in an alley southeast of the Rosewood Gardens Race Track, near an area of heavy violence and looting. Platt climbed from the Ford, inspected the site, looked around. A minute later, back in the car, we were pointed in the direction of the racetrack itself.

* * *

ROSEWOOD Gardens remained closed to the public, but we gained admittance without much trouble. Platt flashed his private investigator's license, explaining that we were looking into the death of a track employee, Nicky Pembrook. That triggered a call to the head of security, who joined us a couple of minutes later. He was a thick, broad-shouldered man about Platt's height, who carried a revolver in a shoulder holster, had the no-nonsense look of an ex-cop, and introduced himself as Mr. Tate. Platt displayed his license again, mentioned his background with the San Francisco Police Department, and mentioned that I was a family friend.

"You're probably meeting the aunt," Tate said. "She's in the employees' quarters, cleaning out his locker. I'll take you down. Tough what happened to the boy."

"Tough what happened to a lot of people," Platt said.

We found Lorna Draper a short time later, standing in front of an open locker, staring into it with a boy's jacket and baseball cap folded in her arms. Her back was to us as we entered the room. Tate cleared his throat to let her know we were there.

As she turned, Platt tipped his hat. "Miss Draper."

She studied him a moment with faint recognition, before her eyes came slowly around to me. She seemed distant, removed from the immediate world. Tate excused himself, telling us he'd be back shortly, to show us out when the time came. As he left, Lorna Draper regained some focus, speaking slowly, in a subdued voice. "Monica told me you found us out—our connection to Nicky. I guess it doesn't really matter anymore, does it? If people know, I mean."

"This is Hercules Platt, Miss Draper. You've seen him

before—he plays in my orchestra. He's also a licensed private detective."

She seemed to wake up a little. "Detective?"

"I'm curious about the circumstances surrounding Nicky's death," Platt said.

"Who asked you to become involved, Mr. Platt?"

"No one specifically."

Platt drifted toward the lockers, his eyes scanning the names taped to the doors.

"Nicky died in the riots, Mr. Platt. That's fairly obvious, isn't it?"

"I'm not so sure about that."

"They found those words carved into his flesh—*Burn, Baby, Burn.*"

"Thirty-five people died in the riots, Miss Draper. Nicky was the only one who was marked with those words."

Her voice grew hard. "He was white, Mr. Platt. That would seem to explain it, don't you think?"

"Several other victims were white. None of them were carved up like that."

"How would you know that?"

"I did some checking."

"You seem awfully interested in Nicky's death." When Platt said nothing, she added, "I don't know what you expect to find here."

"I try not to have expectations, Miss Draper." Platt stopped in front of a locker, studying the name taped to the front. As he turned to face Lorna Draper again, I read the printed name: ANGEL VARGAS. "I don't mean to upset you," Platt went on, "but if the person who took Nicky's life is ever to be identified, I believe it's going to take a special effort. The authorities have a lot to deal with right now, with a fraction of the resources needed to do it properly."

"That still doesn't explain why you're here."

"We wanted to look around, get a sense of Nicky, where he worked, what kind of fellow he was."

"He was basically a good boy, Mr. Platt, who got into trouble now and then. But only the kind of trouble that caused him to hurt himself."

"He apparently was fond of horses."

She smiled. "Oh, yes. He loved to ride them, groom them, talk to them. Did you happen to see *Short in the Saddle?*"

"That would be a movie?"

"Rory Calhoun, 1955. Not the greatest picture, but it was Nicky's favorite, of all the movies he made. At the end of the day, they had to pry him off that mare." A lump caught in her throat and she turned quickly away. She shut the locker door, taking her time, before facing us again, her composure regained. "I'm going over to the stables where Nicky worked. I suppose you could come along, if you'd like."

Outside, we passed the paddock area and followed Lorna Draper into the stables. Roughly a dozen men, mostly Mexicans on the small side, fed and groomed horses in their stalls. Lorna moved among the animals, stroking their muzzles, patting their flanks. "I share some of the blame for Nicky's problems, of course."

Platt drew closer to her. "How's that, Miss Draper?"

"As an orphan, Nicky was always so eager to please, to make people like him. Hollywood ate him alive—Sid Zell, especially. He took what he could get from Nicky, then spit him out like a cherry pit. I failed to protect Nicky the way I did Monica."

A stallion whinnied and she reached out, calming him. "I wanted it to be different for Monica than it was for me.

I kept her out of the movies when she was younger, made sure she got the right training, then brought her back to Hollywood when she was ready. Preparation and experience—it makes all the difference, you know."

"Still," I said, "everyone needs a lucky break."

Lorna Draper regarded me coolly. "I made sure she got the right breaks."

"And Nicky?"

She smiled. "Nicky was a natural, right from the start. The camera loved him—that funny nose, those jug ears, the twinkle in his eye. Because he was a boy, I figured he'd be able to take care of himself. I guess I made a mistake, didn't I?"

"I admire your honesty," I said. "Not everyone is so candid about their role in raising a troubled child."

"I wouldn't give Miss Draper too much credit for candor," Platt said. His eyes were fixed on hers. "I spent several hours at the county records center. Nicky was born in Tijuana in 1947 to an American citizen of Mexican birth, with John Doe listed as the father. The mother's name on the birth certificate was Consuelo Montero. That would be your birth name, Miss Draper, according to certain film resource books."

"You are quite the detective, aren't you, Mr. Platt?"

"That would make Monica Nicky's half sister," I said.

"Congratulations, both of you." Lorna Draper recovered some of her old toughness, though not all of it. "You've discovered our dirty little secret."

I threw up my hands. "But why did you go to so much trouble to cover it up all these years?"

"Nicky was fathered out of wedlock by a man who wanted nothing to do with raising him. I was still relatively young then, still attractive, hoping my career might yet take off. An illegitimate child would have ruined me, hurt Nicky, even tainted Monica. So I went to Tijuana and quietly gave birth, under my old name."

She walked briskly from the stables and stood looking out at the track, where riders circled atop saddled horses, putting them through their paces. We stood behind her, on either side.

"Nicky's gone now and my career is long over." Her voice was hard, bitter. "So tell the whole world if you wish. Lorna Draper was Nicky Pembrook's mother and if they don't like it, they can go to hell."

Platt's voice was subdued, almost gentle. "I doubt anyone needs to know, Miss Draper, unless it has some direct bearing on Nicky's death."

She began to weep, while the riders used their whips and the horses galloped past, kicking up puffs of dust. Hercules Platt gave me a look and we moved quietly off, leaving Lorna Draper to her mother's grief.

I followed Platt back to the employees' quarters, where he tried the handle on Angel Vargas's locker but found it locked.

"Something I can help you with, Mr. Platt?"

We turned to see Tate, the head of security, standing behind us in the doorway. He moved to the middle of the room, keeping a close eye on Platt.

"I was hoping I could get a look inside Angel Vargas's locker," Platt said. "Unless you've already cleaned it out."

"Haven't gotten to it yet, truth be told."

"You have a key, Mr. Tate?"

"You have a good reason to look in there?"

"Curiosity. A hunch that Vargas's death may be linked to Nicky Pembrook's."

"Vargas got his head crushed by a temperamental filly, the best I can figure. Pembrook got killed in the riots. I don't see the connection. Anyway, a detective from the Rosewood PD already went through Vargas's locker. Didn't find anything worth a damn."

"Then it won't hurt for me to look, will it?"

Tate ran a hand over the top of his bald head, his eyes still on Platt. Then he said, "I guess it won't, if you can be quick about it."

He unclipped a ring of keys from his belt, found the master he was looking for, and unlocked Angel Vargas's locker. Inside were a few personal belongings—baseball cap, Spanish-language newspaper, cheap pair of sunglasses— amid some loose trash and other debris at the bottom. Platt rummaged through it, coming up with a thimble-sized object he held up for us to view, pinched between his fingers.

"This mean anything to you, Mr. Tate?"

It was a piece of soft sponge. Tate stepped forward, squinting.

"Can't say that it does."

"Mind if I hang on to it?"

"I suppose it's OK, since the homicide guys already checked off on it."

Platt found a clean tissue in one of his pockets, wrapped it around the section of sponge, and carefully tucked it away. "I guess we're finished here, then. Thank you for your assistance, Mr. Tate."

"Not at all."

*   *   *

I pulled back out into the streets of Rosewood, where tradesmen were prying the plywood covers off their windows, sweeping up broken glass, and putting up signs that said, *Open for Business*.

"That piece of sponge looks exactly like the others," I said. "The ones that were found in Buddy Bixby's tux and a pocket of Nicky Pembrook's pants."

"Not exactly, Damon. This one's covered with dirt and tiny bits of straw, as if Mr. Vargas picked it up from the stable floor."

"Meaning what, Hercules?"

"Vargas was found dead in the stables, his head bashed in."

"Yes, I remember Bob Considine telling me that back in New York, the night before I flew out here."

"In Vargas's possession was a piece of sponge, much like the ones Bixby and Pembrook were carrying."

"OK, go on."

"Think back over everything you've told me, Damon, your various adventures in the last couple of weeks."

"Come on, Platt, I'm in no mood for games."

Platt rubbed his stomach. "I'm getting hungry. How about we get some chow?"

"Damn it, Platt! What are you on to?"

But Hercules Platt just smiled coyly and suggested we find a good rib joint for lunch.

Chapter 33

AFTER A TASTY meal of ribs, corn bread, and collard greens, Platt and I drove west to Manhattan Beach, where Johnny Langley kept a bachelor pad just off Marine Avenue near the ocean. There was no smog out here, no lingering smoke from the riots, none of the urban tension one felt further inland in the asphalt jungle. Out here by the beach, it was just blue sky and careening gulls and clean sand, and volleyballs being batted back and forth over nets by boys and girls with lean bodies and nice tans.

Langley's address was listed in the phone book and we didn't have much trouble finding it. A sanitation truck was pulling away, leaving behind empty trash cans and scattered litter, while Langley loaded his new surfboard into his Woody, with the nose extending at an angle out the rear right window. He was wearing baggy swim trunks and rubber thong sandals, without a trace of fat on his rippled body. As we approached, he was about to climb behind the wheel. It was clear from his jumpy manner that he was higher than a kite.

"Speed," Platt said to me, keeping his voice low as we approached. "That would be my guess. You can surf a whole day on that stuff and never feel tired. Or clean house like a machine, the way so many housewives do who are hopped up on diet pills. Government passed it out like candy to G.I.'s in the Big One, to keep them alert and fighting. Plenty of 'em came back addicted. I'm not surprised it's catching on."

Langley looked Platt over with his dilated pupils as we drew close—the hat, the inexpensive suit, the cop look. I'd met Langley briefly during the filming of *Zombie Surfers from Mars* but he didn't know Platt, so I introduced them, mentioning that Platt was a private eye.

"I kinda figured something like that," Langley said.

Platt removed his hat, smoothed the brim. "I wonder if you could spare a couple of minutes for some questions, Johnny."

"Maybe another time. There's a big north swell coming in at Huntington Beach and I don't want to miss it."

"Just one or two questions, that's all."

"About what?"

"You, Nicky Pembrook—when you saw him last."

"Geez, what happened to Nicky. Total wipeout, man. What a bummer."

"So when *did* you see him last, Johnny?"

"Last Monday, after the film shoot finished up in Point Dume. Why?"

"You two do some surfing together that evening?"

"We came back here. I let him use my board for a little

while, gave him some tips about timing his takeoff, walking the nose. Stuff like that." Langley laughed. "He fell off a lot. Nicky's not too good on a surfboard."

"Nicky's not to good at anything anymore, Johnny."

Langley's laugh died, and his smile disappeared. "No, I guess not. I didn't mean no disrespect. Nicky was a cool guy, for all that."

Platt glanced at the surfboard, then down at Langley's legs, while the surfer popped his knuckles and shifted from foot to foot, revved up like a high-performance engine with the throttle stuck.

"Must be hard on the knees," Platt said, "all that paddling."

"You get used to it. The body adapts."

"I can see that."

Langley glanced down. "We call 'em surfer's knobs. Got 'em on the upper arches of my feet too. See? Bony bump, each foot. Don't even think about 'em after a while. Listen, I got to get going. I don't want to miss that swell."

He climbed into the front seat but when he reached for the door, Platt held it.

"So you don't know what happened to Nicky Monday night."

"Like I said, we came back here, did some surfing. Later, I dropped Nicky off at that motel where he stays with his chick. Maybe you should talk to Vicki, see what she has to say. She must have seen him after I did."

"You didn't go in?"

"Dropped him off out front and peeled out. Had a hot date with a groovy chick. I guess later Nicky decided to go out to the track to check on his horses. I'd warned him that was no place for a white guy, with all the trouble. I guess he went anyway. Stupid little jerk."

"You want to tell me the name of the girl—the one you had a date with?"

"Not really. She's private that way." Langley cackled. "Given how she's got a husband."

Platt's eyes drifted over the roof of the Woody to the other side, where the nose of Langley's surfboard poked a foot or two out a window. "Looks like you got yourself a new surfboard, Johnny."

"Tuesday morning, I drove up to Lunada Bay in Palos Verdes. Great break, man, almost a half mile out. Long ride, very cool. But it's rocky up there, you know?"

"Not really, Johnny. Why don't you fill me in?"

"I busted up my board on a big wave. Got me a new one."

"I can see that," Platt said, but he kept his eyes on Langley.

"Shorter, lighter, easier to maneuver. It's what's happening, man. The big storm boards, they're on their way out. At least along this coast."

"Where's your old board now?"

"Stripped and cut up for the foam. Already been reshaped and relacquered."

"How would you know that?"

"Because I did it myself, in my buddy's shop."

"Why the hurry to recycle the old board?"

Langley's rapid speech came to a halt like brakes locking up. "Why all the questions, man? Like, are you looking into what happened to Nicky, or what's the deal?"

"I'm the curious type, I guess."

"Yeah?" Langley's features suddenly went dark, as if a cloud had passed across his face. "Well, I'm the type who likes to ride waves. Which is what I'm gonna do."

He started the ignition while Platt continued holding the door.

"It's a nice life you got, Johnny. Surfing whenever you want to, running around in your Woody wagon, going out on hot dates with married ladies. How do you manage it, and still pay for a bachelor pad down here by the beach? Rents can't be too cheap down here."

"Movie stunt work, surf lessons for rich kids, whatever turns up."

"Errands for Sid Zell?"

"Beats punching a time clock."

"You like your freedom, I guess."

"I live for it, man." Langley stared at Platt's hand on the car door. "Like right now, when I'm ready to split. I come and go as I please. You dig?"

Platt removed his hand and Langley pulled the door shut. A moment later, he spun his tires, racing away as the Surfaris' "Wipeout!" blared from his radio, down a dangerously narrow alley lined with telephone poles.

JOHNNY Langley was barely out of sight when another vehicle appeared from a side street behind us, coming around the corner and speeding to a stop a few yards away. Two men in gray suits jumped out, pulling guns and flashing gold shields. One was older, bald, beefy, around Platt's age; the younger one was leaner, with a blond crew cut. In seconds, they had us up against a wall, while the litter from the trash trucks lay scattered around our feet. I started to protest but Platt told me tersely to keep quiet and do as I was told. He cast his eyes down, where they fixed on a crumpled letter-sized sheet of paper lying against the wall.

The younger detective held his gun on us while the older

one searched and patted us down. He collected our wallets, going through mine first. He saw nothing of interest, and started in on Platt's. When he got to Platt's investigator's license, he looked over.

"You're a private eye."

"San Francisco Police Department," Platt said. "Inspector, retired."

"I didn't know they had any Negro inspectors up there."

"They don't, now that I'm gone."

The cop studied Platt more closely. "I think I read about you—big murder case, high society, a couple of years back."

"I was involved in that, yes. So was my friend here, Philip Damon."

The cop sighed heavily. "Relax." We took our hands off the wall while he turned to his younger partner. "Put your weapon away. We screwed up."

He gave us back our wallets while we faced him. "I'm sorry, Inspector. We were out of line here." Platt said nothing, just kept an even gaze. "You mind telling us your business with Johnny Langley?"

"I had some questions related to an unsolved homicide."

"You think he might be involved?"

"It's possible."

"Is it in our jurisdiction?" Platt shook his head. "I suppose you'd like an explanation for what happened just now."

"I'd be willing to listen," Platt said.

"We've been keeping an eye on Langley. We know he's been dealing dope—mostly marijuana and speed, but also a little heroin on the side. He's wired more often than not. We saw you talking to him, figured maybe you were making a buy."

"I imagine Johnny Langley talks to a lot of people," Platt said. "You roust all of them too?"

The big cop's face turned pink. "I'll admit Manhattan Beach doesn't have a very proud history dealing with Negroes."

"Is that so?"

"First black family that moved in got burned out. The residents here don't like to talk about it much."

"I imagine not."

"The city turned the site into a public park."

"How thoughtful."

"This all happened quite a while ago, Mr. Platt."

"Really? So how many black folks you got living here now?"

The cop laughed uneasily. "I'm just saying we were out of line just now, that's all. That we could have handled it better." Platt kept his silence. The cop handed him a business card. "We'll be on our way. Let us know if there's anything we can help you with."

They started for their unmarked car. Platt turned in a stoop, picked up the crumpled sheet of paper he'd been staring at a minute ago. As he flattened it out and studied it more closely, the older detective hollered at us from the open door of his vehicle.

"You find something interesting, Mr. Platt?"

Platt smiled mildly. "Just trash, Detective. I don't want to get arrested for littering."

The cop laughed, climbed in beside his partner, and drove off.

I peered over Platt's shoulder to see what had him so intrigued. It was a loose title page from an old film script. Typed in the lower right-hand corner was a notation: *First Draft: November 14, 1938.* The title and author were listed above that, centered halfway down the page.

SURE BET
By Beatrice Gless

Platt said, "It looks like Johnny Langley's the one who thumped you on the noggin the other night."

"Should we have him arrested?"

"I'd like to wait, put together some more facts first. My guess is that Mr. Langley's involved in a whole lot more than burglary and drug sales."

Three shapely young women in two-piece swimsuits walked by, heading down to the beach. They were carrying United Airlines travel bags and had the look of stewardess stamped all over them. Platt followed them with his eyes, then raised his head, as if savoring the clean air and listening to the distant splash of waves.

"Must be nice to live at the beach," he said.

Chapter 34

THAT NIGHT, SHORTLY after dark, Hercules Platt and I
pulled into the Tropicana Motel in West Hollywood,
parking beneath a neon sign that had seen better days.
The capital T—designed to resemble a palm tree—was
sputtering badly, in need of gas, which seemed to go with
the rest of the place. It was a run-down, three-story affair
on a busy stretch of Santa Monica Boulevard, with the req-
uisite swimming pool, coffeeshop, and plastic outdoor car-
peting. We found the night manager on the first floor and
learned that Vicki Hart had checked out in a hurry, leaving
behind her luggage until she could come back with enough
money to settle the bill. She intended to return later that
night, the manager said, but he wasn't so sure she would.
When Platt asked why, the manager said she'd appeared
nervous, maybe even scared.

"You know, like maybe she was running from something."

"Or someone?"

"Yeah, maybe from someone."

Platt left both our numbers, told me to give the guy a twenty, and asked him to contact us if Vicki came back. Outside, Platt made a call from a pay phone, stayed on the line for a minute without talking, and hung up. Platt was moving quickly now, as he tended to do when he was on the scent. I hurried to catch up, asking where we were headed next.

"Palm Vista Apartments," Platt said, "listed residence of Hudley Pinkston."

"You think there's a chance Hudley might still be alive?"

"I never thought otherwise, Damon."

THE Palm Vista was one of those once-proud hotels trapped in a decaying section of town and converted to apartments for Hollywood dream-seekers who either arrived too late or didn't get out soon enough. Its east-facing windows looked down on the busy Hollywood Freeway, which slashed through a neighborhood that had once sparkled with quaint Craftsman cottages and colorful gardens until the freeway decimated the landscape in the 1940s. Now, weeds choked the gardens, the houses needed painting and repairing, and annoying freeway noise mingled with exhaust fumes in the fetid air.

I parked on the street, making sure the doors were locked behind us. Platt and I entered the building through the front, past a sign that read, ROOMS BY THE WEEK OR MONTH. The cavernous Spanish-style lobby was replete with arched doorways, mezzanine windows, and baroque chandeliers hanging from inlaid wood. A restaurant and bar billing itself as the Palm Vista Terrace was open but nearly empty, with a lone bartender wiping up around two or three sleepy drunks. Next to it was a small beauty salon that was closed for the day. Across the otherwise empty lobby, a wizened old lady who might have been an actress or a dancer fifty years ago was scolding a poodle as it took a pee on the discolored carpet. I suppose there was a sad charm to the place, but it still smelled bad.

Platt located the night manager in a downstairs unit off the lobby and told him that we wanted to get into Hudley Pinkston's apartment. The night manager was a dwarf in his thirties, dapper in red suspenders and a matching bow tie, studying the casting call section in *Weekly Variety*.

"So go up and knock on his door," the dwarf said, looking up briefly.

"I called him," Platt said. "He's out. That's why we want in."

"I don't get it," the little guy said. Platt buzzed his P.I.'s license. The dwarf resolutely shook his head. "Can't do that, my friend. Pinkston's been a tenant here forever, long before I arrived. Anyway, the guy scares me a little, if you want to know the truth." He made a tiny fist. "Not that I can't handle myself, if it comes to that."

Platt asked me how much cash I had on me.

"I don't know. Fifty, sixty bucks."

"Give it to him," Platt said.

"All of it?"

Platt gave me one of his looks. I opened my wallet, pulled out a bunch of tens and twenties, and handed them over to the night manager. He hesitated for maybe half a second, then nodded once and tucked the money away. Platt wrote a phone number in his notebook, tore out the page, passed it across.

"This is Pinkston's number. Keep an eye on the lobby. If he comes in, call us right away."

The manager gave us a key, telling us he had to have it back. We rode up to the fifth floor in an elevator that bumped and lurched at each level.

As the doors opened, I said to Platt, "The things you get me into."

Platt was already out, moving briskly down the hall. I'm not sure he even heard me.

THE main room in Hudley Pinkston's apartment consisted of discrete, narrow walkways through all manner of containers—cardboard boxes, grocery bags, rectangular bins—stacked nearly to the ceiling. From our cursory inspection, this maze of material seemed to consist of photographs, newspaper and magazine clippings, and notebooks crammed with thousands of dated jottings. While Platt moved deeper into the apartment, I glanced at a couple of notebooks that suggested Hudley Pinkston had spent the bulk of his adult life tracking the personal activities of Hollywood's most notable celebrities, and quite a few who never made it that far.

"In here, Damon."

I followed Platt's voice down one of the narrow walkways, past teetering stacks of musty fan magazines from the thirties and forties: *Photoplay, Movie Mirror, Screenland, Modern Screen, Screen Romance,* all of them filled with innocuous puff pieces arranged and approved by the stars' flacks. I rounded a corner, into an area stacked with the scandal sheets that had cropped up in the fifties, as a sleazy section of the press had turned aggressive, even vicious: *Confidential, Lowdown, Insider, Whisper,* whose sole purpose had been to dig up and publish Hollywood dirt, destroying more than a few careers in the process. Hudley Pinkston's territory, I thought.

"I've lost you, Platt."

He whistled sharply and I turned in that direction, into a small room that was surprisingly clean and uncluttered. It consisted of a desk; at least half a dozen four-drawer, steel file cabinets labeled alphabetically; a table on which cameras, film canisters, and related gear were neatly laid out; and a small, unmade bed. Platt stood facing a wall covered with dozens of photographs held in place by thumbtacks.

"Recognize any faces?" Platt asked.

"Holy cow."

The subjects—most of them seeming oblivious to the camera—were all familiar: Monica Rivers, Lorna Draper, Nicky Pembrook, Sid Zell, Rock Hudson, Vicki Hart, Johnny Langley. And me.

Platt was on the move again, running his finger down the drawers of the file cabinets. He stopped, as if realizing there were too many to check. He moved immediately to the last cabinet, kneeled down, and pulled open the drawer marked X,Y,Z. He riffled through it, all the way to the back, and removed several files overflowing with photos, clippings, notes, and other documents related to Sid Zell.

We placed the files on the desk and Platt asked me to systematically go through them, looking for anything interesting. While I handled that task, Platt explored Hudley Pinkston's desk, examining the shutterbug's personal and financial records, including telephone bills and bank statements. Not quite an hour later, I showed Platt several pieces that had caught my eye. He seemed most interested in a

Kentucky newspaper clipping dated 1917, brittle and yellow with age.

FATHER, SON SOUGHT IN
ALLEGED RACE FIX SCHEME

LOUISVILLE—Local authorities are looking for a father and son, Samuel Zellman, Sr., 47, and Samuel Zellman, Jr., early '20s, who are wanted for questioning in what sources characterize as a race fixing scheme at the Hilldale Park racetrack.

The younger Zellman had worked at Hilldale Park, grooming and exercising horses, until suddenly leaving his job three weeks ago under a cloud of suspicion.

According to track officials and local police, Zellman and his father, an unemployed salesman and ex-convict, are suspected of tampering with horses before races to hamper their performance. The officials declined to say exactly how, for fear of encouraging similar crimes at other tracks. Both men apparently left town under the cloak of night, and have not been seen for at least two weeks.

Anyone knowing the whereabouts of Zellman and his son should immediately contact the Louisville Police Department.

I remembered something that Beatrice and I had discovered in *Who's Who in Hollywood,* and reminded Platt about it. "Hedley Pinkston was a newspaper reporter in Kentucky before he came west. Which means Hudley must have lived there too."

The phone rang. Platt grabbed it, listened for a second, hung up.

"Hudley's on his way up. Let's scram."

We put everything back where we'd found it and dashed back the way we'd come in, shutting off lights along the way. Platt closed the door behind us and we stepped into a stairwell for hiding, just as the elevator lurched to a stop down the hall.

Hudley Pinkston emerged and lumbered toward his apartment, a camera slung over one shoulder, a camera bag over the other. He looked as repulsive as ever. I half expected to see a swarm of flies trailing after him.

"So Hudley's alive and well," I whispered. "I wonder why Hedley hasn't found that out."

"Maybe he has, and just doesn't want you or Monica Rivers to know it."

The notion stunned me. "You think Hedley and Hudley might be in cahoots?"

We watched Hudley enter his apartment, closing the door behind him.

"I suspect that Hedley and Hudley are much closer than they let on." Hercules Platt slid his eyes in my direction. "Maybe even inseparable."

Chapter 35

PLATT DROPPED ME off at Beatrice's place around ten and drove on in his daughter's Ford, saying he still had things to do.

I had only one goal at the moment: to put my head on a pillow and close my eyes as soon as possible. Beatrice was out—noshing at Greenblatt's with the rabbi—so I decided to nap on the living room couch, where I fell asleep as cats arranged themselves on the softer parts of my anatomy.

It was a windy night and I dozed fitfully. Within the hour, I felt the cats stirring and abruptly woke. The house was pitch dark. The cats suddenly spooked, using my belly for a springboard and dashing in different directions. When they were gone and the house grew quiet again, I heard floorboards creaking on the front porch. Through the window, I saw a figure moving about, peering in.

Beatrice, I thought. *She's probably misplaced her key.*

As I unlocked and opened the door, there was a flurry of motion and footsteps across the big porch. A hooded figure hurtled over the rail and some gladiolas, disappearing around the corner of the house. Impulsively, I gave chase, my lingering anger over the intrusion and violence of two nights before getting the better of my judgment. On the west side of the house my feet found the narrow walkway that led north, down into the canyon. The moon was at three-quarters but the trees were thick with summer growth and the light that reached the path was scattered and indistinct. I saw the stranger ahead of me, pausing to look back, before disappearing again around a crook along the dark trail. Half a minute later, the path ended at a set of rickety wooden steps descending steeply into the ravine below.

I hesitated, frightened, as the wind stirred the brittle leaves and caused the shadows to come alive around me, twitching and jumping like goblins. Finally I gathered my nerve and began a wary descent. But as I neared the bottom, seeing nothing but a black chasm below, I came to my senses and stopped. I realized suddenly how much danger I'd put myself in—the kind of rash, foolish behavior that only happens in pulp fiction or second-rate movies. Beatrice would surely never write a scene like this one, I thought, unless she had Sid Zell looking over her shoulder, ordering her to dial up the action.

I whirled and immediately started back up, wanting to be away from there as quickly as possible, back in the house, with the door locked. But my rashness had put me into even more danger than I'd realized. As I neared the top steps, the hooded stranger appeared suddenly in front of me, looming over me, nearly sending me toppling backward in fright.

"Mr. Damon!" Peggy Bixby lowered the hood on her

jacket, while I grabbed the railing to keep from tumbling down. "I'm sorry, I've given you a terrible fright."

I gripped the wooden rail, feeling my heart pound. She explained that she'd come to the house to make a confession, to finally come clean on things.

"I was about to ring the bell when I suffered a crisis of confidence. When you opened the door, I lost all courage and ran. I feel awful, giving you such a scare."

I climbed to the top step, took her by the elbow, turned her back toward the house. "Let's go inside, Peggy. Frankly, I need a drink."

"THE truth is, Mr. Damon, I went to the Lighthouse to see Buddy the night he died."

I reclined on the sofa, sipping Scotch, while she sat stiffly across from me in an overstuffed easy chair. I'd switched on a single, small lamp, keeping the rest of the house dark, hoping she might feel more comfortable out of the glare.

"What was it you gave him that night, Peggy, that he hid away so furtively?"

"A business card, Mr. Damon. For a drug rehabilitation center where I hoped he might check himself in. I think he was ashamed to have anyone see it, even the bartender." She pursed her lips, looking earnest, regretful. "I would have done anything to get him into that program. To pay for it, I was even willing to cash in the life insurance policy that I'd been making payments on while Buddy was in jail."

"About that insurance policy—"

"That was to protect my parents, Mr. Damon—so they'd have something in their old age. I put it in my name because they wouldn't have let me take out the policy otherwise. They're proud, hardworking people, strictly blue collar. It's a terrible thing to say, but I didn't see Buddy living a long life. It seemed the prudent thing to do, getting some life insurance, since he might not be around to help them out as they got older."

"Why didn't you tell us all this before?"

She explained her fear of getting mixed up in a sordid story of drugs and possibly murder. The publicity, she said, might even expose the "special friendship" she'd had with Gloria Velez years ago, which would surely mean the end of her teaching career, not to mention public ridicule.

Peggy twisted her hands in her lap. "It's not easy for me to sit here and talk to you like this. But Gloria convinced me it was for the best." Peggy laughed nervously. "The truth will set you free, that's what she said."

Suddenly, the cats were stirring again, looking toward the front of the house, where the floorboards groaned out on the porch. I killed the light, told Peggy to remain where she was. For self-defense I grabbed the heavy cane from the umbrella stand next to the door. Very slowly, with the cane poised to strike, I turned the knob, then pulled the door open all at once.

Beatrice faced me with her key out, staring at me like I was crazy. Rabbi Kaminsky stood behind her, a hand on her shoulder, looking equally astonished.

Beatrice expelled a massive sigh of exasperation. "What on earth are you doing in the dark with that cane, Philip? Trying to scare us half out of our wits?"

HEADLIGHTS struck the house as we stood there. It was Hercules Platt, driving the old Ford, coming from staking out the Tropicana Motel. Vicki Hart was with him.

A minute later, we were all huddled in the living room

with the lights on, except for Rabbi Kaminsky, who was in the kitchen, preparing a pot of tea. Vicki sat alone on the couch, looking pale and shaky, her body hunched protectively, her eyes downcast. It wasn't difficult to see that she'd been doing a lot of crying, and that more tears surely lay ahead. Under Platt's gentle coaxing, she gradually opened up, explaining that she'd taken off in a panic, afraid that Johnny Langley might be looking for her.

"Why is that, dear?" Beatrice observed from her old rocker, where she bobbed slowly back and forth.

Vicki Hart looked around at each of us. "After filming finished for the day at Point Dume on Monday, Johnny and Nicky left together in Johnny's Woody. Johnny had promised to take Nicky surfing, further south where the waves were smaller and easier to ride. I wanted to watch but Nicky wouldn't let me—he was too self-conscious. So I secretly followed them in my VW Bug. I trailed them as far as Johnny's place in Manhattan Beach but I was running out of gas, so I stopped there and let them go on. It was nearing seven at that point. I didn't understand why they didn't just stop and do their surfing there, while they still had some daylight left."

"That was the last time you saw Nicky alive?" Platt asked.

Vicki nodded sadly. "He was riding off with Johnny, down that narrow alley behind Johnny's place."

"Johnny still had his old surfboard, the long, heavy one?"

Vicki nodded again. "It was sticking out the back window." She fought back tears. "Nicky was so happy that evening, so pleased that Johnny was taking him surfing. But as I watched them drive away, I felt something wasn't right."

"You don't think Langley intended to go surfing at all."

"I don't like to think bad of people, Mr. Platt, but—"

"But in this case, you felt uneasy."

"It was the way Johnny was being so nice to him. Too nice, instead of bossing him around the way he usually did."

"You think Johnny Langley killed Nicky, don't you? Then dumped his body in the riot area as a cover. Carved him up to make it look like rioters had done it."

Tears spilled over and Peggy handed her a fresh tissue. "I guess I do."

"Why, Vicki?" Platt leaned forward, his elbows on his knees, his eyes keen. "What would be the motivation for Langley to want to hurt Nicky like that?"

She looked down again and began to tremble. Platt moved to her side, sitting close without quite touching her. "Try to tell us, please. It's important."

"I'm so scared, Mr. Platt."

"I know. But we're with you now. Nobody's going to hurt you."

Platt signaled Peggy Bixby with his eyes. She slipped over to Vicki's other side, speaking softly. "Nicky's not the only one who's gone, Vicki. Since I lost Buddy, I haven't known a good night's sleep. Mom and Dad are sick with grief. If you know something, please—"

The two women shared a long look. Peggy reached for Vicki's hand and Vicki let her hold it. "We'll be right here," Peggy said. "You're with friends now. You're safe."

Vicki took a deep breath, swallowing bravely. "Nicky talked a lot about Mr. Zell's gambling problem. An addiction, Nicky called it, just like a drug habit. Mr. Zell had this overpowering need to win, especially at the racetrack. Until recently, he'd been racking up huge debts, tens of thousands of dollars. The more financial problems he had at the studio, Nicky said, the heavier he bet. The more he lost, the worse it got. So Mr. Zell started covering his losses at the track by diverting money from the studio coffers."

"How do you know that?" Platt asked.

"Mr. Zell had checks made out to Nicky for work he never did, for movies he never appeared in. Nicky was still in the studio's accounting system, which made it easier, I guess. Only Nicky never got the checks. Mr. Zell was cashing them himself. Nicky found out, through a bank statement. He went to Mr. Zell and confronted him about it. I warned him to be careful but he said we needed the money and he figured Mr. Zell owed him."

Beatrice stopped rocking. "Blackmail?"

"I'm not sure exactly what Nicky had in mind. But Mr. Zell convinced him there was another way they could make money together—a surefire betting system for winning big at the track."

I asked her if she knew what the system was.

"No. All I know is that it worked, and Nicky was really happy about it, because he said we were going to have lots of money. But then Mr. Zell cheated Nicky out of his share."

"And you think Zell ordered Johnny Langley to take care of it," Platt said. "You think he wanted Nicky out of the way before he could cause serious trouble."

She nodded. "I just don't know how he did it. Nicky always had his gun with him for protection, the one Mr. Zell gave him years ago. Nicky was kind of paranoid, especially when he was using drugs."

"He had the gun with him that day, when he rode off with Langley?"

"I saw him slip it inside his belt, Mr. Platt. You know, under his shirt." She shuddered. "And now I'm afraid Johnny's going to come after me, because of what I know."

Rabbi Kaminsky appeared with a tray and began dispensing cups of hot tea. For a time, Platt sipped his tea in silence while the rest of us chattered around him.

"What intrigues me," I said, "is this perfect betting system Zell came up with that was going to make him and Nicky so much money."

"What makes me curious," Beatrice said, "is how a script I wrote before the war figures into all this, and why someone would go to such lengths to make it disappear."

Platt set his cup in its saucer, then looked around at us. "I believe the answer to both your questions is in the script itself—the clever plot premise Sid Zell came up with that Mrs. Gless can't quite recall."

"I've been wracking my brain trying to remember." Beatrice thumped her knee with her fist. "I wish like the devil we knew who broke in and stole that script, along with all my notes."

"That would be Johnny Langley," Platt said.

Beatrice sat forward on her chair. "You've found my screenplay?"

"Only the title page, I'm afraid, outside Langley's apartment. He apparently got rid of the rest of it with the trash pickup. The title page must have fallen loose."

"Then how can you be so sure the story line holds the key to Nicky's murder?"

Platt reached into a pocket of his jacket, brought out two envelopes, and opened them one after the other. From the first, he removed the single piece of sponge discovered in Buddy Bixby's tuxedo, which he laid on the table. From the second, he dumped the three identical pieces of sponge Nicky Pembrook had been carrying in his pants the night he was killed. From another pocket, Platt extracted a folded tissue, which he opened and laid on the table to reveal yet another section of sponge. This one was covered with stable dirt and bits of straw, the one Platt had discovered in Angel Vargas's locker. It was the first time Beatrice had seen them, I realized, or even known of their existence.

Platt looked up into Beatrice's widening eyes. "Perhaps these will help jog your memory, Mrs. Gless. There's also a phrase you might consider: *winning by a nose.*"

"Of course!" Recognition dawned in her eyes. "I remember now as if it was yesterday."

The rabbi, still on his feet, spread his big hands. "For goodness' sake, Beatrice, tell us!"

"In the story," she said, "the father played the horses, laying down sizable bets. The son worked in the stables, tending to the animals. Before each big race, the boy shoved bits of sponge into the nostrils of the favorites, to impede their breathing. The father placed his wagers on the long shots, collecting big odds when the favorites lagged behind. After each race, the boy removed the wads of sponge from the horses' nostrils, with no one the wiser." Beatrice looked around at the rest of us. "When Sid Zell brought that to a story meeting, I found it quite fresh and promising. Everyone was caught by surprise, because no one ever expected Sid to come up with an original idea of his own, at least not one that was any good. He loved movies and he was a crafty businessman. But like a lot of producers, who can be so adept at harnessing the talents of others, true creativity was not among Sid's gifts."

"I imagine a lot of story ideas and plot elements come from real life," Platt said.

"Most of them, Mr. Platt, if truth be told. We borrow wherever we can, then filter the ideas through our own imaginations."

"Which probably explains how Sid Zell came by this one," I added, remembering the newspaper clipping I'd discovered in Hudley Pinkston's file on Zell. "Before he arrived in Hollywood and changed his name like so many others, he was a young man named Samuel Zellman running race-track cons with his father in Kentucky."

Vicki Hart picked up one of the sponge wads, looking troubled. "I can't believe Nicky could do such a thing. It's too cruel. He loved horses, more than anything."

Rabbi Kaminsky smiled sympathetically. "More than heroin, Vicki?"

Peggy Bixby left us for a moment, then came back to warm everyone's tea from a china pot. "Buddy must have found out what Nicky and Sid Zell were up to," she said as she refilled our cups. "But how?"

"I think I can explain that," Vicki said. "When your brother got out of jail, he came to stay with us at the motel. I'm sure that he and Nicky were shooting up together, although they never did it around me. Nicky probably started talking about all the money he was making—he liked to brag. He probably even showed Buddy some of the sponges, and I guess Buddy kept one."

"As a tool for blackmail," I suggested. "He started calling Sid Zell, making threats, trying to squeeze him for dough. Is that how you see it, Platt?"

"Don't stop, Damon. You're doing fine."

I drew in a deep breath and continued. "Johnny Langley knew both Buddy and Nicky from that movie, *Wheels on Fire*, the one they all worked on together a few years ago. Langley may have supplied Buddy with his drugs, and gotten Nicky hooked about the same time. From time to time, Langley also ran errands for Zell. When it came time for muscle, some dirty work, he was Johnny-on-the-spot."

"And what about Angel Vargas?" Platt asked, as if testing me.

I turned to the others, explaining. "Angel Vargas was a stable hand who was found dead a couple of weeks ago, with a crushed skull."

"And with Buddy's name and phone number in his pocket," Platt added.

"Buddy told us he'd run into Vargas at the track, when he was looking for a friend. The friend must have been Nicky. Buddy told us he left his name and number with Vargas. I suppose that could be true, couldn't it, Platt?"

"But what about the sponge we found in Vargas's locker?" Platt said. "Think, Damon. Put the pieces together. It's a matter of logic now."

I took another deep breath, pushing on. "Vargas found that piece of sponge on the stable floor. He got suspicious, figured out what Nicky was up to, fixing the races. Maybe he approached Nicky about it, to warn him to stop, or maybe to get cut in on the action. Nicky may have told Sid Zell, who had Vargas killed."

Platt raised his eyebrows approvingly. "Not bad, Damon. Not bad at all."

"My goodness," Beatrice said, a hand to her cheek. "This is absolutely heinous."

"If it's true." Rabbi Kaminsky stood and began pacing. "It all sounds plausible, I suppose. But can we really assume that Sid Zell is such a monster that he'd have three men killed to protect a race-fixing scheme? He's got a family, for goodness' sake. Social standing in the community. So much to lose."

"All the more reason to feel threatened by exposure," I said.

"You know how ruthless he can be when he wants something," Beatrice said, "and he lies without a flicker of conscience."

"Yes, yes, I know." The rabbi sounded genuinely troubled. "But that describes a good many executives in the movie business, doesn't it? It may suggest that they lack scruples but it hardly makes them guilty of conspiracy to murder. We're talking about evil here, not situational ethics." The rabbi threw up his hands. "Where's the hard evidence that any of this happened? Where's the proof? And what about some of the other people involved—Monica Rivers, Lorna Draper. Where do they fit into all this?"

All eyes settled on Hercules Platt.

"There's one name we left out," he said. "Someone who's closely linked to the others, and who's done such a skillful job creating a cover for their private lives."

"Hedley Pinkston," I said.

"Perhaps it's time we paid Mr. Pinkston a visit," Platt suggested, "and peeled back a layer or two of *his* private life."

Rabbi Kaminsky glanced at his watch. "Not tonight, I hope."

"No, not tonight." Platt rose, yawning. "Tonight, we should all get some rest, if that's possible." He suggested that Vicki Hart spend the night in Beatrice's guest room and offered to sleep on the couch, as an extra precaution.

A minute later, as Rabbi Kaminsky and Peggy Bixby departed, Hercules Platt set about the house, checking the locks on every door and window.

Chapter 36

THE ANNUAL MOVIE Publicists Association luncheon was held the next day at the Hollywood Roosevelt Hotel, across from Grauman's Chinese Theater on Hollywood Boulevard.

The last time I'd been there, in the late fifties, it had been with Terry Southern to catch Anita O'Day performing a sassy set at the Cinegrill. Today, as Platt and I entered the big lobby, the old hotel looked a little threadbare, though still serviceable. Sofas and chairs—faded but plush—were arranged comfortably among the pillars, while two bartenders served drinks from behind a chrome-and-leather Art Deco bar with sunlight streaming in the big window behind them.

Across the way, in the main ballroom, the luncheon was already in progress. Platt and I observed from a side door, while waiters scurried in and out, clearing empty dishes and serving coffee.

Hedley Pinkston—never more dapper and well clipped— was in his glory, as he was honored as the Publicist of the Year for a record fifth time, and accorded the association's Lifetime Achievement Award. Toward the end of a grandiose acceptance speech, Hedley predicted a "magnificent future" in which personal publicists would gain unprecedented leverage in protecting their clients from a predatory press.

"We'll bring the big magazines to their knees!" He spoke with a grin, drawing laughter from across the room. Yet his manner—excited, increasingly shrill, finger thrust in the air—brought to mind newsreel footage of power-mad dictators rousing the rabble. "It's all about control, friends, and the control will be ours, not theirs. If they want our top clients, then we'll demand the cover, photo and copy approval, even the choice of who writes the story and shoots the pictures. I see a time when the media pays as much attention to celebrities as it does to all the dour and depressing news of the day. It may not happen right away, or even in my lifetime. But mark my words, the balance of power is going to take a dramatic shift, and we are the pioneers who will lead the way."

The audience rose to its feet in an ovation that lasted nearly a minute. Hedley basked in the adulation, smiling grandly as photographers shot photos of him clutching his two glittering plaques.

Up on the dais, Monica Rivers stood next to Rock Hudson, smiling stiffly and applauding with the rhythm of a metronome.

*   *   *

MINUTES later, the crowd was drifting through the big doors and across to the lobby bar, which was suddenly very busy. I grabbed a Scotch just in time, while Platt kept a discreet presence off to the side, taking it all in.

As I joined him, he commented on the surprising number of smart-looking women in the group—no surprise to me, since publicity was one of the few avenues open to bright young women trying to find a niche in an industry dominated by clubby men. Several reporters were also on hand, hanging around to cadge free drinks. There was also a small herd of photographers galloping about, armed with special passes that apparently marked them as friendly and unthreatening. Most of their attention was drawn to Monica and Rock, whose arms were entwined around each other's waist and whose smiles never slipped as the shutters clicked.

Platt allowed Hedley Pinkston to get a drink and draw a crowd in the middle of the lobby before edging up to him. Unsure what Platt was up to, I stayed close, keeping my ears open.

"Congratulations, Mr. Pinkston. This seems to be your big day."

Pinkston turned, looking confused for a moment, possibly because Platt was the only black person in sight, except for the hotel service people. Just as quickly, Pinkston recovered, extending his hand.

"Thank you, thank you so much. So nice to see you again."

"There may be no one better in Hollywood than you at protecting his clients."

"That's very kind, Mr. . . . ?"

"Platt, Hercules Platt."

"Of course. Mr. Platt. Forgive me—where exactly was it that we met?"

"You haven't." Monica Rivers stepped into our midst, her voice as chilly as the white wine she was sipping. "Mr. Platt performs with the Philip Damon Orchestra. He and Mr. Damon apparently just happened to be passing through the hotel." She glared in my direction. "On their way out, I believe."

"Damon?" Pinkston saw me and quickly lost his smile. "I thought we had an agreement"—he lowered his voice— "that a certain distance would be kept."

"This is Platt's show, Pinkston." I raised my glass. "I'm just having a sociable drink. Hello, Monica. You're looking well. You too, Rock."

"I remember you," Hudson said amiably. "You were at Claudette's get-together the other night."

"Indeed. We had quite a nice chat, didn't we? *Rio Bravo, El Dorado*—Hedley, Hudley. You left me rather bewildered."

"I'd had a bit too much to drink. Whatever I said, pal, take it with a grain of salt."

"Actually, I found it fascinating." I turned my attention back to Monica. "When I said you were looking well, Monica, it was a lie. In fact, you look rather unhappy. Not surprising, considering what they're doing with you."

"I don't know what you're talking about, Mr. Damon." Her eyes faltered a moment. She tightened her grip around Hudson's waist, drawing him closer. "I've never been happier."

I raised my glass to her. "Here's to your happiness then."

She raised her glass in return, blinked hard, and we sipped our toast to each other. The reporters moved closer, taking out their pens and opening their notebooks, looking earnest, if confused.

Monica's eyes rested on mine a final moment before they

turned away, finding Platt again. "We're busy here, Mr. Platt. If you wish to speak to Hedley, perhaps you should make it another time, with an appointment."

"I just wanted to congratulate him," Platt said, "on the way he's watched out for his clients all these years."

Monica's voice grew sharp. "I believe you already told him that."

"All of his clients, that is, except Little Nicky Pembrook."

She reacted to the name like a slap in the face. "What's Nicky got to do with this?"

"I always did my best for Nicky," Pinkston said. "The boy had problems that were beyond my control. His passing is a great loss to us all."

Platt lifted his brows. "Problems, Mr. Pinkston? Yes, I'd say Nicky had problems. Some of which were kept secret even from him. Weren't they, Miss Rivers?"

"I don't like this conversation," Monica said.

"I suppose not, especially with so many ears listening."

I scratched my head. "You're losing me, Platt."

Rock Hudson raised his glass. "You and me, pal."

Platt ignored us, focusing on Monica. "It doesn't trouble you, Miss Rivers, that Nicky was murdered?"

"Of course it troubles me. The riots—it was horrible what happened."

"It's much more complicated than that, I'm afraid."

"Perhaps you should be more clear, Mr. Platt."

"I believe someone ordered Nicky killed. The riot was just a convenient cover."

All around us, murmurs buzzed like bees, while the reporters scribbled furiously in their notebooks, flipping pages as they filled them.

"But who would want Nicky dead? He had problems, but he was a sweet boy."

"Someone you know, Miss Rivers." Platt swung his eyes toward Pinkston. "Someone you both know. A man who had a great deal to lose if Nicky continued to make trouble, demanding his share of illicit money gained at the racetrack."

Monica's eyes widened. "Sid?" The word came out of her mouth so reluctantly it sounded like a sharp intake of breath.

Pinkston pulled himself up to his full height, puffing out his chest. "You're making an outrageous accusation, sir. A slur against a great man."

"I believe Johnny Langley can be tied to Nicky's murder," Platt went on, still keying on Monica. "I also believe he's responsible for the murder of Buddy Bixby, for essentially the same reason—to silence him, to stop a blackmail attempt." Platt shifted his eyes toward Hedley. "Johnny Langley was Sid Zell's personal thug, wasn't he, Mr. Pinkston?"

"I wouldn't know anything about that."

"You're much too modest, Hedley. There's not a lot you don't know about Sid Zell, is there? Going back decades, all the way to that racetrack in Louisville, Kentucky."

"I'm a publicist, sir, devoted to my clients."

"Come, come, Hedley. You're so much more than that."

Platt drew Pinkston's silk handkerchief from his breast pocket, dabbed it in his drink, seized Pinkston's chin with his other hand, and began rubbing Pinkston's neck. By the time Pinkston was able to pull away, crying out in protest, Platt had scrubbed away a layer of stage makeup to reveal a distinct purple birthmark just above his collar. The crowd let out a collective gasp, which included my own.

"Hedley, meet Hudley," Platt said. "But I guess an introduction isn't necessary, is it, Pinkston? You two have spent your whole lives together, never a moment apart."

Pinkston put a hand to his neck, but much too late. The shock passing through the room told him as much. The color drained from his stricken face while his eyes came alive with panic. His mouth opened but no words came out.

"When you came out here from Kentucky," Platt explained, "you knew all about Sid Zell. As a young reporter, you'd come across that earlier clipping about the racetrack con, which the authorities had pretty much forgotten about after so many years. You traced Sam Zellman to Hollywood, found him running Premiere Alliance Pictures under a different name—Sid Zell. It was the leverage you needed to get your foot in the door, to get your start in the publicity game. You and Zell made a pact—you'd protect him, help cover up his past, if he fed you clients."

Pinkston raised his hands imploringly, seeking out his friends in the room. "It's true, Sid Zell was my first client, but—"

Platt cut him off. "But that wasn't enough, was it, Hedley? The more success you tasted, the more you craved. So you came up with a diabolical scheme that allowed you to express both sides of your personality—the sycophant who longs to be around celebrities, basking in their light, and the angry loser who resents their acclaim, all the attention they get. As Hudley, you created the crises that only Hedley could contain. Hudley started the fires and Hedley put them out. My guess is, not even Sid Zell knew that there was only one of you."

"This is slander, Platt. You'll pay for this."

"Only now you're faced with something new," Platt went on, "the murders of three men, ordered by an arrogant studio chief desperate to avoid scandal and arrest. How are you going to put out this fire, Pinkston, without getting burned yourself?"

"I had nothing to do with those homicides. Nothing!"

"But you knew what was going on. You helped Sid Zell expedite them. Which makes you an accessory after the fact."

Pinkston raised his chin defiantly. "You can't prove that. You can't prove any of this."

"I can prove you made phone calls to Johnny Langley after each murder. I can prove you wrote checks to him around the same time. You even paid for that new surfboard of his. Your phone records, your financial statements—they won't look good in court, will they, Hedley?"

Pinkston fingered the birthmark on his neck, as if trying to pick it away. His voice became small, pitiful. "That was Hudley, not me. He's the one who does bad things. Hudley's the one who deserves to be punished."

I was as stunned as everyone else, hanging on Platt's every word. Then I realized that Monica Rivers was no longer there. I turned to Rock Hudson for help.

"She cursed Sid Zell," he said, "then flew out of here in a fit, apparently to find Zell at his studio." The big actor smiled pleasantly, the way he had so convincingly all through *Man's Favorite Sport*? "If you'll excuse me, I'm going to be over at the bar, where I intend to get very drunk and pretend I never heard any of this."

I drew Platt aside and told him we needed to get to Premiere Alliance Pictures, on the double.

Chapter 37

〜

SID ZELL HAD never removed my name from the list of cleared visitors, and Platt and I passed through the gates of Premiere Alliance Pictures unimpeded.

"At least the truth is out," I said as we parked and headed to Zell's office on foot. "Justice can't be too far off."

"The script isn't finished, Damon." Platt sounded faintly dubious. "We're in Hollywood, after all, where men like Sid Zell order the rewrites and control the final cut."

From Zell's receptionist, we learned that he was on the remote backlot where the western sets were located, probably along the main street between the saloon and the marshal's office, where a gunfight was to be filmed the next day. Before we headed out, Platt used a telephone in the waiting room to place a call to the police, which left me greatly relieved.

We found Zell standing on the dusty street at the edge of town, gazing out at open land covered with sagebrush and chaparral. Monica Rivers was behind him, giving him a tongue-lashing with all the fury of Mercedes McCambridge in *Johnny Guitar*. Zell swung around as we approached, silencing Monica with a cautionary look in our direction.

"Welcome to the Wild West, gentlemen." Zell smiled with his usual confidence, though his tone was slightly guarded. "Monica's been filling me in on what happened at the Hollywood Roosevelt. Poor Hedley. He must be a wreck, given what you've done to his career."

"His ruined career is the least of his problems," Platt said.

"I do wish you'd come to me first, Platt. I'm sure we could have worked something out. It still may not be too late."

"Some kind of financial arrangement, Mr. Zell?"

"A job, Platt. Head of security, say, at fifty thousand a year? That must be several times what you make blowing your tuba in Damon's band."

"I play the alto sax, Mr. Zell."

"Tuba, sax, trombone—I never could tell them apart."

"And what about Damon? How do you propose to buy his silence?"

"I resent your choice of words, Platt. I make deals, create opportunities." Zell fanned his hands wide, his eyes sparkling. "I see *The Philip Damon Story* adapted for television, a hip new series along the lines of *Peter Gunn*. Philip and Monica as a bandleader and his vocalist wife who stumble onto a new homicide each week. *Mr. and Mrs. North*, only sexy. I've even got a nifty title—*Murder Is My Beat*. Of course, Platt, you'll be our technical consultant on the crime stuff—another twenty-five grand a year."

"Awfully tempting," Platt said.

"The only problem is that Monica hates the idea of doing TV, so we've been having a bit of a spat."

"Are you really in a position to be making such generous offers, Mr. Zell? What about your financial troubles?"

"That's about to change." Zell looked out again on the vast, empty acreage that began where the sets ended. "I'm selling off most of the backlot to developers for a subdivision. I'll convert the studios for TV production. My accountant, Vito, assures me there will be more than enough money to make all of us filthy rich."

Platt leveled his eyes on Monica. "Is that true, Miss Rivers? You and Mr. Zell were arguing just now over career matters?"

Before she could reply, Johnny Langley's Woody appeared up the street, raising dust. Moments later, he braked in front of the blacksmith shop. He leaped out, clad in a T-shirt, swim trunks, and rubber sandals. A layer of powdery brine coated his bronzed skin.

"I called him at home," Zell told us, "and caught him just as he was coming in from the beach. I thought he might be useful to us, now that things are out in the open."

"I don't trust you, Sid." Monica's voice was tight, anxious. "Not for a moment."

Zell smiled like a cobra. "So when have you ever trusted me, Monica?"

Zell placed a hand on Langley's back as he joined us. "Thanks for coming out, Johnny. I hope the waves were good today."

"Perfect tubes, Mr. Zell. I was totally stoked." As usual, his pupils were enlarged, his manner jumpy. He raised his shirt in front, revealing a handgun tucked into his waistband, flat against his washboard stomach. "I brought the gun, like you told me to."

"Good boy, Johnny." Zell turned to Platt, whose eyes were on the gun. "You've met Hercules Platt, I believe."

"Yeah, I met him. He came to my place yesterday, asked me a bunch of questions."

"Mr. Platt has an interesting theory about what happened to Buddy Bixby and Nicky Pembrook. Don't you, Platt?"

"I have my suspicions."

"Please, Mr. Platt, enlighten us."

"I believe you ordered Johnny to kill Buddy Bixby with a hot shot—an overdose. The crime scene photos show odd indentions in the sand where Buddy's body was found, just below the imprints of the killer's knees." Platt glanced down at the bony knobs between Langley's kneecaps and shins. "Surfer's knobs, Johnny calls them. Beatrice Gless was the first to notice them, using her magnifying glass."

"That don't prove nothing," Langley said. "A bunch of stupid pictures."

"No," Platt said, "but it helps build the case." He returned his attention to Sid Zell. "Like Buddy, Nicky was also squeezing you for money, threatening to make trouble. Once again, you turned to Johnny Langley to eliminate the problem."

"No!" Monica stepped forward, sounding as if she was trying to convince herself as much as us. "Sid may be a bastard, but he'd never do that, not to Nicky."

Platt pinned Langley with his steady eyes. "You were seen driving off with Nicky hours before he was killed."

"We were going surfing. So what?" He lifted his shirt again. "Besides, Nicky carried this gun for protection. Everybody knows that. How is it I bashed in the head of a guy who had a gun on him?"

"How is it that you came to have possession of his gun, Johnny?"

Langley opened his mouth but no words came out. He looked to Zell for help, but Zell offered nothing more than a placid gaze and a ridiculing smile. Langley swallowed with difficulty and his breathing quickened.

"He's not the brightest bulb," Zell said.

Platt picked up his story. "You've done your share of stunt driving, Johnny. You're good behind the wheel. As you sped off down that narrow alley with your big surfboard poking out the window just behind Nicky's head, you deliberately swerved into one of the telephone poles along the shoulder." Platt clapped his hands. "Whack!"

Monica jumped, gasping.

"The nose of the surfboard struck the pole," Platt went on, "causing the lower portion inside the car to swivel around, striking the base of Nicky's skull with deadly force. The blow left wax residue at the site of the impact—paraffin that Nicky himself had applied to the rails of your surfboard when he waxed it Monday afternoon, during the shooting out at Point Dume. You drove out to Rosewood after dark and dumped Nicky's body near the racetrack, figuring his death would be laid off to the riots. To get rid of the murder weapon, you ditched your old surfboard for a newer, smaller model."

Monica went after Zell with her nails out, screaming at him. "You killed him! You killed your own son!"

Your own son. The words caused my jaw to drop, although Platt seemed completely unsurprised. Zell grabbed Monica's wrists, looking to me for help. But I was still trying to absorb what I'd just heard—that Sid Zell was Nicky Pembrook's father. Platt pried Monica gently away from Zell. She was putty in his hands, sobbing uncontrollably.

For once, Zell looked almost contrite. "Nicky wasn't supposed to be hurt. You have to believe that, Monica. I
wouldn't order the death of my own child." Zell shifted his
eyes, regarding Johnny Langley with contempt. "I told
Johnny to put the fear of God in Nicky, that's all. Just take
him for a drive, I said, threaten him, give him a good scare
so he knows not to mess with me anymore. But what does
Johnny do? The schnook kills him, just the way Platt said
he did."

"I warned him he was going to get a beating, just like
you told me to," Langley said. "He got scared, pulled his
gun on me. I thought he was going to blow me away. What
was I supposed to do?"

Zell relaxed, smiling again. "So you see, Monica, I have
no blood on my hands. It was this *schlemiel* who killed Nicky,
not me. As for that other business with Buddy Bixby, let
them try to put that on me."

"Don't forget Angel Vargas, the worker at the stables,"
I said. "I imagine you had something to do with his death
as well."

Zell laughed dismissively. "Circumstantial evidence,
nothing more. Let the prosecutors file their charges. My lawyers will eat them alive."

He pulled out a cigar, lit it, pulled on the smoke. Then
he produced three more, smiling pleasantly. "Cigar, anyone?"

MONICA'S sobs gradually ebbed, and she pulled herself together, though her mascara had made a mess of her face.
"You have your facts now, don't you, Mr. Platt? The truth
is out." Her wary eyes moved between Platt and me. "What

you and Philip do with it is up to you, I guess."

"Not quite all the truth," Platt said.

Monica studied Platt in edgy silence. I threw up my hands. "What now, Platt?"

"It's true, Mr. Zell is Nicky Pembrook's father. But what about his mother?"

"Lorna Draper," I said. "We already established that. Yesterday, when we confronted her at the racetrack."

"Yes, that's what she told us—a lie to cover up a previous lie."

"What are you saying, Platt?"

"Come on, Damon, use your head. You've got all the facts. Do the deduction."

"Platt, please. I'm a wreck. Just tell us."

Platt spoke slowly and precisely. "Little Nicky Pembrook was a pawn in a carefully orchestrated plan to pave Monica's way to stardom. In the beginning, even Sid Zell didn't know how he was being used. But he found out soon enough. Isn't that right, Monica?"

Monica applauded, smiling churlishly. "You're very good, Mr. Platt. Quite the investigator."

"This is your big moment, Miss Rivers. The spotlight's all yours."

Monica turned my way, as hard and cold as ice. "I gave birth to Nicky nineteen years ago, Philip. Little Nicky Pembrook was mine."

"SO it was Lorna Draper's idea?" I peppered Platt with questions, while my head spun with all the information coming back at me. "Lorna was the one who set Sid Zell up to become the father?"

"When Monica was sixteen," Platt explained, "Lorna took her to meet Zell at Errol Flynn's place. That's what you related to me, remember?"

"Of course. You had me tell you everything, down to the most insignificant detail."

"Nothing's insignificant, Damon. You need to learn that, if I'm ever going to make a decent detective out of you." I opened my mouth to tell him no thanks, but he picked up his story. "Lorna knew from her own experience that Zell could never resist a lovely young girl. Zell impregnated Monica, with Lorna's silent complicity. Nine months later, when Monica was seventeen, Lorna took her to Tijuana to have the baby. To protect her daughter, Lorna used her own Mexican name on the birth certificate, presenting her passport and greasing the right palms to fix the paperwork. The baby became the leverage Lorna needed to manipulate the kind of career for Monica that she'd always wanted for herself. Zell, who had a family with his wife, Esther, went along with it to avoid scandal—and Monica went along with it for the chance to become a star. Some of the clues were down at the county records center—birth certificates, dates, fingerprints, citizenship papers."

"And Nicky Pembrook? He never knew who his real parents were, or how he'd come into the world?"

"It made him ideal for molding into a child star. Needy, vulnerable, desperate to please. Nicky became Lorna's unexpected bonus, filling in until Monica was all grown up and ready for her close-up."

Monica looked wrung out, miserable; a part of me still wanted to go to her, hold her, offer what comfort I could. "At least Nicky's at peace now," she said, sounding as if she was trying to ease her conscience. "We can take some solace in that, can't we?"

Platt's voice remained tough. "But there are still three

murders to account for, Miss Rivers. Three murders for which someone has to pay."

His eyes slid back toward Sid Zell.

"Look elsewhere, Platt." Zell sounded almost smug as he puffed on his expensive cigar. "There's nothing that physically ties me to those homicides, or even the business at the racetrack. The three most important witnesses are dead and anything Hedley Pinkston might say at this point lacks any credibility. The man's clearly a lunatic. As for Nicky's girlfriend, Vicki Hart, her testimony would be hearsay—if not inadmissible then certainly biased." Zell turned on Johnny Langley. "Which leaves our friend Johnny here, the one with the blood on his hands."

"You can take care of this, can't you, Mr. Zell? You told me you could find a solution for any problem that might come up."

"I'm afraid I see only one way out, Johnny." He reached over, lifted Langley's shirt. "The smoking gun, taken off the murder victim. Now that's real evidence, isn't it, Platt?"

Zell lifted his eyes to the distant sagebrush, looking gleeful. "Here comes the cavalry, in the nick of time." Heading in our direction, raising dust, half a dozen police cars bore down on the movie set. "I assumed you'd call them, Platt, before coming out here to confront me." He winked. "I called them myself, just in case."

Langley stared at Zell, then at the gun in his waistband. "What are you doing, Mr. Zell?"

"It looks like this is your moment of truth, Johnny."

Langley raised his chin, steeling himself as the patrol cars drew closer. "If I go down, Mr. Zell, you go with me."

"The word of a drug-dealing surfer on amphetamines against that of a respected studio honcho? No, Johnny, I'm afraid you'll be facing justice all by yourself. You'll spend the rest of your life in prison like a caged animal. The only surf you'll see will be in *Gidget* reruns, if you're lucky enough to get television privileges. You've taken your last ride, Johnny. All you have to look forward to now is a lifetime behind bars."

The look on Johnny Langley's face was bleak. "I'd rather die than go to prison."

"Yes," Zell said, "I figured that."

Langley stared at the patrol cars converging at the edge of town, then swallowed hard, as if coming to the only decision he could accept. Without another word, he walked away from us, out toward the open land, a solitary figure going to meet his salvation. As the cops braked and jumped out, Langley reached for the gun at his waist.

Platt cupped his hands to his mouth. "He's got a gun!" Then he pushed Monica and me toward the saloon, out of harm's way, while Zell ducked behind a buggy.

Johnny Langley raised the pistol with two shaking hands. A police captain, shielded by the door of his vehicle, yelled at him to put the gun down. Instead, Langley opened fire, shooting wildly. The cops returned a fusillade of well-aimed bullets. Langley went down in a heap, twitched a few times, and never moved again.

"Geez, if I'd only gotten that on camera," Zell said as we all emerged from hiding. He thumped his chest with a closed fist. "Kind of gets you right here, doesn't it?"

Monica shook her head, her face stained with tears. "You're pure evil, Sid. That's the only way I can think to describe you."

"How about ingenious, Monica? Or at least cunning?"

Platt seized Zell by the throat. "You could have gotten an officer killed!"

"Don't be a schmuck. The pistol was a prop."

Platt let go of Zell's throat, backing off. "Langley was firing blanks?"

Zell looked at Platt like he was stupid. "You don't think I'd trust a kid like Nicky Pembrook with a real gun, do you?"

Monica stepped forward and slapped Zell hard across the face. "I promise you, Sid, you'll answer for what you've done."

"Bet you fifty clams I never even get indicted." Zell pulled his jacket together and straightened his tie, preparing to meet the police captain striding in our direction. "L.A.'s a company town, honey. Movies fuel its engine. Big shots like Sid Zell get to play by different rules. And why not? Look at all the pictures we make, all the people we employ, all the popcorn we sell. Anyway, everybody cheats a little and gets away with it. Here in Hollywood, we just do it bigger and better."

"I loathe you, Sid."

Zell blew her a kiss. "I love you too, baby."

"Maybe I'm no angel," she said, "but at least I hurt when I think about Nicky and the way he died. I wonder how your wife will feel, Sid, when she finds out about us—about the kid you've kept secret all these years. I wonder how your other children will feel, when they read about it in the newspapers."

"Think twice, Monica. Sure, a scandal like that could hurt me. Maybe even force me into a nice retirement. But it will destroy you. Your career is all you have left now. You got nothing else, sweetie."

Fear passed like a shadow across Monica's face. "Of course, Sid. You're right." She smiled tightly, laughing a little. "You always are."

I seized Monica's arm. "You have me."

She found a tissue and dabbed at her tears, smiling more

warmly. "Oh, Philip, you're so sweet. But there was never anything between us, not really. You must know that."

"How can you say that? The moments we shared, the closeness we had. I fell in love with you, Monica."

She touched my face, her eyes filled with tenderness. "Don't you understand, Philip? I'm an actress. I'm trained to make people fall in love with me. It's what I'm good at, darling."

HERCULES Platt and I gave our version of events to the police captain, who laughed aloud several times, scoffing at how complicated and preposterous it sounded.

The next morning, law enforcement representatives from various jurisdictions gathered for a joint press conference. Together, they placed responsibility for the murders of Buddy Bixby and Nicky Pembrook squarely on Johnny Langley, mentioning a drug deal gone bad as the probable cause. The death of Angel Vargas, later ruled accidental, never came up. Officials removed Nicky Pembrook's name from the list of victims in the Watts riot, fixing the final death toll at thirty-four. With the media focusing so much attention on the aftermath of the rebellion, the wrap-up on the murders barely made the front page.

By week's end, Hedley Pinkston had been found dead from an overdose of sleeping pills at the Palm Vista Apartments, his head resting on a stack of *Life* magazines that featured Rock Hudson and Monica Rivers together on the cover. Sid Zell issued a press release eulogizing Pinkston as a great publicist and selfless individual, which *Daily Variety* and the *Hollywood Reporter* printed almost verbatim. Then Zell quietly arranged for the body to be sent home for burial in Kentucky, covering the expenses from a Premiere Alliance charity fund for orphaned children.

Chapter 38

◆

THE PHILIP DAMON Orchestra resumed playing at the Cocoanut Grove, but it never felt quite the same.

For one thing, the Beatles hit town at the end of the
month, and the Ambassador Hotel was overrun with mobs
of screaming girls who'd heard erroneously that the Fab Four
were staying there. When the Beatles left town two days
later, we were so inundated with requests for their hits that
I finally relented and added "Twist and Shout," "All My
Loving," and "A Hard Day's Night" to my playlist. Not
long after, the Ambassador announced that Wayne Newton,
a Las Vegas lounge singer, would be appearing at the Grove
following our engagement. Meanwhile, Sammy Davis, Jr.,
was talking about putting together some investors and turning the Grove into a "happening" venue to be called the
Now Club, a prospect that caused my guts to churn.

I asked Hercules Platt how he felt about adding rock 'n' roll to our repertoire. "Beats playing to empty tables," he grumbled, and I knew he wasn't happy about it. To our surprise, though, we began to really enjoy playing Beatles tunes, which were more sophisticated musically than we realized, especially as their songbook grew.

I thought I'd put Monica Rivers behind me, but I was wrong.

In early September, I heard about a memorial service she and Lorna Draper had arranged for Nicky Pembrook, and I felt I should pay my respects. In my heart, I knew I had another reason for attending: the chance to see Monica one last time before I returned to Manhattan, maybe even take a final tumble with her, a memory to carry with me back to New York of a fascinating woman I'd loved blindly and foolishly.

The morning service was held outdoors in Griffith Park near the equestrian ring where Nicky had taken his first pony ride as a little boy. I sat near the back, on a metal folding chair, listening to the eulogies but mostly studying Monica, who sat up front on a small, portable stage with Lorna Draper and Vicki Hart. To my surprise, Sid Zell was among the mourners, causing me to marvel at the man's gall. He'd faced a secret grand jury—Platt and I had been called to testify—which had failed to indict him for conspiracy to murder, citing lack of evidence. For the service, he was dressed in a fine black Sy Devore suit, looking properly solemn.

As the service ended, Monica left quickly, accompanied by Vicki Hart. I followed them toward the parking lot, hoping to get a word with Monica. Before I could, Sid Zell joined them and they climbed together into Zell's big Cadillac. As they took off, I hopped in my car and went after them. Not half an hour later, we were in the lobby of the Chateau Marmont, where I spied on them from a distance as they waited for an elevator.

To my consternation, Zell had a hand on Vicki Hart's slender neck. The elevator doors opened and the three of them stepped in. By the time the doors were closing, Zell's hand had found its way down to Vicki's pert bottom, where she let it stay. Monica glanced at Zell's effrontery, smiling in compliance. I watched the numbers above the doors as the elevator climbed, and saw the dial stop at five. Monica's floor.

I turned away, sickened, certain I was over Monica Rivers for good.

LATE that afternoon, Beatrice woke me from a nap. She was dressed for gardening, and held a small transistor radio in one hand.

"Sid Zell is dead, Philip."

I abruptly sat up while Beatrice turned up the volume on the newscast. According to the report, Zell had died of a heart attack hours earlier while visiting Monica Rivers at the Chateau Marmont to discuss her next film role. After briefly leaving him alone, she returned to find him dead on the floor, too late to save him.

A horn sounded out front on Lookout Mountain Avenue. I stepped with Beatrice to the door to see a long white limousine parked at the end of the walk. A rear door was open and Monica sat just inside, one high heel on the pavement, showing plenty of leg. She climbed out as I strolled down the walk to meet her.

"I just heard about Zell," I said. "You must be heartbroken."

Her smile was perfunctory. "We had a lot of history together, Sid and I."

"I was at the service for Nicky this morning."

"Yes, I saw you. It was nice of you to be there, Philip."

"I'd hoped to speak with you, but you left rather quickly. I followed the three of you back to the Marmont—you, Zell, and Vicki Hart."

"I knew that too."

"It doesn't bother you, what I saw?"

"Sid, with his hands on Vicki?" I nodded. "I don't think you'd hurt Vicki, Philip, not if there was some way you could avoid it."

"You've got everything figured out, don't you, Monica?"

"I learned a few things from Sid over the years."

I peered into the limousine. "Where's Vicki now?"

"On a plane home to Ohio. She's decided to teach school. Peggy Bixby talked her into it. She told Vicki she'd never get rich or famous but that she'd probably be a lot happier. If she really wants to act, Peggy said, there's always the local playhouse."

"You didn't come here to tell me about Vicki's career plans, Monica."

"No, of course not." Monica tapped out a Benson & Hedges, while I took her Cartier lighter and sparked the flame.

"So what happened after the three of you went upstairs this morning?"

Monica inhaled deeply, exhaled slowly. "I told Sid that I needed to go out for cigarettes—a ruse that Vicki and I had worked out beforehand. As I grabbed my bag to leave, the look in Sid's eyes was ravenous. He had his hands on Vicki before I was out the door." Monica dropped her lighter back into her bag, closed it up. "Within minutes, Vicki had Sid in bed, doing things with him he hadn't done in years, driving him wild. It wasn't long before his chest pains started. By the time I returned, he was in full cardiac arrest."

Monica picked a fleck of tobacco off her lower lip. "Not the most original idea," she admitted. "Sid used it as a plot twist twenty years ago in *Fatal Kiss*. I thought Anne Baxter and Robert Ryan were quite good in that one. Did you see it?"

"I'm afraid I missed it."

"Anyway, while Sid was thrashing around, consumed with fear and pain, Vicki left the hotel by a side entrance. I helped Sid dress and got him to the sofa. I left the room for a minute to tidy up the bed. When I came back, I told him an ambulance was on the way." Monica smiled thinly. "The ambulance took a bit longer than that—after I finally made the call a half hour later."

"In the meantime, Zell was dying."

"While he was still conscious and alert I told him what was happening, that no one was coming to save him. 'It's judgment day, darling, and there's no escape.' Those were my exact words. Of course, I borrowed them from *Dead Aim*—the original version, my apologies to Beatrice. Poor Sid—he struggled, begged, tried desperately to crawl to the phone. He actually reached it, bless his heart. Sid was a real fighter."

"But you grabbed the receiver and held it from him?"

"Tore out the phone from the wall, tossed it across the room."

"Ah—how clever."

"Not really," Monica said. "Lana Turner did the same thing in *Eternal Damnation*, back in '52. That's where I got the idea. Anyway, when Sid's pulse was finally gone, I waited another few minutes, then re-plugged the phone and called for help."

"Why are you telling me all this, Monica?"

"I figure you deserve to know, after all I put you through. You were awfully good to me, Philip, when things were rotten. I owe you this much, at the very least."

"And if I reported what you've told me, you'd only deny it, anyway." Monica merely smiled, exhaling a cinematic stream of smoke. "I've never met anyone quite like you, Monica. You're so convincing. You lie so remarkably well."

She pecked me on the cheek. "You say the sweetest things."

"I'm curious about one thing, though."

"What's that, Philip?"

"Jerome Kern's 'All the Things You Are.' Is it really your favorite song, like you told me when we were driving back from Palm Springs?"

She squeezed my hand, smiling as warmly as Julie Andrews in *The Sound of Music*. "It was then, darling—when it needed to be."

THE limousine whisked Monica away and I went back into the house. It was the cocktail hour and Beatrice was preparing drinks. As she mixed two gin martinis, the phone rang. It was Bob Thomas from the AP calling to get a personal comment about Sid Zell, if Beatrice was up to it.

She looked pensive for a moment before she spoke. "I knew Sid Zell for nearly thirty years," she said, speaking slowly and carefully. "He knew how to make movies and he knew how to make money. He was also a cheat, a scoundrel, a con artist, a bully, and a thug. Anybody who tells you different is a damn liar. And you may quote me."

Beatrice hung up, smiling grandly. "My, that felt good."

She slipped a Buddy Bixby record onto the turntable and adjusted the volume. Buddy's slight, plaintive voice filled the room and drifted beyond, crooning "Good Morning, Heartache" sadly but sweetly. Beatrice suggested we take our drinks and join the cats out on the veranda, put our feet up, and watch the sun settle over the canyon, which is exactly what we did.